CFD

Mary Blindflowers

THE BLACK STAR OF MU

ANTINOVEL ANARCHO-SURREALIST

ISBN : 978-1-911424-33-8
SKU/ID: 9781911424338

All Right Reserved. No part of this book can be used or reproduced in any manner whatsoever without written permission from the publisher, except in the case of brief quotations embodied in critical articles or reviews.

Editor: Wolf Graham
Translation: Francesco Saverio Maione

Cover and Book design: Wolf

in cover
"LA STELLA NERA DI MU"
by Mary Blindflowers
oil on canvas

Publishing Company:
Black Wolf Edition & Publishing Ltd.
4 Rogart Street, Glasgow G40 2AA, Scotland
www.blackwolfedition.com

Copyright © 2018 by Black Wolf Edition & Publishing Ltd.
and other respective owners identified in this work.
Designs and Patents Act 1988
All rights reserved.
First Edition 2018 - First Printing 2018

EDITOR PREFACE

After reading the manuscript of this surrealist NOT-NOVEL or as the writer Mary Blindflowers underlines, "antinovel anarcho-surrealist", I was impressed by her way of describing existing issues of today world using also a holistic philosophical paradigm.

A captivating and pungent writer, sometimes eccentric in her writing.

As an editor for the publishing company Black Wolf Edition & Publishing Ltd., I always evaluate convincing texts, innovative even if written differently. The manuscripts I choose to be published need to have a real logical thread even if they can have a beginning and an end falling into a vicious circle like a LOOP, as I found in this manuscript.

I fully agree with this critic review about her: "Mary is elusive, refined and pungent as her works that set over the dilemma of the contemporary human being wrapped in the melancholy that often becomes rage to the powerless of action...in her I can find consideration and questions that call other questions nourished by a reflection to which an ordinary person is not prepared to go beyond the wall of social conventions... I like her a lot, as writer and as person..."

I add that it has been a pleasure working with her during the proof editing and finding an author who promptly and consistently defends her text.

A book to read in full to understand the clear and absurd connection between surreal and real that the writer highlights using esoteric symbolism.

A novel differently written, cleverly introduced by the author herself with her poem "The Gold".

Wolf Graham
(The Editor)

THE GOLD

Delicate Chrysopoeias[1],
gold of unbesmirched alchemical illusions,
the witch leads over alpha and omega,
she composes night hemistichs,
disordered memorials of poetry
and bitterness faded clouds,
she is suddenly and cruelly thirsty,
the witch grasps
a new pledge into the darkness,
enchantment to know things,
to break the old decaying
time-worm,
destroying hours, minutes,
seconds,
reaching a decent euphoria,
idyllic parallel worlds,
from the deep essence of nothingness...

---

[1] from χρυσοποιία (onomatopoeia, prosopopoeia, pomposity, pharmacopoeia). The choice of Chrysopoeias is a poetic licence.

Mary Blindflowers

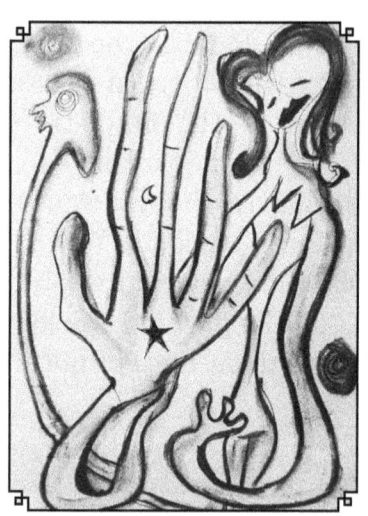

WALKING MAN

The air is static, unreal, an ordinary day of a seemingly ordinary man that does the same things for years, he shaves his beard, he puts his shirt on, having a shower, brushing his hair, having breakfast and finally he leaves.

He leaves home and he loses himself completely into that static air, into that unreality existing outside.

The path is like a dog hanging tongue, long, slimy and lonely. The houses look small and empty, their windows ravenous mouths watching towards the empty. The nothingness fills the gaps, leading and ruling over empty spaces, swallowing the grey and cold cement, impetuously devouring day and night, the music and the song of any present and future life.

That man is alone. His loneliness is not only physical, it is definitely an inner sorrow, an indefinable anguish, deep as a grief that goes into the stomach, a weight on the shoulders, harming his own gut, that creeps into his breath, into his head and it really hurts.

He comes across to a stray dog which has a yellowish and suffering glance. He thinks and quivers inside. Luce shivers, with no sense, purely emotional. No voices around there, not even a breeze or a single gust of wind. An unreal, metaphysical silence shrouds everything, every instant and breath.

It's still too early, too early to live and too early to die, too early in every sense, philosophically and temporally. The sun hasn't driven away the night shadows yet. Hands of darkness despairingly grab the houses facades with their black and sharp nails sunk in the soft flesh of some roofs.

Fast and cold feet of darkness run, trying to avoid the first burning hot and destroying rays from a rising sun, so they will not turn into dust and ruins of gloom, forgotten ashes. The night, as everyone, does not accept to fade into grey tones and then to die into the full cruelty and indecency of the light.

Meanwhile the man is walking, with a burden of his work bag, with a burden of his age, of his prolonged silences and personal complexes, taking around his soul into the unenthusiastic plasticity of the terse atmosphere.

Here it is the creature, facing him, standing, gorgeous, regal, as usual. Not even a wrinkle on its face, not a white hair, it doesn't get old, it can't get old and no one knows if it's a good thing or not, it's simply like that. Unreal and timeless beauty.

That man smile becomes a bitter sneer. The creature is the pain, the bond, the start and the end, the poisonous honey of the destiny. Whilst the man goes down three steps out of nine that are in between him and the creature, he says loud its name: 'Luce!' A word that drives away darkness and nightmares. Luce...

That name rolls over the hard silence of the steps, over the little houses, over the ancient stones polished by the elements. Shout and thrown suddenly into the world, this name falls down like a rock over the overcrowded and exhausts darkness, faded by the cruel and deadly dawn.

Luce turns around, as this is a powerful name, it's a key, a magic word that opens mysterious worlds.

Her shouted name strongly echoes into the air. She slaps the ancient dust, whilst the darkness changes its colour into a brighter purple. Luce arrives, going up three steps, she is so close that the man can smell her scent. She smells like indefinable wind breeze, bruised roses, wild moss. She is white dressed, long ebony hair, silver white nails that blind, like ready-to-fight blades. Her eyes are instead black empty abyss, deep as ancient wounds, movable black islands into the very white aseptic sclera. Big eyes, sad as cliffs into a lost sea and now drained by some spell, never got wet by salty tears.

The man looks at Luce, sailing into those black petrol deep pupils, a thick, sticky ocean.

There aren't any boats, neither arms, not mussels, and not even human emotions, that would understand that indefinite black petrol with no start and not end, whirl which has seen parallel universes, and brings the indelible and dark mark of them.

That man cannot make it done, he is weak, similar to the darkness that changes colour into grey fading in the air. Luce wins over him, she is stronger, not human, she has better skills and different world muscles and blood. Her silver nails are just sinking into the man flesh, the grip wounds his arm and ideally rips his heart, reducing it into a small pieces.

The man is bleeding, the warm blood that comes out his arm is blending into her cold skin. Here he is, the man grabs as a weapon a sharp bit of his useless, pathetic and weak heart. He throws his heart with his words, hitting, and hitting the creature with his tongue that is used as a weapon and then with his hand. Now he grabs a really sharp paper knife. He hits. Luce is injured, she falls down.

The creature let herself fall down without loosing control over the things.

Is everything over like this? Just with a falling wound? Where is the story then?

We don't know it yet, we will not be able to know it until the end. The creature is not scared, basically she would never fear because is superhuman, she knows the secrets of the black and white. She feels loosing grip beneath herself, she knows that she will fall down, that she will hurt herself, maybe. No one can foresee how much. The stone is hard and black like her double-pupils witch eyes. The stone can wait. The stone is waiting to challenge against the strength of the creature flesh and bones, the stone is waiting to drink the blood from the recent wound.

Luce is always late. It's an old habit and old habits die hard. The rock is greedy, it is thirsty, but the body is strong, weightless, and because of a strange spell it becomes light like a feather. Her silver nails shine under the sun now big in the sky.

The man looks down at the creature, he is scared about what he did, stunned, he closes his eyes, tired, he looks horrified his piece of sharp heart, now pale, ex-sanguine, with no destination anymore. The heart and the hard metal paper knife are one. He damns himself and tries to grab the creature hand, to not make her fall down, to tampon the wound. Even Time stops, he takes a chair and put it on the floor and he takes a seat as a quiet spectator, he is curious.

The show starts. The time that an item takes to fall down. This story lasts that enough time.

Luce looks at the cement whilst falling down and underneath the cement she sees the dark soil and underneath the damp of the ground she hears people steps, warm breaths, words and thoughts. Mu, a specular universe, mysterious and flooded of souls, a ground fancy of freedom. Mu, the eternal, the Underground Earth, the black and white space.

Luce can hear sounds that others cannot hear at all, she perceives the underground river flow, the river of the rituals into the windless space. Many times when she was a little girl, she has beaten the waters with a rod to rule over the spirits of Nature, when she used to sink a vase full of stones in the water, she prayed to hail with double execration words, because the Earth, the human being one, specular to its Underground World, would have seen still cold and fresh water coming from the sky. And the sound of her invocations of witch sometimes made fall down ice stones over the Upper World. Lightning was striking over the human houses and water on the roofs, for days, for whole nights, with no rest. And the sea was bellowing as an ox led to the slaughterhouse drooling on terrified cliffs. The Upper World was a huge experiments laboratory which it has been useful to Mu to test its power. Whilst over there a mad storm was striking, a little noise could be heard in Mu, like the rain was softly hitting the roofs. Looking her eyes through the mirror, Luce would have imagined the Upper World and everything happening over there. Mu is a world full of surprises in where dark and big coelacanths and rhino-grades crowd together, curious species nowadays extinct in the Upper World. There is no wind, no moon, no sun, no rain, only sharp stars sharing a metallic smile. The air is aqua green, temperature is unvaried, quite warm, without the stressful outrage of the four seasons, with no vacuous surprises, not even bad harvests.

Just the air is full of new fragrances, of summer, enchanting fruity aromas.

Mu, the Underground Earth, has seen Luce born on the 28 June 6666 post Matrem, Mu's Calendar, starting from the date when the Great Mother would have given her eter-

nal heart to Mu.

Luce is not a human specie. She is the Black Star of another world, underground and free.

According to a legend from the Underground Earth, every 606 years, a baby girl with a Sign, a black star shaped spot on her palm, was born in Mu. In that occasion a moon appears in the sky extraordinarily and then sinking down back again after 9 hours.

Luce was born without heart. When her midwife used to hold her, the little baby mouth could not cry. Her very light and deathly pale appeared dead. But her parents wept tears of joy when they noticed the mark on her defenceless palm.

Corax, Luce's father, wrapped thoughtfully the girl into soft white and black linen blankets so her future strengths would have been boosted up. As he left the house, he went towards Hilde's house, the ancient heart pulsing only for Mu since 606 years ago. Hilde was a perfect machine which would never get sick, not even getting old, not feeling pain.

The house that was hosting that ancestral and mysterious heart was plain, with a black sloping roof, milk coloured facade and a little garden full of strange plants which were moving as they would have been alive. Hilde was feeding the plants overnight with flies, pieces of meat and other little insects. Some of them had large white mouths black-streaked with some wreaths of thorns that were looking as teeth, other were showing off big flowers which were dazzling flare and little man shaped moving roots with neither eyes nor faces. There were wool trees with black and white cotton balls that were in reality small carnivorous sheep in miniature, hanging upside down as ripe fruits. Sometimes it can be heard the bleating into the air. They used to open their starving mouth asking for some food. Everything was alive in Hilde's garden. Black and white blades, mixed, had big eyes similar to man ones and lips which they used to whisper some words seeking the wind, but the wind wouldn't have heard them because it escaped from Mu looking for new colours. So the thin blades ended up fighting each other, the white blades against the black and vice-versa, swearing about revolutions, anathematizing, declaring war to each other loudly. But it was only a big noise for nothing, because the poor ones could not move, as they were clung so strongly to the ground. Then they were cursing at the wind itself which wasn't there and it would have preferred, the traitor, the infamous, the coward, the Upper Earth, leaving them disabled, paralysed. They were cursing their own inert roots and they were dreaming to go away from Mu, although they did not know exactly where and how, because they never had to walk.

Not even that big black and white-striped toad parking over the stone dwarf of the garden knew anything about it or maybe it was pretending to ignore it. No one seemed to care too much about the Unknowable Beyond. But the blades had ears and they could listen things, they had mouths and they knew how to whisper. They were saying that Hilde only once got closer to the abyss of the Unknowable Beyond. That spot is just after the entrance of Mu, a black vortex which nobody ever did go beyond, no one that history or legends could remember about. But someone could possibly have been there. Hilde can feel it. She can feel it when doing some rituals affecting the Upper World. When she looks herself through the mirror and she can see into that bottom depth of her eyes. She sees the Upper World people, the human beings. Maybe some Black

~ *The black star of Mu* ~

Star during the time has reached the Upper World o maybe other forgotten worlds, perhaps... It should be satisfying watching the rain dripping on her hair before the time has come... And feel the touch of the sun on the skin. Hilde sighs. She knows her destiny already. What about if the legendary Upper World would not exist? What if that was a fantasy from poets and sophists? No no... It definitely exists!

Lot of books talk about it and then the eyes see everything and reflect the worlds and when they cannot watch things they listen, they feel. It's a shame that they cannot change the destiny.

A Black Star has to be a solid wall with nerves of steel, a Black Star does not have doubts or uncertainty, it is dangerous. Dark energies could stick to the grip of doubts, finding a way to destroy Mu. Black and white must stay always in balance.

Now Hilde changes her expression. Did she see anything? Yes, here we go, it is more than that, it is everything. A pitiful silence is widening into the air. All the alive creatures of the garden have understood, like feeling the extraordinary of this event. Somebody knocks at the door. The blades are desperate and they all shout as a chorus: 'Who is there? Let's open the door. No, no, no! Damned wind, traitor and coward... We cannot move, there is no wind. Although somebody must have been into the Upper World where the wind is or maybe into other impenetrable universes...somebody would have been beyond the chasm, the Unknowable Beyond... Ah if we could move on and walk... Goodbye Hilde, goodbye...'

Corax smiles now with this cold heartless bundle between his arms in front of Hilde's open door. She exchanges the smile and nods: 'I had a dream which left me breathless, and I have seen the moon, beautiful, full, shining. And I have seen a dense and vague light. I was scared, do you know Corax? Welcome to my house, welcome to Mu's time. Everything is done already now. Birth and death are entangled sisters of a not successful delivery. We can not avoid our fate. Even I who I am the Black Star can not avoid it. Mu must survive. I was waiting for you, come in. I am ready and what about you?'

'I am scared, honestly.'

'You don't, come through the doorstep, I will tell you exactly what to do.'

After they walked over 3 stone steps, they get into a warm room which smells of indefinable aromas. The light is greenish, like everywhere in Mu.

'It is the time now.'

'I am afraid.' Corax puts his head down.

'Not too worries. It's written. Nobody could resist to the Mother's Law.'

Hilde leads Corax into a room which has milk-coloured walls, and she talks to him quietly, after inviting him to take a seat on a really dark black stone bench, the only furnishing there, where there is a book. Corax will be waiting there. He nods. The woman takes the girl, bringing her into an oval space where a light gets through from a small glass opening from the ceiling. She puts the powerless bundle gently over an ancient table, round, made of concentric layers of woods carved into curious and cryptic symbols. The table feet are like open jaws of strange unshaped horned animals. Hilde slowly and gently unfolds the black veils and then the white ones from the girl's body, those veils that symbolize the knowledge of the good and the evil, she says double words which were unintelligible both straight and upside down. The air gets dark, then bright with some variations which are astonishing and it creates an atmosphere again unreal and dreadful. The creature body is lifting over the table. Hilde puts her hands underneath her. After that she gets undressed slowly, turning her palms up. Her left palm has a mark, a black star identical to the girl one. Now the star burns Hilde's palm which is getting fiery. The witch sinks her sharp fingers into her own chest. A small incision opens the candid flesh. Her fingers go deep beyond the wound, they extract with surgical precision the ancient immortal and still pulsating Hilde's heart and they push it into the girl chest after ripping her soft flesh up. There is no blood at all. Her wounds heal in few seconds. Everything happens in silence, with no sobs, with no tears. Through the secret of that oval room life and death are arranged through.

After that Hilde, the witch, born with that mark, dresses up, she opens a trapdoor, taking the girl with her. She has to go downstairs into the darkness, slowly, only her and the little girl. In the meanwhile, Corax will be waiting without moving into the static air of the other room, he will open the book on the stone bench and he will be starting to read loudly and clearly, slowly, pronouncing well any syllable of each word.

His words will resound loudly beyond the room, into the alive plants garden, through Mu's streets, through the pearly Grand Mothers path and Mu citizens will wake up and cry and shiver and touch the flesh of their candid arms to make sure they still have feelings.

Corax is reading: «At the very start there was the Nothing and the Nothing was Everything, the Real Existent

Uncreated, the Mystery, the Androgynous hermaphrodite primordial irrational Chaos, self-reproducing in different reflections or emissions. Surrounded from the Nothingness tears, boys and girls get assigned to their world. The first ones will lead over the Upper World. The fall from the Nothing eyes has stunned them and they don't keep any memory about themselves, about their existence purely reflected. The girls have Mu, the Underground World where there is a certain awareness about the Nothing. Both Underground Earth and Upper World are part of the Not Existing Glare because only the Nothing really exists. There are really far reflections of the Uncreated, into the Dark, which is better not to keep memory of them, obscure presences, unusually shaped and elusive. They live in unexplored lands, beyond the abyss of Mu, The Unknowable Beyond from where nobody came back yet. There are some reflections really close to the Mystery, into the light, very strong energies which is ideal not to deal with, scourge would be death or the eternal lunacy. Nothing is taken for granted. It wouldn't be said that the Dark is Evil and the Light is Good. That's a human concept of those who cannot remember the Nothing, who don't know even about the existence of Mu. Reflections are relative and some malicious and benign presences could nestle into the Dark, the same happens into the Light. Between Dark and Light there is Mu which ensures a perfect balance. The weighing needle is its Black Star. Above Mu, specularly, there is the Earth inhabited by unaware human beings. Two opposite reflexions in tension. After 606 years the ancient heart of Mu is renewing. Leave your warm and safe houses and listen to ancient voices, reawakened, they whisper and bustle and remember. Remember you too Mu citizens, hear and remember that you are only reflexions, you do not exist. Now more than before you have to fear about Mu. The Black Star will come down to our world borders. Let's wait for what's happening.'

After these words a deadly silence suddenly comes, like falling from the sky or maybe from one of those parallel worlds populated with presences mentioned in the book. Nothing can be done; just waiting that Hilde makes her trip.

Hilde's Journey

Hilde has to complete her mission to make Mu still surviving, so the Great Mothers could murmur in their pearly pathway, in order that everything is fine and the windless, nightless, stormless and rainless land will keep on its life cycle which is carrying on since millions of years with no interruptions. The manhole in the middle of the oval hall has been opened, like a mephitic and disturbing abysmal eye, like a hell engulfing ideas and feelings. Hilde, as well, is searching through the dark aperture, a cold and mouldy air runs over her throat. She has to move on. She cannot carry on too long without her heart. Her bare feet feel the stone steps moisture. She is shivering whilst holding Corax's newborn daughter, the new Black Star who will take over her at Mu. It's freezing! There is no time to waste thinking about own body worries. She has only 9999 steps to do until the end and she does not even know what will happen, she knows only that she has to carry on. The walls are slimy because of the indefinite moods of the Earth. Hilde's really white skin is so bright into the dark cave, it lights up eyeless insects, baby dragons, grey shell beetles, hairy centipedes, long poisoning clawed black scorpions, empty snail shells.

Hilde's delicate feet trample on big salt grains, then sand. She comes down step after step, beat-less. During the route she has nightmare visions, seeing unimaginable creatures, three-headed ones, with their stunning beauty although their obscene deformity, coloured and grey. She feels on her skin kind of hellish heat and arctic freezing and the Mothers voice whispering and encouraging her to follow her destiny. That voice resounds in her brain, it is in her skin. The light alternates with the darkness, continuously, but it needs to follow the Mothers whispers. They blow arcane syllables through the heart of the small baby who becomes more and more hot. No ordinary Mu citizen has ever been into the Mothers Path. Only the Black Stars or Mothers are allowed to go there, the ones like Hilde or the baby, born with that particular mark. It is in this mysterious place that everything starts, everything ends... The road to get there is short and long, cold and hot the same way, bright as stars fragments, dark and primal as a moonless night. Because the Mothers Path is the reflection of the Everything and the Nothing and the Nothing is the origin of the Everything which is a reflection as well.

Hilde knows it very well and she smiles whilst resting her feet over the frozen rock. That stone slowly, imperceptibly sunders into various stones which become warm and fragile over Hilde steps. Those rocks are eggs now and the Black Star foot tramples on them, breaking them. The candid and black shells smash and they show the reddish yolk, the slimy yellowish white albumen. Hilde is worried to fall down and she comes forward slowly breaking egg shells then she slips into the empty space as the egg shells pathway vanished, so she is alone in the dark, as suspended. The silence is tough for few minutes, impenetrable, profound, as coming from another world never explored, never inhabited. Hilde does not know what to do. She simply stands by, closing her eyes. Anyway she does not know where to go, so she is waiting. She feels Luce's heart getting warm underneath her ribs and the small chest heating up.

In the meanwhile Corax gets back on reading the book and loudly, following the instructions, starts to read: 'Regression will allow progression, because only who has seen the bottom can communicate to someone about the life in general. Only who knows about darkness can understand the light. The backwards is ahead, the past is the future. The present would live at Mu within an intimate connection to what has been because memories and flesh stay together, because the dead time would flourish into a live present, avoiding the memory decay.

Mu citizens, mindful reflections, please avoid the oblivion worm, listen to the warm siren voice of the Mothers which are waiting for their sacrifice. Your ears must feel very soon the arcane strength of their words. Please hope that what is hiding will be showing soon, that Mu's heart gets warm, that Mu's bones get recovered, that Mu's mouth would talk with living and death people and would breath the black and white and will survive over the Upper World, like the soul survives against the body, like the thought goes over the speed and the energy of the flesh. Now, the wait.'

Just pronounced those words to Mu the greenish sky starts moving into a strange way and it's getting darker turning into a vortex. Just minutes and a dark night shows towards a petrol-coloured sky full of bright stars like disquieting daggers, intense like deep eyes. Now the moon shows and it is like a thin and sharp sickle ready to sever the world off, mistress and ruler of the sky. There is no God that could hold it in his hands without injuries, not even heart that could warm its cold unreal nudity. Recumbent into the funereal blanket of the sky, the moon is waiting with an ancient ice-stone steadiness, like a weapon ready to shiver. If Hilde would have completed her travel successfully, the moon had propitiously disappeared from the sky, and Mu will turn back to live. If Hilde would have been unsuccessful, if she would not get to make the ancient and precious Mu's heart being back again, the pronged moon would come down and it will mow down the Underground Earth, and Mu citizens will be bleeding upon the Upper World, which will be flooded and completely suffocated.

That's the Law. No one knows who wrote this Law not even where Hilde's book comes from which she has given to Corax for reading. This book is full of energies from unknown worlds. Mu citizens say that this book was born from the Mothers whisper. However it does not rule over their own destiny. Its words need only to remind Mu about the Law, to make Mu citizens comfortable during the wait whilst the sharp moon is staring at them from the sky. The sound of those words is really hypnotic and powerful, giving to Mu citizens the chance to feel for their first time the breath of mystery, to understand that beyond the perceived there is the arcane essence of unknown and cryptic worlds.

Corax talks louder whilst reading, 'And the sky is now dark, mysteriously mellow, a killer moon is waiting for its sacrificial prey like final purpose of its travel. The Black Star shouts its name into Mu's womb. 'I am Hilde, I am the living voice of the Mothers, the carnal connection between Mu and the occult darkness of its womb...'

Hilde and Corax pronounce the same words in unison. Hilde sees a grey shadow breaking off the darkness. It is sitting opposite to her, upon a white table, on her head strong lights and moving images projections, images of the Upper World men and stars and planets, visions of a young Hilde, of her parents when they discovered her mark into her white hand.

The shadow talks, 'Who are you?' Its voice is hypnotic,

intense and horrible at the same time.

«I am Hilde, the Black Star of Mu, I am the living voice of the Mothers, the carnal connection between Mu and the occult darkness of its womb, I am the elected, the chosen one, the reflected emanation which has reminiscence of the Androgynous Chaos in order to get marked. I, the only one, the favourite of the Uncreated, the black, the radiant, the inviolate, the unemotional balance between the Two Worlds, the Upper and the Underground...'

The shade gets a bit nervous. 'Do you know, my darling, who I am?'

Hilde doesn't know it, but she closes her eyes and she hears Corax voice that on the stone bench is reading the book repeating, 'You are the dark desire that is revealing only through a Pindaric flight of a dream. You are the instinct, the beast that pushes its natural and sharp claws against the deceiver artifice of the good education. You are the tooth that bites and makes bleeding the flesh of the conventional appearance. You are the primitive light over a sweet and suffered explosive path of impulses. You, feral, bestial, passion, you are hands and feet and various buried eyes. Pleasure vibration, collective and personal jumble, images, sounds, colours, cryptic masks and complicated sunsets that reveal the true colour of the sun. You are not good nor evil, you offer life and death on the same little dish. All the artists count on you, they don't care about the world and they walk smiling at you step by step towards destinations of free parallel worlds. Subconscious, they call you like that.'

The shadow smiles, 'Exactly. And I will lead you my dear Hilde, until the first human instinct and the world that you know will melt over me and for me which will be your eyes until to the end of the day and the night. We will flay the time that without skin will have no sense, empty and inane shell. We will kick it on the heavy edge of the night ad nothing will have a sense except for the destination.'

'And which is the destination?'

'We will find the way together. Give me your hand, Hilde, trust me and you will never die. You will be a diamond with one face and you will scream your imperishable name through the Mothers Path. And the strength of your name will be stronger than any other nonexistent god.'

'God…'

'God is a universal key of male genre, a phallus which open every door, an Upper World invention to employ power, a mean that moves wealth and soldiers, crowds seduction, deceit, men vanity, business. And this God has got a big house, inside that there are his proponents who fill their own pockets whilst preaching charity and humility and they have on their necks the golden weight of their Lord image delivered by Virgin Mother, which has been printed on t-shirts, calendars, flags…'

'Odd.'

'So this God would have created the man as boss and the woman as servant.'

'Pfui!'

'And the sky, the Earth and what is in the middle.'

'But it is impossible! The Androgynous has created everything.'

'Who knows. We say the Androgynous, the Upper World citizens call him God. Everyone has his own different dish to offer, fantasy meals, irrational whoppers, honey balsams and sad panacea.'

Corax closes the book, he puts it on the cold rock.

Hilde whispers, 'Do you doubt over the Androgynous?'
The shadow holds its head in between its hands. 'You doubt it, me too because you are myself and I am yourself. What do you believe Hilde?'

'Earlier I said that I have reminiscence of the Androgynous, but it is not true. I was repeating the words from the book, the one that they have taught about since generations. Always the same story. Repeating with no knowledge, without reflecting about it. I don't like this. I don't know anything about anything and I look into the dark, but I cannot see anything. I am blind and I would like to see something, I am deaf and I would like to hear something. Do you know which is the genuine truth, uncontrollable?' The little Luce into the strong arms of Hilde seems to move a little bit and shivering because of those words sound. It can be heard a hiss in the air interrupted by extended hiccups. 'I haven't got any certainty. I only believe into the common nothingness. I believe about the not-divine, the absence, the emptiness which its value is equal to zero.'

The shadow laughs. 'The Empty? Why?'

'Because I can fill it up with everything I want and the willing is power which is waiting to get transformed in action. I would have been going into the Unknowable Beyond. I was very close to it, you know, I touched the bottom. Now I feel an incredible meaningless inside.'

'Let's go to fill this nothingness up with a meaning then. Don't you know maybe that in the Underground World called as Mu God is dead? Not even born, to be precise. The Great Mothers are not goddesses. They are the voice of the freedom which fill the empty up with a meaning.' Hilde holds Luce in her arms. The dark absorbs again the shadow of its subconscious. Now is all black. After few seconds the darkness changes colours through a transparent atmosphere, turning into an inexpressible absence.

Hilde walks, she looks at her feet, but underneath them there is nothing, there is only the empty and her body is suspended into the nothingness, fluctuating. So she closes her eyes and thinks. The floor is not even so cold anymore and it seems pulsating like a living creature. Her thoughts materialize below and above her feet, some images flowing into the air, the trees of the complex are growing, clawing at the transparent air with their branches, drawing clearly their outlines, loaded with bitter fruits. And those fruits are falling down and seeding and they make other plants growing up that become a wild tangled woods. Hilde struggles to walk through it. She manages to reach a candid open space. The colour of this open space is made from billions and billions baby teeth. Every step that Hilde makes those teeth thin out. Those feet got pinched and wounded by a multitude of cut nails pieces. It is painful to walk over them. Then the path becomes soft slope because of a soft carpet of eyelashes. Misty eyes appear now, hands and heads of wounded dolls, childhood relics now useless, massive piles, sacrifice of lifeless victims. There are shoes, small size clothes, moulded worm eaten cakes and milk and cookies piddles. The path gets more narrow and it leads to a tight cavity, humid and warm. Hilde walks but her feet are in the water, a strange silence. The water is calm and there is the dark again.

The shadow appears again plastically separating from the darkness. 'Who are you Hilde?'

'I am a small girl which cries!'

Hilde walks through the water since being fully immersed. Into her ears a heart beat, maybe the one from small Luce who seems to move her arms and getting even smaller. Whilst Hilde is coming forward through that warm and watery universe she feels very hard to breath while Luce gets smaller and moves around, float on her own, she snuggles up.

The shadow persists, 'Who are you Hilde?'

'I am a seed thrown into the deep calm sea and I cannot love anymore your desires because I have no heart now, I have lost it into Luce's body.'

'Keep walking then.'

Hilde comes out the water, her foot draws a black print upon the whispers of a really thin dust, along a spiral-shaped pathway. Gradually her body starts to dismantle, slowly, painlessly, adding dust over dust. Her voice whispers blending with the other innumerable voices of Mothers.

'Who are you Hilde?'

'I am an idea, mixed up with the nothingness, I am dust into the Great Mothers path and I will whisper forever the arcane strength of my free name.'

'Who are you Hilde?'

'I am power incarnated into Luce's body, day and night, I am the eternal alive, the absence of crying, the ancient heart of Mu throbbing through the fibre of being. I am the visceral result of the Mothers, the endless freedom of infinite possible worlds, the eternal doubt, the rigid hesitation that breaks the veils of the world.'

It can be heard very loud a baby cry. Luce was reborn alive. The ancient heart of Mu now is in her chest and is beating furiously, like a horse at a gallop.

Corax gives up the stone seat, he leaves Hilde's house, going through the live plants garden and going back home whilst the Mothers' voice is still whispering through Mu's streets. And whisper after whisper the Great Mothers make blowing up the sickle of the moon which disappears towards Mu appearing to the Upper World.

The crying of new born Luce let Mu citizens out of their houses. They are just going through the greenish paths of Mu. They are happy and loud. The heart of the Underground Earth will pulsate for other 606 years more. Mu is safe now. Destiny has been done. The hopes have been realized as expected. Although there is still something strange in the air, like an out of tune note, a feeling of not-happiness.

Iris, Corax's first daughter, is 6 years old. She knows how to read the future with her double pupil and she can see things that others cannot. She stares at the greenish air as she feels scared. She puts her hand on her new-born sister chest, closing her eyes and feeling her sister's heart beating under her own palms. The beat is strong, like a lightweight punch, but irregular, disordered. Luce will draw new ways for Mu. She will create new adventurous world, climbing over the night. She will go through the Unknowable Beyond. She will pass the imposed limit to the ones born with the mark. She will be braver than the tradition would allow to her. Iris knows it. Into Luce's heart Iris feels the apprehension of who dares to destroy. She takes her hand off Luce's chest, shivering. She does not say anything to anyone.

Mu, the eternal

Mu is a huge land, full of tunnels, stable temperature, with big and really busy cities full of night life. The capital city is *Dailorg*. Mu citizens are pale, smart and gorgeous. Mu's tunnels are very high, similar to long and huge caves that likely cross each other. They could be travelled on foot or with particular shuttles similar to isosceles triangles, with their tips ploughing through the air forward, aerodynamic. If someone walks through there, a soft ground made from really white dust can be touched, similar to talcum powder, which sometimes has pink tones. Traditions say that the white ground comes from the Great Mothers' breath. Mu's ground smells of milk and a walk is really pleasant. If somebody is in a rush or maybe there are long distances to cover, a shuttle can be used, a silent triangle, capable to fit up to 9 Mu's passengers. The shuttle fluctuates in silence and metallic through the soft and windless air of Mu. There are few of them at Mu, available for anyone wants to use them. They are really cosy and spacious inside. Soft, black velvet seats. In the newest models there is a hall where some music can be listened whilst travelling.

Travelling without any shuttle is really hard because Mu is a really huge planet. Each city is divided in zones.

In each city there is a main zone, the Omega. Generally there are some white houses with some black and clean roofs. Entering into some houses, there is a feeling of going back into the past. Shiny, ancient walnut furniture, windows with coloured glasses reproducing scenes about Mu's traditional story. Mu citizens love the warmth of the wood

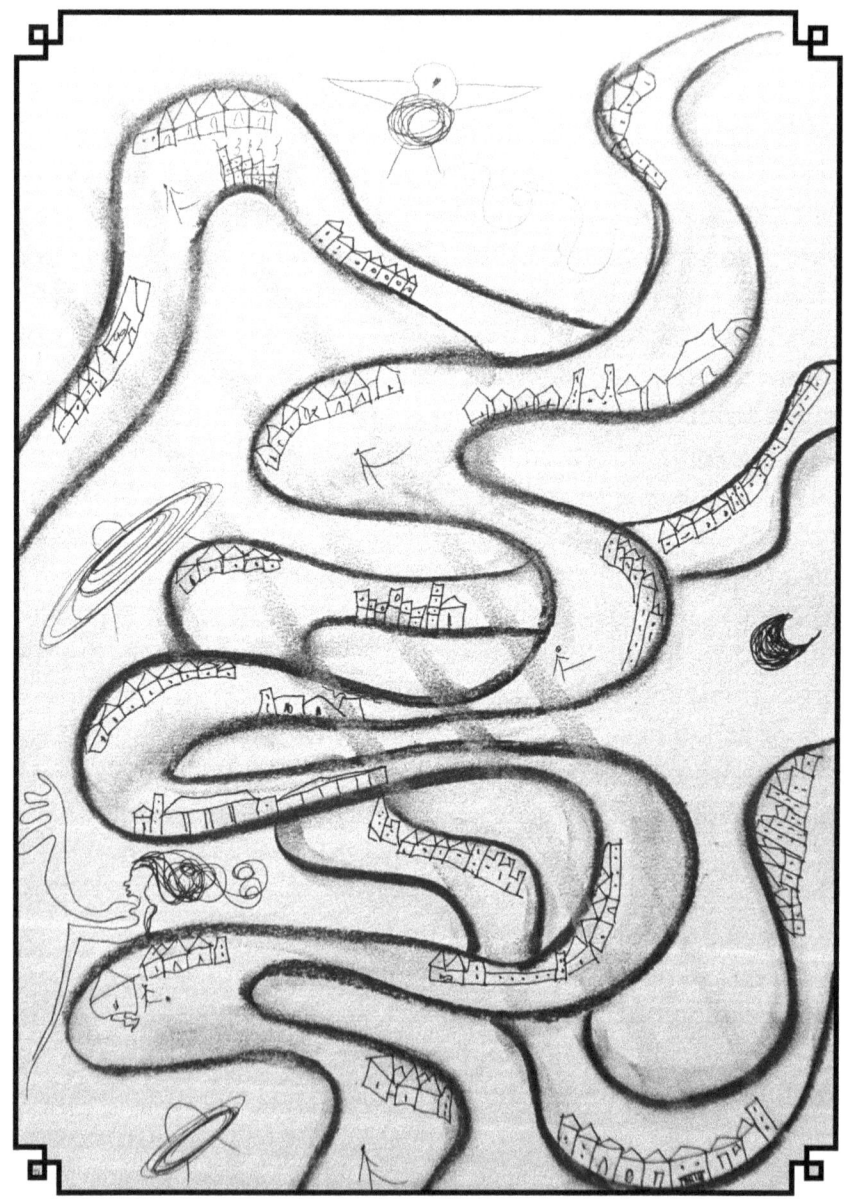

and they hate plastic, even if they are IT innovative. Mu is ruled by the self-regulation principle. Each Mu citizen knows his own actions against others turn back again. Mu people have a very strong group identity. But they are not generous naturally, they are not selfish for necessity. It is the right Mothers Law oppressing their consciences. Who kills his people will lose centuries of life because the Mu person killed absorbs the energy from his killer, transforming him into an hideous creature which will lose also the freedom too, the most important thing for Mu's. So, before someone innocent could be even touched, Mu citizens reflect over life and death evaluating pro and cons. The corrupting money which is so important for the Upper World doesn't exist at all at Mu. So there are no banks at all. A soft and fertile ground produces good and nourishing fruit enough for everybody. The stable and warm weather allows people to wear lightweight and strong clothes. Mu people breed rhino-grades, a kind of mammal unknown into the Upper World. Really appreciated by gourmands is the *Nasobema lyricum's* meat which has a lot of noses that uses for moving around. Its long tail is capable to grab food really distant from the animal body. The *Jumping-Noses*, that instead use their huge nose to hunt, to jump and to capture their preys, are appreciated as pets. They are friendly and nice and they take to their owners quite a lot, giving everything to him, even life if necessary. They have a really smart sense of smell, they are able to smell the small crustaceans hiding underneath the sand at Mu's beaches.

Mu people like animals and they don't rush to accumulate goods because they are immortal. The physical maturation of their bodies stops when they are around 25 years old. After that age they don't grow anymore older. Only a traumatic event or maybe a violent action could cause their death.

Birth and death at Mu are really rare events. Mu people can spend half of their day into zone Alpha. There they could collect the fruits of the ground which grow up naturally in big quantities. In the zone Beta there is plenty of flax and cotton plants enough to make all the dresses a Mu person would like to. The zone Gamma is helpful to the soul pleasures, the arts and the music. There are enormous libraries full of rare and precious books. Public art galleries full of paintings and sculptures. Concerts halls open to everyone, which music fills people heart with wonder and ecstatic astonishment. The goods are for everyone, so whoever would like to steal something it would have been something stolen to himself, definitely not worthy.

There are no alarm systems, not even keys and locks. People don't need them. The power of the Mothers is so big to avoid any crime. It has been said that they live upon the mouth of the night. Although no Mu people, except the Star before dying and melting into their pathway, can touch and see them. Luce, Black Star of Mu after Hilde, is made of the same qualitative substance of the Mothers and after 606 years it will become dust over their pathway feeding the power and the life of Mu. Nobody knows exactly if the Mothers were the souls of the whole Black Stars of Mu. Luce represents eyes and the ruthless hand of the justice. The Black Star lives beyond the feelings and can access to the forbidden zones to the common Mu people. This because she was born with the mark and her body contains the big ancient heart of Mu. There is someone who says that her heart is made from iron, others say that is made from steel. Really nobody is sure about its material, maybe made of the tears and the breath of the Mothers, an unknown substance, alchemical and mysterious, but so powerful to be able to lead a race.

Luce, whilst growing up, has learned to know. Great thing learning to know. The knowledge of the Beyond, the skill to understand what is behind the veil of the appearance has a cost. Luce is on her own. The perfect Star, which could have influenced the thunders and the music of the Upper World's clouds, which closes her eyes and dreams about swirling parallel universes, she should feel only the sense of her own duty towards Mu people. Luce shouldn't have heart really, not even feelings. Mothers' voice not even taught her how to make the rain and the hail coming down into the Upper World, it has inoculated to her kind of insensitivity. But something has gone wrong during her second birth. Luce's skin feels things and it could shiver too, her heart fears and her body and mind have their doubts over life. Hilde probably, before becoming dust has been doubting and something of her is kept inside Luce, a black dot, a stain in her heart, into the perfect mechanism turning which every 606 years will be reborn.

Luce when she was 15 years old has completed her education. She knows why the fruits of the land grow up naturally. She can go beyond what can be seen. She can see what is underneath the roots of the plants, she knows what feeds them, although at Mu doesn't rain. She has learned slowly and step by step every single thing. The ancient heart of Mu should be stronger than her, ruling over her, making her impassive and unbiased. That heart beat has to lead over the rhythm of her long life, the dance to follow, precisely, without any kind of rebellions. That's the way she has been taught. She nods, although she knows that something happened. She looks at her sister Iris into her eyes and smiles. Iris holds her hand.

Both know that her heart has lost the control for a moment and Luce in that moment has shivered. For one second she has been pushed over the Unknowable Beyond, the forbidden.

THE HOUSE

When Luce was 15 years old, she left her parents house to go to live at Hilde's, which house belonged to the previous Black Star, back to her descendants, since to get to the first Black Star which has not been left any memory at all.

The house is deep in the silence, quiet, it looks sleeping, resting like a tired body. The black and white blades of grass into the garden are slightly warped out, gloomy. The living plants look dead. When Luce goes through the wooden gate, everything is changing. Plants get back to life again suddenly , blades of grass come back straight on their own, some smart open eyes just observing the new Star. Luce goes into the house. Into the room Hilde's bed is untouched. She lifts the heavy curtains to let some greenish Mu's air get through. In the dining room a huge ebony table is full of carved figures and inside the impressive fireplace are on display two cast iron majestic andirons.

Solid furniture made of strong wood is there to last long. The house is pretty, really cozy and friendly.

There is a small laboratory too, through a trapdoor. Luce lifts hardly the lid pulling a very heavy bronze ring. The hatch open leads to a room full of different scents. There is in the middle of the room a big incense burner from where a big cloud of smoke comes through, in the right corner a huge fireplace with the cowl held by two columns: experience and intellect. A table opposite the fireplace is full of musical instruments because life is harmony, like Mu's tradition says, the mouth plays parables. On the walls there are ancient prints and on the left an alchemical oven, a still sitting upon the oven with a snake inside, half white and

half black, perfection and imperfection which are going together through the matter.

Luce would ask her sorceress friend Niobe for a tip about how to use the laboratory. She will definitely give her some precious suggestions.

At one point the Star sees on the floor some dried bread waste and a water bowl into a corner. A sneeze. Someone or something sneezed out. Here again. From that dark corner, there is someone hiding which has a cold. Luce gets closer to the corner trying to look through the darkness density. Then she spots a strange creature. She takes a piece of bread and she put it next to the shade. A paw comes out from the dark grabbing the bread up.

'Little one, come here!'

It is a Jumping-Nose left in that room.

'You are hungry, gorgeous, come here! You must be Puck, Hilde's Jumping-Nose.' From her bag Luce takes an apple out and she offers it to the animal which grabs it with its three-fingers paw. It swallows it, chewing it, and then it spits the core and seeds out on the floor. Then it collects them and then it holds on there.

'What are you doing here? Haven't you got your kennel into the garden?'

The creature comes out the darkness and it starts smelling Luce's dress, still with its paws dirty from the apple waste. The Jumping-Nose jumps backwards towards a bin and it throws the apple waste in there. Luce laughs.

'Little one well done!'

The creature is black and white and it has big sharp eyes and huge ears similar to a bat. Instead of the back paws it has got a long tail which makes it well balanced, as it uses only a huge nose to stand and to jump backwards.

'It's weird, you shouldn't be here. This is the laboratory beyond the trapdoor where it has been said that the Black Star's travel would have started from every 606 years. Puck, come here.'

Puck, shy, gets closer. It emits a light hiss, but prolonged, full of positive vibrations. It licks Luce's hand. Its tongue is small and rough, like the cats one. Similar to the feline is its body size and its eyes which can see through the darkness at night.

Puck knows the dark and the light so it has been like burnt by them. On its paw there is a strange star-shaped scar. Luce has seen it one day that she was walking on the beach, whilst Puck was digging out with its paws underneath the stones to look for small molluscs good to eat for itself. That scar is really similar to the one which she has got on her palm.

Luce strokes its head, like humans do with their dogs, then she takes it upstairs. Puck is a rebel, it doesn't like its kennel into the garden, it prefers the soft white mat into the bedroom. During the night, then, while Luce is sleeping, a jump, and it comes to the bed or over the pillow, close to Luce's head, lightly and sensibly, agile and it purrs like a cat.

When it is nervous it is continuously hissing from a kind of hiccup and it moves its tail spasmodically.

They knock at the door. Here we go, now Puck is nervous.

Who could be at this time? It's 4:00 in the morning. Luce wakes up, lazy. She opens the door. She is not scared. Nobody would dare to touch the Black Star. Mu would be devastated.

A shapeless creature asks to get in. It has the skin as

sandpaper, the hunchback and two thin arms which come from its huge trunk in where is possible to see its ribs. Its curved and yellowish legs complete the framework.

'Is the only time when would you kill people?'
'Sorry, Luce. I need to go into the Radicale.'
'I can see it. You look definitely tired.'
'Let's go together! Before Mu people wake up, before they would see me in this way.'
'Would you have thought about it before, would you?
'It has been an instinctive reaction, a brawl.'
'A brawl? For what?'
'Take me to the Radicale, please.'
'For what?'
'For what for?'
'The brawl, idiot, is there any reason?
'A lady from Mu.'
'What is your name?'
'Thomas.'
'This lady from Mu must have been gorgeous to force yourself going this way.'

'I was not involved in this, I have never seen her before. She has been the cause. She was staying with her friend. As soon as she has seen me, she pointed out myself with her finger, I don't know for which reason. She whispered something into her boyfriend's ear, his name is Chemako, if I am not wrong. He went just over me very hungry. I had to kill him for self-defence. Its blood dried out all my beauty and energies.'

'And the Mu lady?'
'I don't know, I haven't seen her anymore. She was tall and very blonde, with some blue reflections on her hair and green eyes, but I don't know who she is.'

'Let's go!'

Luce walks into the windless space, pushing strongly her feet on the floor, one, two, three, eight. Puck follows her sniffing the air and he enjoys hissing. Thomas just follows Puck out of breath. At the ninth step the ground breaks showing a really thin white dust. Luce is like sucked in and suddenly she falls underneath the ground of Mu next to the ancient roots of plants and herbs which Mu people eat since various past generations.

In theory, only the Black Star and the guilty ones can go up there, although Puck is with her. Even himself it has been touched mysteriously by the mark. He smells with his big nose the roots of the plants. Big muddles draw intricate and creative wefts where some misshapen tearing creatures are hiding underneath. They are perennially bowed down among the arches of the muddled roots, they have humpbacks and heads recessed in awful and grimy bodies. From Mu is only left the face, with big and shiny eyes because of the continuous crying, whispered, stimulated by the thorns of the roots that sting the skin, fiercely.

Thomas greets Luce and then he joins them.

The eternal tears of those assassins feed the strong roots so Mu would have its nourishment into the mutual garden of plants and fruits. And they are Mu people tears condemned to cry because they made crimes. Their only meal is a piece of root really bitter. They have no toilets and no beds. Restless bodies forced to move through the only space left between each root. Their excrements fertilize the ground. No chains, no bars. Mu doesn't have prisons, it's not necessary. The penalty for those who break the Mothers Law is the crying into something called Radicale. So the evil doesn't get wasted, but used as nourishment for the good. The Radicale does have no start and no end, no doors, no windows, no sky. It is a no-place, an absurdity because there is nothing more true and terrible than something absurd.

There are no courts of justice at Mu, no lawyers, not even long and expensive trials. Thieves do not exist, simply because they would steal from themselves. Every good is for everyone and stealing doesn't make sense. Anyway whoever makes any crime will become awful and misshapen, and his deformity is more according to the seriousness of the crime. A guilty killer becomes awful, after the killed one has absorbed all the killer's positive energies. So the assassin, feeling shame, knocks to Luce's door and he ask her for the travel together. Luce invites him to follow her and she brings him through the dark zone. Nobody knows how to get there; nobody can escape from there too. Only the Black Star can enter and exit from that no-world, the bottom of the bottom, the dark Radicale.

By virtue of the Mothers' power the land of Mu does not know the burden of rigid chains, not laces or keys that lock the bars. It's said that the Mothers go everywhere and they know everything. Power and knowledge, entangled twine.

Nevertheless Luce when born had felt an anxiety towards the unknown, a desire to know forbidden things.

So now, that she is 15 years old, she keeps asking herself questions. If Thomas would be right? If he would have been involved with no guilt? Maybe the system is not perfect. The power of the Mothers should know it. Questions, always questions. Those are part of her flesh, of her Mu's blood, of her womb. Answers. Here it is what Luce needs, answers.

Mu has huge libraries full of books of every kind, kingdom of silverfishes, dust and words. The admission to the main libraries is free for everyone, no controls. Maybe in the library there are some answers.

Luce meditates often about life and death; she would like to know more. After she has been into the dark Radicale she often goes to the library. Subconsciously she links the two worlds and reflects on them. Maybe in the library there is a book about the power of the darkness, about the reason why Mu people are like that and they cannot touch other worlds. Maybe about why she felt torment for Thomas and she instinctively believed to his words, to his sight that seems genuine.

DAILORG LIBRARY

The biggest library in Mu is in the capital *Dairlog*. The building is huge, spiral shaped, shelves full of books bending through an incredible spiral structure with huge steps that go down to abyss of sciences. Slowly going downstairs you would find the rarest and most ancient books, *dulcis in fundo*.

The greenish air at Mu looks watering down through an ochre yellowish really sweet upon the light of big Liberty lamps, really art masterpieces. There is silence and peace. Luce loves to go down to the end, in the last room and then touching the slightly cracked backs of the old yellowed books and sitting and thinking.

She looks something in those ancient pages, a sign that will remind to her own early torment. She browses and searches, browsing and reading, consulting. Hours spent in the library. Live hours when books speak their own special language.

Her agile fingers turning pages which are full of free words. The index stops with a sentence *the knowledge is a weapon of power, it is useful to control, to influence the social consciousness...bio-power, politics, Government, civilization, servants...rebels*. Mu does not have any kings or queens, no parliament, no laws. No Government. Total anarchy. There are the Great Mothers... Luce is puzzled. Why does not the Great Mothers' power reach the other Worlds? For example the Upper World... Do the Mothers have a real power there? Maybe are they only a symbol? Basically at Mu there is no official power. Luce knows that she is going too far and those books wouldn't answer to

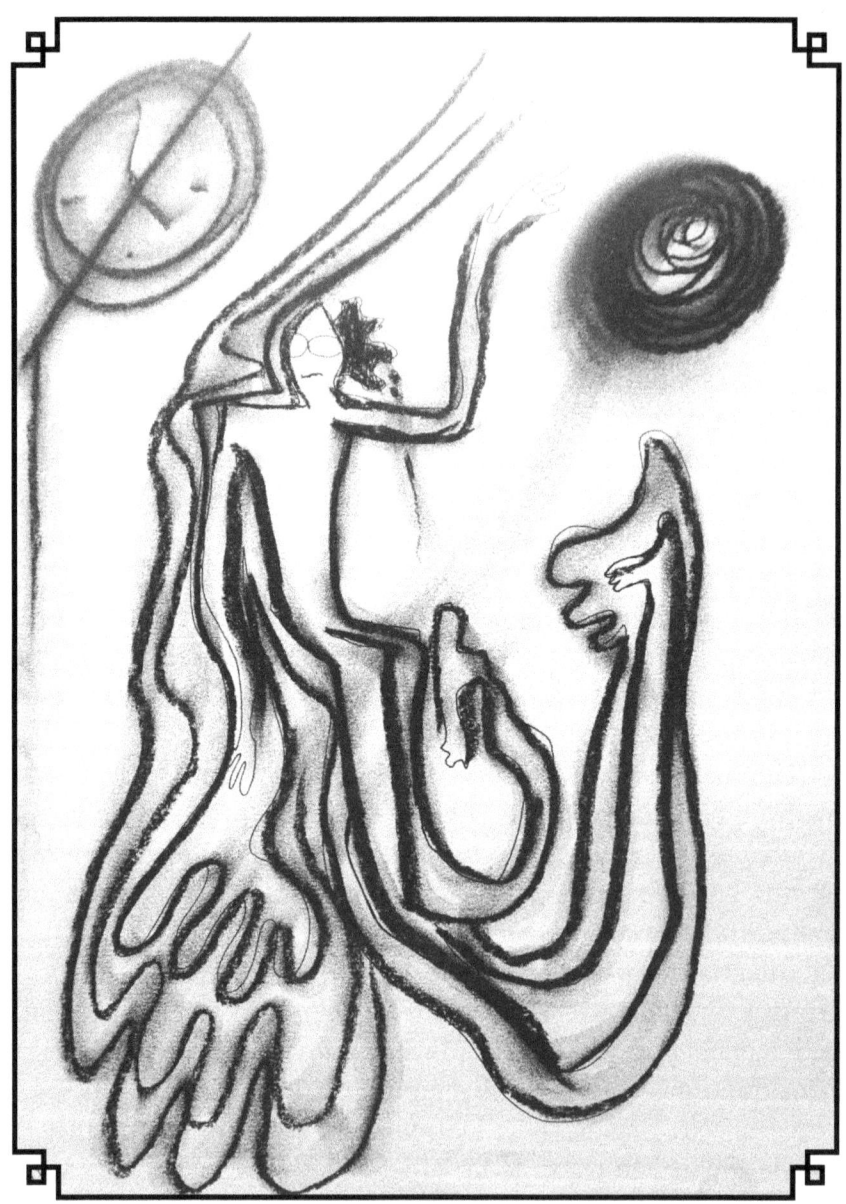

her intrusive questions. Nobody has ever thought to investigate over the Mothers' essence. Nobody knows why they exist and how they were born and which substances they are made from. No books say that, it is useless browsing volumes over volumes, pointless investigation, disappointing too. Not everything is on the books. Maybe someone intellectual knows a bit more. It needs to investigate about this matter.

Luce stands up. In the last room of the library there is a wooden and metal door, impressive. A woman figure carved on the door is divided in two parts when a visitor opens the door. Once the door is open, firstly there is darkness then a feeble light enlightens three steps going downstairs. It needs to be careful not to slip over. Few metres along a bright corridor which is enlightened from the top. There is no ceiling indeed, looking up the sky and lightly clouds around can be seen. Left and right, whilst Luce walks around, marble statues, wisely carved, bi-facial figures with long and meticulous hair, goddesses that let fly arrows, inebriated Maenads with one head in their hands, ancient utopian mirrors with golden wood frames and filled up with moving figures, fluctuating around. There is no point trying to look in the mirror. Any reflected image through the mirror is not matching, it is someone else's image which is unknown. Mu people say that the mirror doesn't reflect the shapes but the thoughts about someone would wish to be. Only the Black Star of Mu, being perfect, should reflect herself as she is, exactly the same, but Luce doesn't actually. The mirror reflects one image which is not her real shape, surprisingly masculine. She looks at the mirror and what she sees in there is a man. She goes over, those lucid surfaces make her nervous. She feels a bothering anxiety inside herself. At the end of the corridor three more steps and finally she can access to the zone where all the brains are sleeping, because of Mothers' willing they are stored there to be preserved from the putrefaction. A long multitude of white brains comes out from the bottom of a salt lake, bodies are under the water, resting, quietly and nicely. They are thinking and sleeping. All around them mountains with trees which have magnetic eyes and gnarled trunks like knuckles ready to punch. On the top still no ceiling, but glasses with a toothed crescent moon painted over, bitter laugh into a greenish sky. The white brains have blue and reddish veining, and they breath like living creatures inside open skulls with no skull cap. Luce is inquiring, she walks around the sleeping lake. She points out her finger towards the painted moon which enlightens the lake through a fierce light.

'Hey, you!'

The brains shake by her voice and through the sharp rays of the painted moon. Once they have been humans and they used to live in the Upper World and they used to eat, to breath, to love, long time ago. The Great Mothers, after those brains death, have chosen them to answer to the Mu people's doubts which can question them about everything. They answer in turn. Each brain questioned expresses his free thought. When alive, they used to believe about the existence of Parallel Worlds. They have a superior intelligence and foresight, those brains never ruled out the possibility of other worlds' existence. That is the reason why the Great Mothers have given them the chance of the immortality. Their eyes are closed because their vision about the words is not affected by the sight, their bodies are unarmed because they don't need to touch to believe or to move for travelling. They travel sidereal distances only with their thoughts. Theoretically it should be like that, although practically lot of Mu people got a bit puzzled by their answers.

'Hey, you! Yes, I am talking to you! I have doubts, puzzlement, maybe you can help me, there are some things not written in books, missing things, something which I don't understand.' Luce has a pleasant, young and silvery voice.

Brains are moving from the left to the right.

'Who does know about the life and death's theorem? Words as *power* and *knowledge*? And I read about the story of the Upper World's men, but I did not get quite everything, some things are strange, mechanism of which their nuts and bolts are hidden, massacres, killings, wars, absurdity.'

The answer is not late to come from a brain with big reddish veining. It moves like a living thing, its face comes out the water. Its mouth is a hole where sounds and words come out. 'Maybe I can help you,' its voice is clear, loud.

'Who were you?' The inquiring tone of Luce's voice is all around the air.

'I was almost God and I used to have power.'

'Man or woman please reveal yourself.'

The skull lifts up as an open shell even more with its talking content. It lifts up until a woman body shows. It goes towards Luce, where the water is lower. It wears a white coat crusted with ground, roots and salt. Its eyes could not open, they are sealed. Its body is pale, but its brain inside the open shell of the skull is living and it looks palpitating.

'I was a woman, I used to have power to save lives. A surgeon. My hand over their wounds, taking decisions, taking decisions in few seconds, lethal moments. I used to be God.'

'God does not exist,' another brain just comes out from the water. Its masculine body is almost naked. Only its hips are wearing a white cloth.

'God was my heart and my hand and my eye and He was leading over me sometimes leaving me disappointed. Moments, people lives were in my actions. When someone died under my eyes I used to die a little bit as well, every day, slowly. Taking decisions is draining, having power is wearying, a self-destruction,' the woman says.

'Power? Which power?' The naked body has a strong and warm voice.

'The power to save them!'

'Illusions of the Upper World, deceptions. No one dies for no one, no one lives for no one, it is the cruel rule, bestial and unvaried of every known world. Power is a really wished elixir, and it's not all about taking hard decisions, but to make the others being subjected to them, and it satisfies whoever has got it, like the blood feeds a vampire, like the flesh feeds the wild beast and the animal feeds the parasite.'

'No, no, you are wrong, you rant and rave! I was wore up, although I still had power of life and death, I was giving orders to the others, I used to cut, to operate, with my hands, I used to take decisions in behalf of the patient, I was deciding for him, I was him.'

'You were nothing. A woman with a role. You were only following the law, you were doing your duties. Between duties and powers there are shades of meaning. You got carried away with your things until you got confused the life with a surgery room, till the extreme act to practice the power of the scalpel on yourself. You don't know the true power, no. It has eaten you like the worm does to the apple, infecting yourself too.'

'You are crazy! You don't know what you are talking about! Try to see everyday wound people after a crash, try to touch the blood still warm and the viscera and the beating heart... I was tidying up, opening, closing down, it was me... if you were wounded, would you like to have someone taking decisions for you?'

The naked brain now is silent, it looks suffering.

The other urges, fiercely. 'You don't answer, why? Answer me!'

Silence.

'You never say anything, no answers, never, there is a beginning of rebellion in yourself, a labyrinth, a super-human cosmic empty space, a refusal of the facts, an absurd willing to do.'

Luce just says, 'It is more than enough. Leave it alone. The emptiness is the precursor of being, it is the pure space for the creation, it is the white page. Please retreat, I do not need you. The power is weapon that it can be handled, it is not an alter ego, a friend that can be referred until death, not an exhausting love, destructive. Who leads over the power usually keeps the right distance, it cannot be so worn out. I need a brain which has eaten the power and it is satisfied now, enjoying it, which knows its small secrets. Maybe the half naked brain knows more than what it said.'

'No, I know nothing, we know nothing really. Although I knew the power. Nobody would be able to manage it, the power leads over every game. It is a demon, the smartest and fiercest. Water flows under bridges and wears the mountains out, the rain digs the soil, rivers dry, men become white skeletons stripped from their flesh and veins, but the power does not change the essence, its own evil substance. The power is a demon which takes possession of bodies. Those bodies deceive themselves thinking to lead over the power, to decide over everything, but they are nothing, only pawns over a chess board. When a man dies, the power becomes other human flesh, after a generation, a party or a group dies, the power personifies into other groups, other generations, other parties. Power is immortal because it feeds through us, through our flesh. Nobody has really this power, because the demon uses and then throws away bodies and destiny. Centuries ago, I felt strongly its bite, the 15th December 1969 according to the humans' calendar. Long time ago. Defenestrated. What a curious destiny. You know, Luce, if it were a shape, the power should have been a dusty corner, dust over dust, enduring. It cannot be cleaned, it's really hidden through that corner, concealed filth, plots and conspiracies, puppeteers, dust, dust. Impossible to remove it. Faces over faces. Devil takes on human form continuously, but never it shows its real face, because it doesn't have one really. And whoever has power makes confusion this devil with a god and it will be ending up with a fanatic illusion. The power is a cancerous corner, thousand corners, a billion of corners, trillions and trillions of dusty and dark, sticky and jumbled corners. The devil has its own emissaries, specks of dust spread all over the world to diffuse terror. Crazy cells, sharp splinters. A man could know a corner and ignore the other ones. We are zero. The only thing that is important is the freedom, running naked and purified from the horrific grip of the power, escaping unarmed, innocently, idealistically and pure-hearted. And if guilty and corrupted hands would throw us through the window of the time depicting us like crazy suicide victims, it does not really matter, because what is important is the message, the priceless freedom that we have affirmed against the corrupting dark power and we won't die like the others, because we are free. I died as a man with no chains because of the power, not for the power, there is a lot of difference. And I never deluded myself to be God.'

Luce looks at him sadly. 'Naked, what is your name?'
'Do names and labels really matter for you? I was a distracted one, died because of distraction and I spitted into the fierce eye of the power thinking about it could have been a safe escape from. I was definitely wrong... Nobody could do this and then muddling through the ordinary life, no one. Look at me, Luce.' Nudo lifts up his eyelids. 'Did you see it? I can open my eyes despite the other brains, I am the only one who can do it because I have always watched things beyond the reality, a Stateless world, the world of Mu.'

Luce is 15 years old and she doesn't understand very well things. She enquires.

'The Great Mothers can do everything, though.'

Nudo laughs. 'I see, did you ever see them?'

'No, never, nobody could see them, although their voices could be heard at nights over the pearly pathway, strong, persistent, like a sirens' chant.'

'Who told you that those are the Mothers' voices?'

'Legends say that, everybody says it.'

'Everybody who?'

'Mu people, all Mu people.'

'How do Mu people know about it then?'

'It is what it is, traditionally.'

'Why? Who decided it and when?'

'I don't know it. Books don't say about it. Something is missing, although I read a lot. I go to the library everyday. I would like to know more things which I don't know, but the Mothers say that is not good, that is better some things being kept secret.'

'The Mothers?'

'Yes, when I start walking over through the pathway they say to me that is not good looking forward to know

about too much.'
'Do you know where do those voices come from?'
'No, I do not.'
'Maybe are they moving around like snakes looking for their shelters or maybe do they come from outside yourself and you do not realise it?'
'What do you mean? From myself?'
'Yes, from inside yourself. I am tired, Luce, I ask for a permission to rest please.'
'No, please. Nudo please wait!'
'I am really tired, we will talk another time. Please remember that it is very good doubting even about oneself. Everything could be under the eye of doubts, even the plastic myths.'
'But there is no doubt about the Mothers!'
'Really?' Nudo laughs just before closing its eyes. It dips into the water again leaving out only its brain.

Luce now is more doubting than before. That Nudo is maybe crazy, an odd brain, being there for a strange reason. She thinks over and over it whilst she goes away from the library walking toward her house.

It's night time now, the greenish sky becomes darker, as proof that is bed time now. Luce is not sleepy. *Doubting about the Mothers... The ancient voices of Mu... The beginning and the end... It is like denying that something exists in the world... Doubts over the pure essence of Mu...*

The bedroom that Luce shares with her sister is comfortable. The house is silent, not even a ticking clock. At Mu there are no clocks, not even alarm clocks. They are useless. The sweet voice of the Mothers which vibrates in the empty of morning creates melodies that reawaken calmed senses, pure archaic deep sounds of abyss and bright skies. The Mothers... The Black Star takes her shoes off and tip-toeing she enters into the bedroom. Iris that came along with her at Hilde's house, sleeps, a light sleep, a feather light breathing. She has thin hands over the blankets, unarmed, red cheeks, thin closed eyelids. Iris is blind, but she feels things that the others cannot see. She opens the double eyelid over Luce. 'You are back, it is late.'

'I am sorry to wake you up.'

'I was not sleeping even.'

'I spoke with a kind of brain in the library and I was a bit puzzled. Have you ever seen the Mothers?'

'Nobody has ever seen them.'

'So how do you know they exist then?'

'I don't even see you, although I think you exist.'

'You think that I exist, that is the point.'

'Which point sorry?'

'The existence is only a thought. Something is like it is just because we think that is like it is, tall, short, thin, pretty or ugly, although is not guaranteed that is really like this.'

'Indeed, nobody can say that. We know nothing really.'

'Strange.'

'Strange what?'

'Nudo's same words, *we know nothing about it*. What if I would like to know more about it?'

'Luce go to sleep please, it's better.'

'Sleeping? Don't you think you are wasting your time sleeping rather there are so many things to know about?'

'You have to follow only the Mothers' voices, nothing else matters.'

'I think you are not even sure about it.'

'Yes, of course. I think so. It could be dangerous snooping through the darkness. The dark is a sticky magma. It just sticks on your soul trying to investigate it. What is the point then? Are you not happy? You live in a country with no war, no banks, no hanger and no thirst, no avidity, no parliament, not ever king and queens or corrupted princes. No monarchy, not even sick democracies. There are no lords not even servants, no awful palpitation wake up, no shrewd ones. Assassins are kind of idiots that have been put into the Radicale. There is no money. There are no door locks, not even padlocks because Mu people know to have everything and nothing. This bed, this house, those paintings, the books, we will not take anything with us whether we will get sick and the Mothers' voice should call us to feed the dead ones. And then the life, with no accidents, is so long that we can give ourselves the luxury to live in peace of mind.'

'We are almost immortal, sorry, you are, because I will only live 606 years, then who knows?'

'Then your flesh will melt like dust into the pearly pathway of the Mothers and your voice will join theirs. You will live for ever, Luce, you are the Black Star of Mu. The ancient heart of our land beats in our chest.'

'Yes, they say so. We don't know anything, that is the only thing I know.'

Luce couldn't sleep that night. Too many concerns. Good thing that there are no schools at Mu with rigid timetable to follow, otherwise Luce would have been late to any lesson that morning. Mu people anyway don't know what is a lesson in the human sense of the word. Nobody has to go to school. Although everybody can read and write, they know what is the planets movement, they admire the art masterpieces and they have an eye for arts, they know lot about life as well. All that because of the huge library which is not an ordinary place but it is the heart of the town. They teach literature, writing, arts, philosophy, history into the various classrooms. It is located in Dairlog city centre, it is like a spiral full of books over different floors. Each floor has different rooms. From the top to the bottom, first, second, third floor and so on, lessons taught are more complex, different levels that Mu people can attend at their pleasure according their skills, the age and the preparation. There are lessons at any time before midnight. The library is never closed. Moreover from the bottom centre of the building there are some tunnels which go towards the other towns of Mu like rays. Those tunnels can be travelled on foot or on board of some shuttles which can be parked easily outside the library. Everyone can access the library, with no restrictions or cards. Billions of books and prints, sculptures and art masterpieces. Nine hundreds rooms available for everyone where all the knowledge of Mu is kept.

Luce loves the Planetarium Hall. Enormous. A big glass dome on the top shows stars and planets. The ebony wooded walls full of books and ancient volumes seem to whisper old legends. And if there is a perfect silence, sitting on a stool in the centre of the room, a warm and smooth light will spread over. Looking at the top, towards the glass transparent dome, it can be heard noise of the planets. Arcane and very deep sound of acoustic vibrations perceptible by hearing, deep and modulated harmony which seems to come from an unknowable abyss. A poem which makes vibrating the empty giving it a lot of inexpressible meaning. The sound is similar to a god's voice that opens his mouth and creates worlds, shouting and creating and making to shiver the foolish inconsistency of the Nothing.

Luce spends hours listening. And, if the hall is empty, even better. One could concentrate better, one could think easier. It's not about Mu people being loud, but the empty loneliness welcomes parallel worlds and it makes them vibrating upon the far beaches of doubts.

Questions arise. Library could only answer to some of those questions. There is the Art Room where it is showing sculptures and paintings and stunning antique prints and books explaining the styles, techniques, the colours... Although there is always something that has been missed. Not even into the Brains Hall everything can be sorted out. Instead, doubts are increasing while there is an investigation, new connections are discovered. The mat hides the dust, but the dust was never born on its own, someone created it spreading it even in the spots with no easy access. There is a dark bottom. Nudo doubting about the Mothers, not possible! Who is Luce then? Who is anyone? Doubts, power, darkness, confusion.

'You are again here, indeed.' Nudo looks amused.
'Yes, I am back again.'
'What do you know about Mu and the world and...'
'Nothing, I told you. Nudo knows nothing.'
'How did you dare to doubt about the Mothers?'
'It has been said...'
'I can feel them as I can feel the planets movement into the Planetarium Hall.'
'I do believe it.'
'Can you hear the Mothers' voice?'
'Sometimes. At night I can hear some lonely and sweet whispers.'
'The Mothers.'
'I wouldn't know...giving a name to your feelings is hard.'
'Do you know the story of Mu created by the voice of the Mothers after the Androgynous Chaos had allocated the worlds?'
'Yes, somebody told me this story, I know it.'
'Although you still don't believe it.'

'No, sorry.'
'Is there anything you believe?'
'I believe about everything and nothing.'
'What does it mean?'
'It means that what I believe for it doesn't count then.'
'I don't get this point, sorry.'
'I believe about you, I can see you and talk to you. Are we chatting, aren't we?'
'Yes, of course, Nudo, let's talk.'
'But is it really this way?'
'Of course!'
'No, there is nothing sure. Who is giving you the calm certainty of our real existence?'
'What kind of question is this?'
'Who is saying that we are existing?'
'Well, I can hear and see you.'
'You can see and feel a dream too.'
'Although who does tell you we don't exist, that there are no other worlds beneath us, more skies over the World of the humans, upper or lower or maybe on the right or on the left, parallel, hidden, not recognized by us?'
'But this is a universal doubt!'
'Yes, a universal doubt. The doubt is the dangerous salt.'
'Nudo, I pinch myself and it hurts, which means I exist in the world.'
'If you pinch yourself, I don't feel pain, your feeling is not connected to mine, it's on its own, like a castaway lost into the immensity of the ocean.'
'Even a drop is a proof of the existence of the sea.'
'What if even the drop is purely an illusion? If we were a dream? Only a utopia? A strange tale?'
'It's sad, I would say.'
'It could be a possibility.'

'It's not impossible. Nothing could really exist.'
'Or maybe everything.'
'Yes, nothing or everything.'
'Especially Mu, an ideal world, unreal, self-determined and free. The world that does not exist or maybe the only one possible to exist.'
'How can we discern the true against the false, the real from the unreal?'
'I think it is not possible.'
'There must be a way, a solution.'
'Conglomeration of eternal insolvencies. I don't know solutions, truly because of your physical and moral position you can see things differently, illusions indeed, words. Ah, can you see that brain over there?'
'Yes, who is it?'
'It is the only man-woman which has challenged the deceiver illusion of the words and now it doesn't know whether having jumped into O of doubt what is living now is still illusion. Stand up. Adamo!'

Adamo wakes up. 'Only words!' His emaciated body lifts up from the water and starts to talk. His voice resounds. 'Nudo is right. In my life I was a woman with a male body, an ordinary creature and I have been slave and victim of the words, of the definitions. I would like to tell you a story, whether there is enough time.'

Nudo laughs, 'Time doesn't count, it is a watching boor. Who cares about the time? Soft clock, useless popular whore. Are not we so brave and strong to challenge it, me and you? To tear its hair off to make it callow. The time, pffh! Mu's library doesn't have opening times, it is never closed, because time is zero for who lives forever.'

'I was not human in my terrestrial life, through a primitive status of being, not integrated, not done, like a set of shoes with no laces, a cream-less cake. A shameful limbo, not soup nor roast. As it was said. Whispers, bad words, hypocrisy, fake righteousness. What was I doing? Where was I going to? Really ridiculous. During the family meetings a fish out of water, in the world like a homeless turtle. Uncles, aunties, fathers and mothers, sisters and brothers, strangers were talking each others, greeting up with kisses, leaving lipstick signs and saliva on my well shaved cheeks. I hated them and they used to hate me too. Their words were becoming effective, previously little little, almost like shy newborn babbles, then bigger, more savage, ravenous, superb, voracious, ready to swallow, to eat the world. Words... And they were crying over the body of the poor uncle, who has always been a bastard mean. Although they weren't honest down to the bottom, instead. But they didn't say the real story... "A generous man, real good man, friends with humans and animals, smart and...rich..."

Wealth is often sand hiding cat drops. Explain to those people who I used to be, nice and bravely, telling everyone was walking into a parallel world of shocking sounds, of meanings that nobody meant nor perceived anymore into reality.'

Adamo takes out the water where he was immersed a mirror. 'Wake up, idiot, instead of staying here to stare at your face through that mirror. Obviously you cannot see through. Lift yourself up and move away from your supernatural status towards you travel to, get away from the parallel universe where you are fluctuating. Where do you live? Use the empty shell of the meaningless word, distractedly pronounced, just to say something, just to be in the world, an infinitesimal vibration which is going into the air, bland, born from nothing and dead into nothing. Say that your uncle was good, that he was a jewel, say it, say it!

Eh, no. You are not there, I know it, you don't want to be normal, the inanity of the emptiness is horrible. You should know that the meaningless is the true life itself, the word just said, innocent and diabolic distraction, like during the sleeping, lost in thought, it is everything. We are the word; letters and syllables rule over the world, man is their slave. You don't want to be subjugated by that brutal power that leads over the universe, close your eyes and feel. I close my eyes and I feel, I can see beyond this mirror and all the words of the world. How could I get explained it to those bumpkins? I knew what they were thinking even before they started thinking, and I am lonely. They believed that was a magic trick and I let them do, indulging them, I had to do this way, to look like them, "ordinary". This is the word they use. Like it has a deep meaning for real. Ordinary, a group of syllables with no measure dictated by fake and bastard gods. Being free is really hard, a continuous test for your strength. I knew, although everything else, inside myself, to have the only thing that counts for real, the freedom of mind against the defining slavery of the definitions, of the empty words. Now I stop doing smirks on the mirror and I start to remember something.'

Nudo laughs, 'Yes, tell us please.'

'Before going out, everyday I had to clean my house. My bedroom in the morning used to be full of ultra-bodies, letters and exclamation points. Every morning when I woke up vowels and consonants pronounced unconsciously during the night became real, I don't know how, nor why. I only know that I used to find loads of letters piled up when I woke up, everywhere, mainly on the pillow around my head and at the end of the bed. Even on the door, like the words tried to escape overnight to go somewhere, to conquer some far island and then they died during the escape, maybe climbing the walls and falling over the naked ground, over the white cold marble floor. I hated that floor. Since that drama of the dematerialisations, as it has been named, I used to keep the door always shut. I did not want that letters and numbers which started to invade my house together with interjections, full stops and semicolons, would escape. They could damage something. I preferred to leave them into my room, then in the morning, when shadows were dissolved away, I used to pour alcohol over them, so after a little while they died, then I used to sweep them away throwing them into the rubbish. Alcohol was the only thing able to kill them. Really hard work, sometimes they used to fill the whole room, preventing myself to breath properly, they were all around the window, almost like they want to break the glass to invade the world, like strange pulsating animals. Better not, world wasn't ready for the assault of raw letters through their concrete obviousness and maybe it will never be, it is not ready for receiving free thoughts, with no gag, letters, semi colons without inhibitions. There could be chaos. To avoid this chaos and to save all the streets of the town from the jams ideally created by those letters, which were coming out my mouth becoming real, my house used to smell of spirit like a hospital. A deep smell everywhere, embarrassing, sharp, nauseating. Neighbours sometimes used to complain, they said I had to stop spreading spirit everywhere, which was awful. I replied to them that it had been useful against the bugs, excellent disinfectant, the best so far. I could not say certainly the truth. Saying that when I am distracted whatever I think comes out as real letters and dots, vowels and consonants that swarm into the room, extraneous and bulky objects, like pests. If I have said the truth, I would have been sectioned by them straight away. The problem got worse during the night time because I used to talk whilst sleeping. Letters materialization started to show when I was 40. Suddenly, with no notice at all, like a fatal disease. First time that happened I was at the *Gnam*, a posh restaurant, with my ex-girlfriend, good for her that she is my ex-girlfriend now. The poor girl was talking to me and I only replied to her lost in thought, yes, no, maybe, of course, just to make do with an answer, without understanding what she was talking about. It has been really awful. In a moment all my yes, my no, my of course, my agree, they all became real items, around my body, over the dishes, over the food, inside the glasses, under the table. Those objects all invaded the hall, waiters got nervous and the customers were thinking those items were animals, a big group of animals just appeared like this, maybe from distractions, falsity. They were biting the ladies feet with their fake teeth, the ties of the fat rich-men with their branded silk shirts who were chewing silly crispy salads. The materialized items, dots, commas, vowels and consonants and even numbers, were moving around like living things. From that day the hell. I could not think distractedly about something and then saying few words lost in thought, with no chances that those could materialize into letters and living numbers. And the exclamation marks were throwing themselves towards me like lances, the Os were looking at me with a question mark next to them. It is absurd but I really felt like they were watching me, I perceived their empty eyes over myself, and the circles were getting wider, like they wanted myself to enter a parallel universe. Even the gaps in between the A and B fonts and the other letters got wider, surprisingly broadening, like an invitation to go beyond that empty space, that absence. The Zero then was even attractive, looking for absorbing myself into the dark nudity of his empty room. I was always scared, I am a natural coward maybe. My legs were shivering just thinking of going beyond the letters emptiness, the Beyond, the Unknowledgeable.'

'The Unknowledgeable...' Luce feels her back shivering.

'Sometimes I was tempted, but the panic should have blocked me, stubborn, anchored to ground. Initially it has been though, I didn't know what to do. I thought even to be crazy, to have been creating my own fantasy. I imagined myself suffering of a kind of mind alienation, a disease to be reported to a psychiatrist. If it had been this way, maybe I would have been a visionary, a schizophrenic! A bit of therapy, some medications and not maybe healing but at least I would have a relief from the hallucinations. In my case, however, it was not about fantasy visions. It was all real, even other people could see those materialized letters. At the restaurant everyone could see them. The worst is that the story made news, because one journalist was sitting at the table there. That busybody published an article with an appealing title: *"Ultra-bodies at the Gnam"*, highlighting that initially it was thought about a cockroaches army which came out the kitchens, instead the customers better looking at them, they realized that "living and free letters", with no control, came from somewhere, who knows for which reasons. Then I started to give myself a continuous control over my words, every syllable should have to come out after a deep thought, a big self-control, a massive focus, indeed, to avoid the worst, to avoid to be crowded around by meaningless words materialized around my body, everywhere I would have gone. Indeed materializations would have happened only when I was talking distractedly, without thinking, with no control over the strength of my words. Those words, unrestrained, used to atomize in front on me and the others naturally. They could not declare myself mentally ill since the letters were invading concretely the bareness of any empty spaces. If naturally I would have kept secret this thing initially, after the restaurant episode, it has not been possible anymore. Everybody was talking about it.

The continuous effort of concentration, which I would have to make to control my words with the strength of thought, was exhausting all my physical and spiritual energies. At night I used to jump into my bed literally exhausted. It was the only moment where I could relax although I used to talk while sleeping, with no awareness of what I was saying. I could not do anything about it. My words materialized and my room was getting full of demoniac letters. In the morning I used to kill them, fiercely, desperately, washing over them with alcohol, hitting them with the broom, squashing them with my shoes, like bugs. What could I do in that case then? I wasn't ready yet to go beyond the empty, I was weak, a wretched weak little man. Although, awesome. Before going out I was recounting myself through the mirror, I was washing myself in front of this mirror, shaved, perfumed, combed, here we are, a flower, white teeth, maybe big nose, but well balanced with the rest of my body. I have always been an awesome man. I wished every time that my dear cousin would not have been drooling on my lips, saying that she was a bit blind with a small sense of distance.

I knew the way I am inside, I could close my eyes and I could see my internal organs, perfectly, even now I can trace walking along the movement of the blood flowing inside myself, like I am following a stream, and then I jump over the kidney and intestines. I can call the conscience really loudly, but no answer, it looks to be inside a cave, there is a noise of dripping beads. It's not enough to know how we are inside ourselves, it's not enough to section our body to see inside it, there is something more, more mysterious and depth, and strange. But to know this mystery is either dangerous and hard. I could not talk without my words would have been transformed in letters spread like insects in the world, so I decided to be mute, stubborn. For years I was pretending I could not talk, slave of the word. I moved to another city. Silence has been a mandatory cure. The only way to avoid letters and numbers pronounced distractedly to materialize around me. But that cure wasn't sweet, only a standstill. One day I screamed and from my mouth just came out whole words that encumbered the world and brought the chaos. Then I saw the word DOUBT floating in front of me in the air. The O was calling me, appealing, and I made the big jump in, I jumped into the O and now I am here. Where am I? I am here at Mu, in the big brains room. I thought to be an ordinary man and I was, I swear, a pretty ordinary male with a female heart. But I jumped in. It's not a joke. I believed in other worlds. Everything and Nothing. But which is the real life then? This one or maybe the one that I was living in the Upper World? I don't know. I don't get it. Nudo is right, to discern between the truth and the false is almost impossible. We live in the dark. One thing, indeed, is common to all the brains in here, isn't it Nudo?'

'Yes, Adamo, the jump.'

'Everyone has always jumped and we arrived all together at the same time, cancelling the distances of time and space, because we believed in our illusions and disregarded the power, me first, and nobody then regretted.'

All brains got up from the water and whispered, 'No one, no one of us has regretted it.'

The voices go through the library rooms, surrounding the statues, dusting the old books never opened, they make the nothingness vibrating, touching doors into darkness, the monstrous eyelids of the Unknowable.

Luce loves the brains, there is something in them, beyond their creepy appearance, which attracts her and frightens her at the same time. Everyone with their history, projected to Mu because they were brave to imagine the Beyond. And even the Great Mothers should love them, if they allow to doubt about their existence too. Maybe they admire their bravery, their challenge to the conventions, their escape from power as useless mask, livid daemon which is better to avoid because you would die and be subject to the darkness powers.

THE WIZARD DEFEATING THE FROGS

A Black Star, moreover, should recognize the daylight and the darkness and maybe taste crumbs of dark, the same gloom that brains hate.
 When Luce was 25 years old, she has completed her education at Mu meeting Dr Scuro.
 It's midnight. In the Art Hall, Luce sits opposite an extraordinary painting. One hand on a dark black background which grasps a soft clock that seems melting because of the wind. Luce feels the breeze on her face. She touches her own face to check. Weird. At Mu there is no wind not even inside a Hall, impossible. Silence. A that time nobody's in the library. The Hall is empty. The floor now is fragrant grass and the wind is stronger. The clock in the painting has been liquefying on the glass. The Hall disappeared.
 Trees and houses, a black sky instead of the ceiling and the wind blows stronger, arrogantly, stinky and irritable. It looks willing to uproot everything. Waste paper coming from any whirlwind around. Human profiles are showing in the storm. Their clothes latch on themselves, showing the shapes not always awesome of unknown bodies. Luce's very long hair, like crazy black strings, is anxious to hook some clouds in the sky. The dust of the street gets into their eyes. Noses and mouths of those snotty kids, that cannot go out, latch on the window glasses, giving to their faces monstrous shapes.
 The women, like dark shadows, wrapped in their flying fringes black scarves, rush their walking. They are scared that wind of the hell would take their souls away.
 Luce doesn't know where it should be.

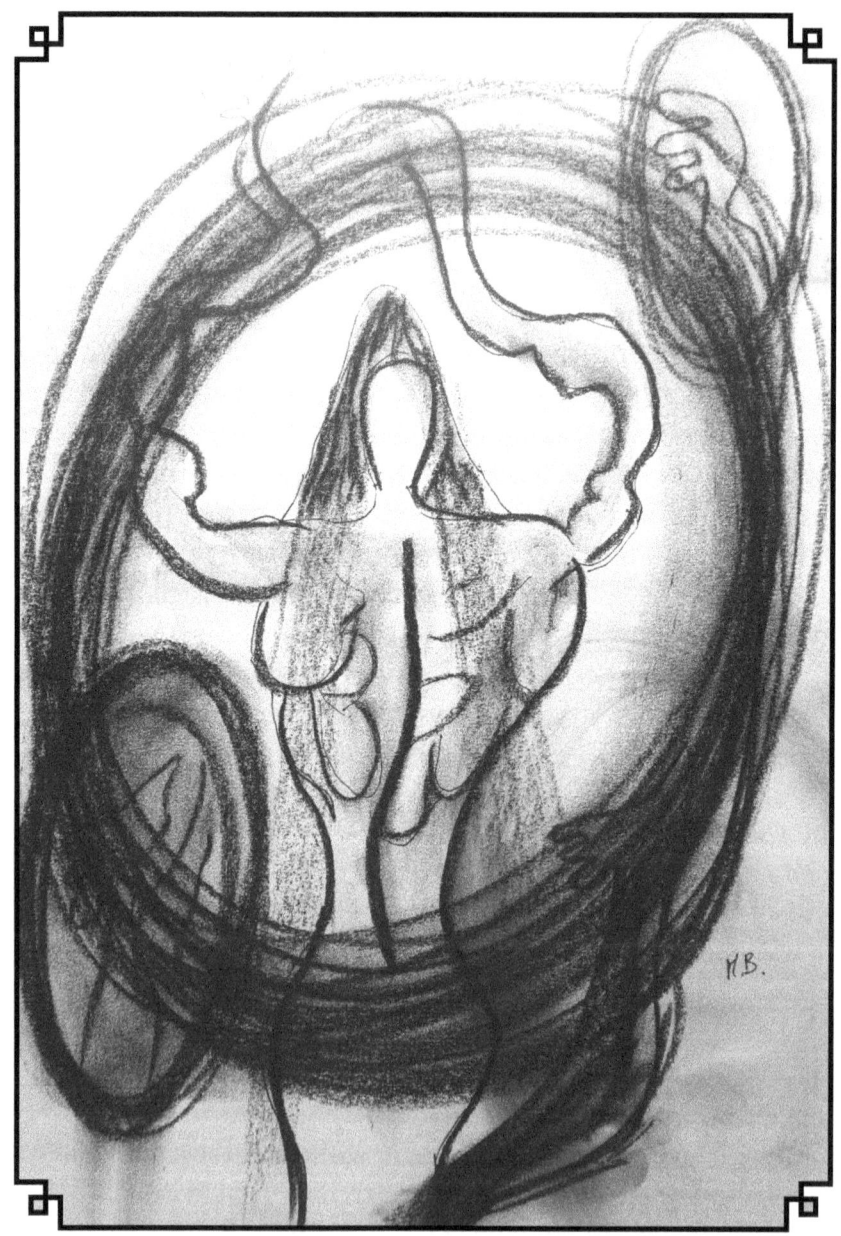

~ *The black star of Mu* ~

The sky on top has lost every green tones, it is black, crowded by yellow globular lightning cruelly intense. Thunders appearing suddenly, they follow a strange zigzag route. Sometimes they go through walls and windows with no damage and they disappear with one explosion smelling of sulphur and grey ashes.

Even the ground seems shivering a bit, hit by the thunder noise. Flowers, in the country, pull down their fragile corolla, similar to tired penitents. Stray dogs yelp can be heard through the night.

The starless night comes down from the top of the mountain with a huge rucksack on its shoulder. It walks over covering the pathways with some black snow layers, took out from the rucksack.

Black snow! Black like tar, everywhere. And like tar it has even the viscous elasticity and the same colour. One metre and half of snow. It does not easily melt not even within contact with Luce's warm hands.

It follows a muddy and rusty rain, reddish coloured with a bitter iron taste.

Luce does not know what is happening and she is just waiting, with patience, with no fear.

After the intense rain, the melted clock on the floor gets covered by spiderwebs. Silky strings in every corner, piled up, they dismantle under their own feet like candyfloss. It is possible to touch their thin and weightless texture, weaved by million invisible spiders. Of those spiders, no sign. Luce cannot tell where those spiderwebs could possibly come from.

She walks alone, now, through a soft path made of spiderwebs. Because of the strong cold she cannot feel her feet inside her lightweight shoes. Her hands are hurting and they are slighting shivering. She has to come back... She would try to escape, indeed... No, no, useless, the magic darkness will catch her back again. These are dreams which she cannot escape from. It's written in the Black Star's destiny. Bringing the light means to know the darkness and nightmares. Never escape... Corax, her dad, told her that she maybe go through parallel worlds which no one knows deeply about. The most important thing is to come back once darkness has been seen.

A dark shape comes out the shadow reflected by a tree. That shape is a man, really smart.

'I am Dr Scuro, nice to meet you.' The voice of this man is strong, like a metallic sound.

'Where are we here?' Luce notices that Scuro's shoes creak over the grass which whitens at his touch.

'We are into the nightmare, my dear, into this nightmare, just come with me please.'

'Are you real?'

'True and False, nothing and everything, who knows? I am the man that defeats the frogs and I am powerful, I am the event, the system, the State.'

'Nobody has power.'

'We'll see.'

Dr Scuro holds her hand. The wind now is a scary whirlwind. Shapes disappear. Completely dark. Through the dark a door opens from where a dazing light comes out. They go through it. There is a white hospital bed and one nurse. Scuro vanished. The nurse has an old fashioned cap and a withered face, having bags under her cruel eyes. She says silly things, no sense. She points out that Luce is late, hitting her watch with her nails.

She would have referred to the doctor. Referred what?

Laughing showing her sharp teeth.

She is awful, horrible witch. Still talking about nothing and time which is never enough. Her watch is clicking and it is getting hard and harassing, through the whole room.

'I will refer to the doctor, I will refer it to him, I will refer...'

She is free to say everything she'd like to everyone. The oldie woman makes Luce swallow a sedative pill and then disappears whilst locking the door behind. Her steps make noise through the corridor, then silence. Jailed. The only window has bars too. It's freezing now. Those blankets on the bed are not enough to make her body warm. Teeth-chattering and shivering. Her leg seems to walk with no control, going somewhere, without Luce's willing. She hits her leg to make sure that is still there and it hasn't left to some far places, away from that silly place looking as a room, away from that forced prison. Luce doesn't sleep, it is impossible. Her thoughts fight in her head. She tries to rule and divide them, to have a break. Useless. She has no power over them, no attention at all not even a break. It's better this way. The nightmare has to be indulged and lived in every intimate feeling, to understand and to get back.

She is sweating, unbelievable. The Black Star never had been sweating in her life and now she is sweating copiously and all the sweat has been freezing on her body, like a dress of suffering. Then every light goes off and she is in the dark, alone, like an abandoned castaway in the middle of a stormy black water ocean. She shouts. Her voice's echo comes back to her hears louder, through a lacerating rumble. The door opens and a glimmer of light just enters into the room. She gets up from the bed where she was earlier, having her elbows over the pillows. A shadow. Luce is not crazy, it is her shadow that separates from her and starts moving around. Autonomous and independent gestures. The shadow leads towards the door, standing out completely, identical to Luce, but shadow, pure and simple shadow. Luce has forgotten it somewhere and now it is there and maybe is watching out. The shadow moves toward her again, little silent and stealthy steps. Asking to be followed, beyond the door. Luce thinks it is a good idea. The shadow honir is smart and it knows its stuff, trustworthy and responsible, one other Luce, but stronger. They go together through a tight corridor, a kind of guts now dark and now bright. The honir disappears into the darkness and then it appears through the light as well. It's only allowed to walk in single file, silent. Only the noise of breathing could be confused with the persistent rhythm of thoughts. Luce feels a vague apprehension, the same she felt when born. Not knowing what is happening improves your sensations and reawakens the sight too. That hateful monster white dressed has disappeared with the watch. The nightmare is silent now. Dr Scuro is nowhere.

The shadows speaks saying that Scuro is unpredictable and dangerous bastard. Luce has to nail him, forcing him to give up, although unarmed. Luce doesn't understand a lot. The honir doesn't make it clear. It is too enigmatic and detached. They are just about to go up. Their feet are slippery. There is little oxygen and it was totally dark. Only after 10 minutes they could see a light.

The shadow follows her with no hesitation at all.

It comes from a cave enlightened by few torches and candles. From inside a strong smell of sulphur. Voices can be heard. Crawling inside the cave and they stop into a place not illuminated, making sure not being seen. At the centre of the grotto a boxwood table with a zodiac signs silk tablecloth, a stave and other mysterious ideograms.

Over the table two candelabras glow silver under the torches. Two incense burners spread a bitter smell around that, together with some sulphur steams through the air, gives a kind of euphoric dizziness. On the floor a soft shiny white mat and different magic tools here and there with a planned mess: a perfectly straight hazelnut wood stick, cut with a luxury metal sickle before the sun rises, under a waxing moon; the sword, the cup and the pentagram; a perfume box; a coal box; a bowl with some lustral water; oils candles, plants and incense burners. Around the table are five Mu people and one man. The first ones are different from the man because of their height and skin colour which shows a bit greenish over the candles light. The man, dressed completely black, tall, skinny, stands up and grabs from a green bowl a white clay paste and he spread it all over his face. Someone from Mu unbuttons his dress as it falls slowly on the floor. Here there are the man muscles, the hard and compact gluteus, wide solid shoulders when naked, perfection.

The man spreads over himself a lot of clay until becoming ghostly white. He wears on his head porcupine tails and a bright red feathers crown. Then he turns this way around. The light illuminates him straight on his face, but underneath all that clay make up, hardly Luce could spot the face of Dr Scuro.

She recognizes him by his eyes, dark, vulgar and penetrating, eyes which browse inside and catch the smell of a naked soul.

And now, there, in the middle of that cave, naked, ritually covered by clay, he is almost motionless.

Suddenly he throws on the floor seven anklebones, trying his luck.

He goes towards a bowl full of nuts and he starts to eat them, one by one, chewing silently. The others do like him, chewing silently.

The cave is cold, although the wizard and his followers don't even realize it.

They start to burn some herbs with a deep, warm aroma. A mixture of coriander, apium and hyoscyamus. And then they add some hemlock.

Luce feels herself trapped, stunned.

The wizard suddenly becomes a skeleton, with no flesh at all, except for his eyes, so black, deep and voracious.

The cave is full of presences. Mu people dead and alive. The wizard, once grabbed a long knife with a mother of pearl handle, cuts pieces of arms to Mu people just arrived. The knife goes through the diaphanous body of the dead ones and wounds the alive ones whose blood has been drunk by Scuro. He offers it to the dead ones that drink it avidly. Then a shout comes from the necromancer. The cavern goes shaken like a whirlwind would do. One of Mu's people whose blood the wizard has eaten, puts a black ball on the table next to a white ball. The two balls melt into one, that becomes grey, because inside there is the death and the life, the light and the darkness.

Scuro screams. His voice resounds through the cave and splits in various echoes, like a glass fragments from a broken bottle.

His perfect body could be seen beyond his skin, solid and compact muscles fibres, blood movement through the veins, lungs inside the chest, and a small black heart which is pulsating continuously.

His heart beats become even harder, resounds through the ears, stunning, it can be heard all around the cave.

Luce cannot talk, not even move, hypnotized by that primitive and fierce sound.

Dr Scuro's voice gets metallic tones, not human, like a robot.

Dead Mu's bodies start to spread a strange smell which feels like a ripened and spoiled strange fruit, a deadly sweetish perfume around.

At one point Dr Scuro moves towards various aggregation of soil that Luce hasn't noticed earlier. When the wizard nodded two Mu's people were starting to dig, extremely slowly, digging, digging deeper with some golden spades.

They don't look being tired, they have crazed expressions, like androids with no consciousness following instructions with no need to understand what they are doing. And everything in that opaque and suffocating air looks meaningless, by now.

The two androids, in the meanwhile, are increasing their digging velocity. Tac, tac, tac, their spades tips hit something hard. The wizard gets closer to the hole and he observes the white grave that is inside, the still shiny wood, damp for the wet soil. Dr Scuro nodded again. His two servants jump like springs. In a second the grave gets uncovered. A black body is lying there. The corpse has been taken to a stone altar and covered by dried and twisted branches. The wizard sets them on fire. Their ashes are collected into a container where they add a kind of green liquid. One of the two androids brings some flat lupin beans and he adds them to the liquid together with an herb called inula, bovine bile, soot and other bitter herbs.

Everyone gulps down this potion in silence.

The honir disappears, the cave too. Dark. Luce appears over a really high ladder. She goes down. The Art Hall is there, the painting with the melted watch too. The dream has finished. Luce's eyelids open again. A nightmare...

Outside the stars shine like nothing ever happened. Luce for a moment hates their indifferent beauty.

~ *The black star of Mu* ~

NIOBE

Luce decides to ask Niobe for a tip over the nightmare. It's said that Niobe was born with Mu. She lives since centuries into a house in the valley. One side of the house has been painted all white, half side white, according Mu's habits.

But Niobe is very precise, so in the black side everything is black, mat, plants, lamp, the stick and even the cat. In the white side everything is obviously white. Between the white and the black, the intermediate zone where the sorceress spends most of the time to prepare magic potions and herbs and roots concoctions.

The night when Niobe decides to go out there is a black greenish sky and layers of clouds which were flying cold through the sky.

The sorceress wears a cloak on her shoulders, leaving through the doorstep. She walks for a good half an hour, ignoring the far dogs bark.

The tall and fresh grass is full of damp dew.

Niobe bows, putting her cloak on the ground, she wears two ear-taps and she starts to dig all around a big root with a small golden spade. When the sun rises she grabs promptly the vegetable tearing it off the ground strongly. The roots make a terrible sound. She gets the mandrake finally. So she can come back home. She throws some coins, some bread and some salt over the place where the plant used to be before and then she leaves.

Luce waits for her on the doorstep. Puck is with her.

'Such a long time! 365 days, sixty minutes and twenty seconds, precisely, eh eh... Oh, I can see that you are not

alone. It is Hilde's jumping-nose.' Puck jumps on Niobe and wrapping her neck warmly with his tail, he licks her hand.

'Yes, yes, I know, you missed me.'

Luce is almost jealous. 'Puck, behave! I see that you know each other.'

'Indeed. Hilde used to come often to visit me.'

'Why?'

'Whys and wherefores, we were friends. She used to be very curious and myself too.'

Niobe's laboratory has not changed at all.

The huge table in the middle of the room contains cans, phials and vials, mirrors, pieces of ancient fabrics, dusty books, disgusting potions with a weird colour.

Luce grabs distractedly a can. Slightly greasy. She reads the label: *fatty wax of a right elephant ear*. She immediately put it back. What disgusting! Niobe is still the same. While she is talking, she takes out her handbag a strange root. She starts slicing it with a big knife, incising it like with the butter. The vegetable emits whispers and shouts under the indifferent eyes of the sorceress who submerges pieces of the mandrake into the boiling wine and then she is waiting for them to cook for a while. Once the root is cooked, she takes one skimmer and she takes some pieces off the wine.

Luce did not want to ask what is that potion used for.

'I know why you are here,' Niobe is serious now.

'Through the air it can be smelt a deadly and unusual scent. I can smell it now that you are close to me. I feel it... I feel through the convulsive shudder of the night, dark presences, shadows that should be buried, vague ectoplasm, like re-born cancers, evil excrescences.'

'I dream.'

'Maybe nightmares.'

'Yes, nightmares that look real, during the day, suddenly.'
'Does it happen more often?'
'Yes, especially in the library, but I cannot avoid to go there.'
'We cannot avoid our ego. All started when you were born. The ancient heart of Mu had new beats in your body, a bit rebellious, a bit sad and puzzled. Luce, you are different from the other stars. You'll contradict yourself because there are lives and universes inside yourself, and fears and doubts.'
'Doubts.'
'The dragging strength of the rebellious doubts is an overflown river, leading to overtake the pearly white river bank of certainty and the warm breath of the Mothers and the laws of Mu and the power of any terrestrial phallocentric gods. You can see Beyond, Luce, you feel it.'
'I should not want to see neither hear.'
'Impossible. You have the gift and you cannot get way from it.'
'Who's the wizard that beats the frogs?'
'I don't know exactly who is this wizard. It's been said sometimes, few centuries ago, *vox populi*, that a parallel world would have been existing, inaccessible, a certain necromancer, an expert in the art to re-invoke the dead ones, a powerful man with the gift of ubiquity. Lot of people had seen him and everybody knew him as the wizard that beats the frogs. He was instilling in the souls some fatigue, wishing to darkness, a frightening folding over beating the cross. It's been said that they could affect our world and seeding back the evil, trying to obscure the Mothers' light.'
'How?'

'He was spreading with his magic the idea of State and power, not existing at Mu yet. Although it is only a legend.'
'I have seen him, in my nightmare.'
A moment of silence. 'You must face him then.'
'I cannot.'
'You have to, I fear it is necessary.'
'But how?'
'We have to go to the library, in the Music Room.'
'Doing what?'
'Evoking the nightmare, to understand better all.'
'But I don't want to step back to that world, on the other hand.'
'I can only help you to understand, I don't have the ability to modify the ancient heart of Mu. The nightmare starts from there. You don't want to rip your heart off your chest. It's useless to escape. You need to challenge your daemons.'
'It's hard, indeed.'
'It's the only way, let's go.'

The music room is empty at that time, silent, huge, really high ceilings, many various musical instruments, 15th Century parchments, miniature of *antiphonarium*, ritual drums and bells with strange shapes.

Niobe takes a big drum hourglass-shaped with the resonance bottom containing a ritual skull under the lifted skin. Tam tam. The sound spreads around all over the room like a wave, a superhuman vibration. The rhythm goes faster, Niobe's hands beat the parchment with calculated strength, no stop. A light smoke comes out from her hands. The drum now is heavy of souls, even heavier. Next to Luce the *honir* comes back from the nightmare, her shadow that holds her hand and leads her away from the drum and the musician. Luce closes her eyes and Niobe's hands now are the hands of a busty man. Her body becomes bigger, muscular, clothes are ripping off. Now Dr Scuro appears. The wizard for the moment doesn't hit the frogs, but the drum. The smoke that comes out his hands gives shape to faces, hands and bodies of people that Luce has seen sometimes between the roots of the Radicale. The hall now is dumper. The walls with their instruments and books will vanish through the nudity of the rock. Dr Scuro is in the centre of the cave with his drum and gathers the souls.

His body becomes so transparent to be able to see through it. His heart beats like a living crazy animal, shaking his ribs. Intestines have bright purple reflects. Heavy bodies materialize around him, his white clay face.

The wizard stops playing and the bodies go down their knees all together in circle, around the ritual drums. The wizard's voice resounds through the cave and echoes.

'My dear shadows, my trusted subjects, my dear dead ones we have to vote before to act.'

Those bodies nod like robots. The black land of the cave seems to move and taking the shape of a two-headed dark body. The body lifts from the ground and, with a transparent bowl in his hand, invites everyone to experience the decision. 10 black balls and only one white. The mystery of the Mothers that converts the darkness into a white has to be substituted by a dark creepy government also at Mu, like anywhere else in the world. That's settled!

Given the bowl to Scuro, the body goes back to the land, it's like absorbed inside it.

Scuro celebrates, 'Time ago we tried to reverse the anarchy of the Mothers, useless. The ancient heart of Mu was strong, regular, but now we could try again, there is a bigger hole, a stronger doubt inside the new Black Star. When she was born her heart had a more irregular beat, from there we will go inside, to devastate the quiet and impose our power.'

Luce and her *honir* shiver, hiding inside a ravine in the cave.

Scuro starts to play the drums again, which becomes again heavy of souls. The hands of the wizard beat the parchment strongly. The sound goes lost through the humid air of the cavern and re-absorbs the dead ones which are re-transforming into smoke, entering through the drums. The gathering is over. Luce observes Scuro's hands, intensely, thin, delicate, light. His body becomes graceful. Niobe shows again. She has never stopped to play the drums. Now she stops. She is tired.

In the Music Room again is silence.

Better go back, it's late.

The day after Luce walks through the streets looking for answers that she could not find around the calm greenish atmosphere of Mu. She looks down for the triangular shuttles following strange geometrical routes, randomly, like a spiderweb.

Maybe Nudo could say to her something more about Dr Scuro. She feels confused about what she heard into the nightmare cavern. In her heart there is a gap where darkness could go through and arrive to touch the Great Mothers destroying Mu, its principle of freedom and self-determination.

The nightmare could assume concreteness now.

Who is the wizard, where is he from and why does he want to destroy Mu's freedom? The balance on the scale of the good and the evil is so perfect that nobody can offend.

The wizard wants to load dark souls over the Good plate, affecting it and then making lift up the Evil's plate.

Niobe can identify with Scuro, entering inside him together with other souls, hiding among them, but she doesn't have the power to control it. Scuro has absorbed for sure powers from the world of dead ones and there is a risk that he will go from the unreality of his world to the concrete and real universe of Mu, destroying the foundations and the balance. And the mean is her, indeed the Black Star. Her ancient heart has received an offence, maybe Hilde shivered while doing the path, she maybe feared before becoming dust over the pearly path of the Mothers. And Puck, which follows her everywhere, how did he resist 15 years in that room without starving? Only when she turned 15 Luce went to live at Hilde's house. Before that nobody knew about Puck. Maybe because of that mark that he has on his paw, he cannot die or get sick, although no living creature could stay without eating, not even at Mu. There were pieces of dry bread on the floor. Someone would have to feed him. Luce was full of doubts and unanswered questions and even fears that she's hiding like sharp mirrors through the bottom of a water filled bucket, ready to reflect the True and False, everything that comes by, evil and good skies, close and far ones.

Nudo is not at his usual place that night. He is busy reading at an antique poems book into the Poetry Room. He wears a white tunic that makes him looking like a ghost by the lamplight, elbow on the table, his head down over the pages. Luce finds him still there.

'*Odi et amo. Quare id faciam, fortasse requiris.* Ciao, Luce.'

'*Nescio, sed fieri sentio et excrucior...* Vale, Nudo.'

'You spend more time in the library than at home.'
'Oh, yes. It's here that I have got my friends.'
Nudo smiles. 'Friendship goes beyond any possible world, because it exists beyond the tangibility of the universes, exactly as hate and love. They are music which moves the empty off.'
'Nudo, do you know someone called Dr Scuro?'
'I don't think so.'
'The wizard that beats the frogs.'
Nudo looks Luce intensely. 'Did you ever see him?'
'I have nightmares.'
'And can you see him?'
'Yes, I can. Why?'
'Beating the frogs is just an expression that indicates willing to power. Your wizard wants to get a chance.'
'What do you mean?'
'Maybe he found a way, a small dark hole through the ancient heart of Mu.'
'I don't get it.'
'You, Luce, can choose between two options, conformism or doubt. The first one is a confident, warm and comfortable path, no thrills. You obey. It's the way through the calm and quiet mediocrity. But you, Luce, you are different. I know this since I met you. Through the black you don't see only darkness, but thousands grey tone. Not everyone does. You have chosen the harder and more dangerous way, the doubt. No quiet certainty then. Doubt has a divine charm, but it is full of tricks and pitfalls. Demons and presences are in it. And you are on your own, the only one that wants to understand. *Cogito ergo sum*. For this reason we both agree over things. Revolution is nice, so big and proud, magnanimous, full of ideas, but so fragile. Anyway

the non-government of Mu has to be protected. Mothers allow to worry, no chains. We are free. Luce, do you know what does it mean? Nobody, I say nobody has to stop us. Who tries to do it has to be executed with no mercy. This is an ideal world, perfect. And whether it does exist or not, philosophically talking, for us it is everything. We are Mu. Nobody would dare what has been created. You have to face your nightmares.'

'Niobe also told me the same.'

Nudo puts the book on the table, pressing very well the pages. A human face lifts up from the right page and starts saying the lyrics of the immortal and unhappy Catullo.

Nudo, Luce and Puck down their feet, are listening for hours, until they don't get surprised by the daylight that crazy and fast goes through the window and awaken them up. The book gets shut, night is over, dissolved by the improper vanity of Mu's light.

'Let's go.' Nudo stands up. The white vest makes him looking ghostly.

'Where?'

'We have to know how the nightmare has affected Mu's heart. I believe you need to sleep.'

The road that takes to Niobe's seems longer than usual. At that time of the morning there is nobody in the street. The greenish standstill air offers a slice of silence and anxiety. Luce does not want to experience the nightmare again. But Nudo does not give up. It's necessary to understand. The Black Star is not an usual creature. Legends say that her calm and unflappable heart is exempt from nightmares because Mu is beyond any disorder and lives her immortal and calm destiny since centuries, with no surprises. Nightmare is not allowed. Something does not work properly.

Niobe is in her laboratory between jugs, glass and hobs. She wears a grey dress while she takes out a bottle from a bucket containing fresh horse manure. She cleans the bottle under the water and she watches it in the light that comes through the window. A viscous and gelatinous substance rests on the bottom of the bottle now.

'Ah, marvellous, the experiment is successful, the spectrum of the rose. It only needs to be exposed tonight over the moonlight and then warm it up to see inside a wonderful rose, either its ghost.'

'Just about ghosts we wanted to talk with you,' Nudo says.

'I know why you just came here. Am I or not a sorcerer? I was waiting for you,' throwing a cake to Puck which swallows it in a second.

'We do have to understand what is happening to Mu's heart.'

'All fine, but it wouldn't be the easiest thing. Come with me.'

Niobe goes upstairs to the loft. Nudo, Luce and Puck follow her. There is heavy dust and a bed covered with a thick plastic bag. Niobe takes the plastic off and ask Luce to lay on the bed for her. The quilts are soft and smell of roses. From Niobe's throat comes out a vibration of hypnotic dirge, repetitive. The sound thickens through the air, filling the empty, chaining up the senses bringing them to an unknown dimension. Luce's eyes go deep through the dark, fluctuating into a strange blue sky, hitting against each other, like crazy marbles. Her face appears together with the eyes, fingers and then the whole body. The space doesn't exist, it's all sky, convulsively fair. A gelatin of cold clouds pours water over Luce's body which is suddenly in the sea.

The salt pinches her nostrils. The sun warms her skin. The foam brushes her feet, lightly. There is even Puck, little and dirty. Luce has a bucket in her hands now. She puts Puck inside it covering him with sea water. The little animal has got big eyes, huge ones, open wide under the water. Puck now is a cat which goes out the bucket very clean and he becomes bigger and bigger and starts multiplying in lot of himself. Now the space is full of black cats, big, little, medium sized, with huge yellow eyes. They split in two until leaving the room of a road to travel. The only one possible. At the end of the road a gorge. Luce falls down. She opens her eyes. The bed smells always as roses. Nudo and Niobe sit next to her. Niobe has drawn a circle around the bed. But in the middle of the room there is a huge hole that was not there earlier, one hell-hole from where daemons go out. Their strong hands with long nails are grabbing the floor. Weird heads of strange creatures overlooking the hole. They have roosters' crest and really smart eyes, reptile's jaws, some drops of reptile cheeks, human hands and silk hair finishing with snakes head. They smile at Luce. They open their jugs emitting a sound. The chasm now is a huge mouth. Luce gets sucked down. She grasps to the blankets with no success, to Niobe and Nudo's hands. Her body gets swallowed by the core of the chasm. The dark changed through the green of the grass. There is a lawn and one stream and a rock. Dr Scuro is over the rock. He is blue-dressed, a kind of weird uniform with black boots. He takes out one of the boots a dagger. He nods to a woman standing next to him. The woman has a mask that covers half of her face. She loosens her long hair showing a blue lock. She leaves and comes back after few minutes with a black buck, pulling it with a rope tied to the body of the animal. Scuro puts his hand over the animal head, pulling it upwards and he pierces the blade in its neck, firmly, confidently. The scarified jumps, kicking and its dark blood goes on the white stone. The rock touched by the blood produced some greenish smoke.

Scuro strips the animal after extracted its eyes, thrown on the grass backwards. He breaks the beast skull with a marked axe and then he eats its brain still warm claiming death against his future enemies.

Mu people dead time ago appear. The wizard makes them going down their knees and they worship him. Then he gets closer to Luce touching with one finger her right hand. Somebody shakes her so she reawakens. The Black Star wakes up for real now. Nudo seems relieved now. In the loft nothing has changed. Only Puck shakes a bit under the blankets that smell of roses. He whines licking his right paw where there is a mark, like a fingerprint.

Nudo and Niobe are really sad. Luce's nightmare is able to pierce the reality. The mean is Puck. For this reason somebody fed him for fifteen years. Through the little rhino-grade Dr Scuro can touch Mu.

Niobe is crying, 'We have to kill him!'

'No, never!' Luce won't be allowing this.

Nudo also says that is necessary to eliminate the body as mean which allows Dr Scuro to access to Mu. With no material body his hands cannot touch Mu. Basically Dr Scuro is not from Mu. To penetrate through the materiality of Mu he needs a raft which would ferry him to this world. A body.

'No, we cannot kill Puck and then, why him? Maybe you are wrong.'

Niobe is sure. 'At the same point where the wizard has

touched you, Puck has a scar, Scuro's fingerprint.'

'It is a violated *Nagual*.'

'The warden animal cannot be violated.'

'Scuro has done it. He could wound him, as you can see. He will reduce Puck in pieces, believe me, and he will drink his blood which he will take to Mu. We need to kill him.'

Puck looks at Luce with two big cat-eyes, grasping her neck, licking her hand.

'I cannot do it! There will be another way, I cannot, you see, you will take him, if you dare!'

Nudo goes one step back. 'It's not my duty, I would not know how to do it. Niobe, you will sort this out for us.'

'Me? I don't think is the right thing to do. Tradition says that the Star has the duty to get rid of every perturbation.'

'Are we talking about a storm maybe?!'

'Nudo! You got me! Disorder, indeed, no good things, troubles, matters!'

Puck starts purring like a cat.

It's the end. None of the three ones could eliminate that trouble, never.

One thing is sure, indeed. The wizard is not from Mu. Parallel worlds exist that no one can touch in perfect balance in the universe. Mu is one of those, the Underground World. Who was not born at Mu cannot access to the Underground World. Only the superior spirits can do that. Brains, for instance, that made the Jump. On the Upper Earth, devastated by hedonism and rationalism, they were brave to believe in something else, passing with their pure soul the Unknowable Beyond, the impassable limit which divides the Worlds. Dr Scuro would have already jumped if he could do it. Definitely he has not a pure soul. He has been denied access. The Beyond doors are shut for him.

With the power of his magic he tries to force the jambs. A material mean would be useful in those cases. He took the purest Mu inhabitant of the whole Underground World, Puck.

Through the nightmares that Luce would experience, Scuro sucks the blood of the rhino-grade, like a vampire does with his victim to acquire strength and purity.

Mary Blindflowers

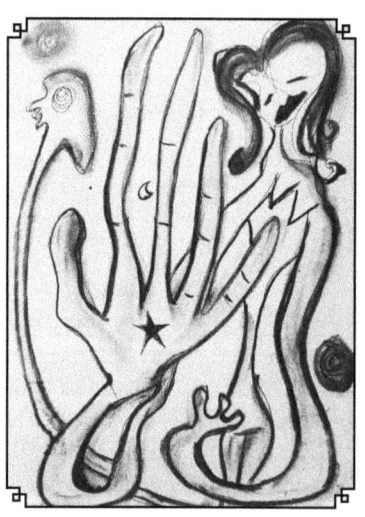

CHEMAKO

Mu's cemetery is not like the ones in the Upper World, none of sad willows on marble graves, not even wreathes nor candles. Only a lot of good light and a lot of water stones, bright, with their purplish and blue tone. They are transparent stones like ice, but hard like diamonds, eternal like Mu, cold. They reflect the sunrays and make the environment really bright. Beyond the stones there is a white and bright beach with silver sand and the sea really clean and transparent.

Mu people supposed to be immortal, but basically they can even die because of traumas, wounds, accidents. And when Mu people see the soil drinking their sons' blood which has made the last breath, those people melt like a suffering mother will do during a mourners singing.

The air gets full of sounds. Around the dead laying on the bed two Mu people sitting check their instruments. They brush their strings, the antique wood of their *melodicon*, strange lyres with carved wood as flowers shape and full of bright black gemstones. Melody spreads out destabilizing the reality, hypnotic draw of absence. The sound pierces the unresponsive instinct of the day, cutting the time arteries. The buzzing of two *mirliton* players approaching the dead is mixing together with the vibrations through the air. The instruments made from marsh canes and leaves vibrate through ancient sounds. While the time is running, more instruments are adding which take the sorrow away, over a different space perspective. The horns brush against abyssal depths. The maker, a master, used an ox horn, waiting for the natural detachment of the bone. The cleaning of the interior has been given to patient ants which had eaten any waste of flesh. The boiling water finished the job. The softened instrument has been shaped and shined properly. Now it is sparking under the light that comes through the window and produces a sad low vibration. With the horns there is even a *bena*, a kind of cane flute, with the bottom made of half carved pumpkin. The women loosen their long black hair, shaking their bodies and they scream following the rhythm of those instruments. The dead is laying indifferent, with his ashen face. At the end of songs and sounds he gets covered by red ochre to give him back the blood lost, to avoid that he'll ask for it to the living ones. Then he gets cremated and his ashes scattered over the beach with the water stones, the only place where the wind whispers and lives in Mu. Tradition says that the breeze is really given by the souls breathing which talk continuously.

The Mu's one killed by Thomas recently rests on the silver beach together with the other dead ones of Mu. In his honour Mu people are dancing on the beach. Their bodies are complaints towards the unknown, their shout lost voices in the empty air left by who is not there anymore. Their back bending in clever contortions. Their hands dig into the silver sand through an agonizing grip, a mimed pain. At night, when the air gets loaded with greenish darker moods, dancers come back home after they left a simple rice meal over the seaside.

Luce, Puck, Niobe and Nudo are waiting for the dead one to come at night to eat his meal in the night silence, light shadows rest, disembodied. And the continuous breaths of the wind like silken strokes, move Luce's dark hair, the white tunic of Nudo blows up. Niobe shivers a little. The water stones have strange colours of fire. The sea is calm, breathing like a living body that dances and smells of deep mystery The water, indifferent goddess, is cold and just watches without getting agitated the fish hunting of fishes eating other fishes, life and death, through a never-ending continuous loop.

A shadow gets closer to the rice plate. Mu's hands plunge their pink fingers into the candid meal bringing it to their mouth. Chemako is silent. His feet make footprints over the silver sand.

Nudo just starts off, 'Vale.'

'What are you doing here?'

'You must help us.'

'Me? Help you? Sorry I just died little time ago, at least I have been told so. What do you want from me?'

'What was your name?'

'I cannot remember it, I cannot remember of you as well. Total blank.'

'Who did tell you that you are dead?'

'Some voices. People I have just met now. Bit strange ones, kind of, if you touch them your hand goes all the way through their bodies. Going through them, ha ha. The way they look like maybe they are right. I must be dead. How and why I am here I don't really know. I cannot remember anything and I don't know anything, it looks to be a good start really.'

'How do you feel?'

'I cannot feel anything. My voice only I can hear and I am starving, everything else is like I wasn't here, you see. Like when you don't feel your leg. I tried to hit myself as well, although I think seriously there is nothing to do about it. Never mind.'

Nudo offers him some fruit.

'Thank you my friend. Dead thanks for this. But who are you?'
'Mu's people.'
'What does it mean?'
'Mu's inhabitants!'
'Is it food maybe?'
'You don't remember anything at all.'
'Nothing. Is it food this Mu?'
'No, it's not food, Chemako.' Nudo gives him a pear.

Luce says that Chemako is a nice name for a dead person with no memory, *that one who doesn't remember things*. Niobe likes it as well. The dead one doesn't complain about anything, he is peaceful. It looks incredible that a kind of Mu person like him could have been killed during a scuffle. After he bit the pear, he says that Niobe is familiar but he cannot remember who she could be, he is not able to tell anymore.

'We hope that his heart is beating next to the Great Mothers spirit and he could help us to understand,' Nudo is sad when he pronounces those words. There is a moment of silence. The silver sand sends lunar glares. The wind whispers unintelligible words. The waves are singing a sweet chant similar to sirens, to abyss creatures, travels, reflected worlds. The white foam smiles, eroding the cliffs.

Chemako eats his pear. He chews it cheerfully. Luce is curious, 'Do you feel its taste?'

Chemako laughs, 'No, I don't think so.'

'It looks like you are enjoying it.'

'No, I have a memory of it.'

'What do you mean?'

'It's hard to explain. I mean that while I am chewing it I can remember its taste and I still can enjoy it.'

'A reflected pleasure.'

'Exactly, like that. That's the right word for it, it has been used by them too,' behind the dead some moving shadows appear. Luce shouts to them not to get closer, her words thrown as stones against their skin, hitting them, and they just sadly pull back. Chemako shows the pear to them shaking it and he winks them. Niobe orders him to stop and asks, 'What do they say?'

'Reflect, yes, reflects here and there... I don't get them. They chatted my ear off as soon as I arrived.'

'What about?'

'It's all about the unnatural origin of the reflection, how they say. So technically, if I am not wrong, they know to be reflections of being, of truth and of all this silly philosophical things, various bla bla about being and not being...good this apple.'

'It's a pear stupid!' Niobe looks irritated, 'Come on! Carry on!'

Nudo puts his hand over the sorceress shoulder, silently inviting her to calm down. Niobe goes on, 'Come on!'

'Basically they feel themselves a bit discriminated.'

'Who is discriminating them?'

'Who knows? One of them is definitely sure about it... Can you eat this?'

'No, you can't eat the core, although you are free to do it anyway, it doesn't harm you.'

'How do you know it?'

'Know what?'

'That I won't harm myself.'

'Come on!'

'You joke darling. Maybe it won't be hurting myself directly, but with my memories I can say that I had abdominal pain and suffering. If I eat and I can remember about the taste and I like it, it's that the case...and I always had problems to digest apples. Once I have eaten chickpeas pasta with pork, a huge rhino-grade steak and sorbet, yes I think it was sorbet.'

'I cannot believe it, Niobe puts her hands into the hair.'

'Why not? It was sorbet, I swear, to digest maybe. After the sorbet I was feeling really good, I eat the apple and I start to feel abdominal pain. Isn't it marvellous?'

'What? Your pain?'

'No! I am just remembering! I remember now all the things I have eaten. Although, I have to say I cannot remember where neither who I have eaten with, when, how or why. Indeed...'

'Let's go to the point.'

'No, this one does not have a kernel, it has those small bits...'

'Seeds.'

'Yes, we are to the seeds now.'

'Gah, what is this story about discrimination?'

'Those ones.'

'The dead ones.'

'Yes, indeed, the dead ones feel disappointed because of their reflections or kind of.'

'Please explain this clearer as I don't get anything when you talk!'

'Basically, because they are the kind of reflections which you can go through their body with your arm trying to touch them, like shadows and so on, they really don't count as matter of fact.'

'Where don't they count anything, referring to what, what matter?'

'I don't know. I have just arrived. They will tell me, I suppose. Or maybe they already told me about it and I don't remember it. I was hungry. When you are hungry you can't think clearly. Who knows? Now because they are not counting, nobody take them seriously and they are disappointed.'

'You must tell us everything.'

'I don't know anything else.'

'Listen, we will bring you food sometimes, but you, indeed, have to give us something more than that.'

'Do I have to be a spy? No, never! It's something could not be done, it is betrayal, indeed.'

'It is important.'

'But is not ethical.'

'It's for a good reason.'

'It's always like that.'

'To save a population, your people, Mu's citizens.'

'Really?'

'Yes, indeed you are from Mu.'

'I can't remember anyway I won't be a spy, no way.'

'So you are going to fast, let's go.'

'No, no wait! Fasting? I could ask for some information around.'

'No, you must listen, that's all.'

'For Mu.'

'Yes, for Mu.'

'Can you bring me more apples, please?'

'Yes, more apples, loads of fruit.'

'It's a deal. Apples to me. Please bring them in big quantity. Maybe some other food. Beans and meatballs, tiramisu, fried chicken and onions and aubergine and...'

'Yes of course, as you like.'

'I have to eat, do you understand? I am starving; I'd eat

the world if possible. I will do everything, but I have to eat now, because hunger is like a monster suffocating owns consciences. I don't have body although I feel the bites of that beast like I could feel them really on my stomach. Basically I only can remember and I feel bad.'

'Reminiscence.'

'Remembering tastes and feelings, nothing else, darkness. I don't know even who I am.'

'You are and you will be forever from Mu, even if you died.'

'They said I haven't.'

'The dead ones?'

'Yes, they say that once you died you are nothing anymore, that you have finished. No one more cares about you.'

'They're lying.'

'Why?'

'Because one from Mu is always from Mu, either dead or alive. Remember this.'

'I will try my best to remind it, thank you.'

'Good, you can go if you want, Vale.'

'It's worthy, friends, indeed.'

When the shadows go back it's dark. The air is green moss colour. Niobe is angry. She feels that something happened. Luce and Niobe read through her eyes fear and anxiety. Puck jumps over the sorceress looking at her whilst he grasps her hands with his tail. In few days he lost weight, only vomiting. Like a skeleton. Only his sight has the same calm sweetness as usual.

'Let's go, we have to free the little one.'

The ritual

Mu has huge forests full of ancient trees with the shining foliage showing through the greenish air at night. Niobe and Luce are scratching the cortex of the age-old oaks. They collect the pieces of cortex within white small bags. Over the pebbly river bank of one stream Nudo collects some plants with yellow flowers and small black seeds, *Hypericum perforatum*.

In to a sunny corner huge Aloe Vera plants show themselves, which their very long and thorny leaves pierce the air.

Collecting all the necessary has been hard, but at the end everything is on the sorceress table.

Aloe Vera leaves are religiously deprived of their thorns and conveniently squeezed out. *Hypericum* flowers ground into the aloe juice and pulp, look like big floating islands into a jelly sea. The cortex is pulverized and added slowly. The mixture has to be left overnight. Still the main problem to solve. Make it swallow by Puck. The rhino-grade does not want to listen at all. Luce and Nudo have to hold it whilst Niobe opens its mouth trying to make him swallow the mixture. After two hours bottles and jars of the laboratory are all broken in pieces, still upside down on the floor, lamp shade cracked, books are stained, table is scratched, Niobe, Luce and Nudo all dirty, although a big part of the potion is in Puck's stomach.

The animal makes strange contortions, red pupils. Tongue out. Puck stays like that a good two hours. His tail hits the ground. He jumps on the light which is still getting damaged. After calming himself, he vomits out a button, a metal key, that concoction waste and a snarl. Now puck is quiet, he looks happy. Niobe caresses him showing him a black stone. She forces him to swallow it is a small obsidian. Puck lays on the floor while Niobe takes a black leather string from where a protective symbol is hanging: ⚑ .

The poor rhino-grade vomits again the obsidian. Niobe washes it through a pure water jet and she makes him swallow it again. This happens 10 times. Puck moves his tail really nervously. He jumps irregularly and ridiculously pointing his big nose to the floor, turning upside down, spinning around, drooling, yelping like dogs, meowing like cats. Then, like caught by syncope, he crumpled. For three days he is like stunned, without eating and drinking. After four days he opens one eye, then the other one, slowly. He stands up and starts again to interact. He spits the obsidian out which is bigger now, like absorbing some energy from him. Niobe grabs it and she puts it over a small white pillow, under a thick glass case, with a small locker. The sorceress shaped it matching the key spit by the rhino-grade. Indeed with that key which is on her neck now like a talisman, she locks the clear shrine. The dark stone absorbs all blues reflections, shivering a bit over the white nudity of the pillow.

'So what now?' Nudo is curious.

Niobe has only transferred the evil from Puck to the stone.

'The wizard is powerful. He has got hands like tentacles that can reach everywhere. His magic is strong. It cannot be won easily. I feel that it is getting stronger. We have to find out more about him.'

'A retroactive nightmare?'

'Nudo, it's really hard to create!'

'We could try.'

'Don't think so, it's absurd. It should be leading through a new time slot. And even if we could do it, if Luce would be successful with that, it won't last that long, few minutes. Not enough, too less to understand.'

'But we could try it,' Luce is firm.

'It could be dangerous.'

'Dangerous for whom?'

'For you.'

Luce laughs. 'Why? Do you think that whether Dr Scuro would success to enter to Mu, I will be safe?'

'I don't know.'

'Then let's try it, I am ready.'

'It needs an ancient soul to do this job. A soul that has lived many lives, a sibyl which would bewitch the time with her sight, distracting it. A woman that would find a lamp of jade into a dark street during the dark green night at Mu.'

'Iris.'

Iris has got both eyes with an unreal green highlighting over a metaphysical black of her blind double pupil. A strong deep black, challenging the obsidian locked up in the shrine. Her long and thin hands touch the thick glass.

Iris has got a firm voice, 'You are wrong.'

Niobe, Luce and Nudo have a puzzled aspect.

'Indeed, you have done a really good job, but not enough I have to say. This stone does not contain the same power as Dr Scuro.'

Niobe is disappointed. 'I have loaded it with all negativity which invaded the poor Puck. We could not kill him, we could not do it at all.' Puck starts purring grasping Luce's neck.

'Thank God. Killing him would be useless as well.'

'He would have to resolve the problem from the roots instead.'

'Not at all, Niobe. The evil cannot be all in one side. The wizard is smart basically. Puck is only a distraction. Indeed you have been committed. The stone is really big. But whilst you were looking after the small rhino-grade, the wizard was widening the door to enter through Mu.'

'How do you know it?'

'I heard it when my sister was born. I've put my hand on his small chest. Luce is not like the other Stars. She was born with the seed of the doubt and this seed produces bad and good fruits. It is the gap, the flaw of the whole system of Mu. In Luce the ancient heart of Mu has been contaminated by doubts, by not accepting that matter.'

Luce blushes, 'It's my fault.'

'There is no merit and no fault. Mu lives since Centuries over accepting the Law of the Mothers. Everybody obeys passively to the tradition, except you, Luce. Although it is your right. Mothers do not forbid doubts. You are the Star who wants to touch the Unknowable. Exploring, investigating, understanding. It's not a crime. But looking to know other worlds is still dangerous for Mu. Parallel universes should never meet up, to avoid the whole system collapsing. Concentric circles, perfect. Being not knowledgeable guarantees other worlds not to be discovered. In this way everybody is safe. Mu's freedom wouldn't be contaminated or affected.'

'But Nudo has been in the Upper World and he jumped!'

'Nudo is a special creature, which has been chosen by the Mothers. His jump has been accepted by the Law of the Mothers. His soul is pure. Dr Scuro has got only the awareness of the evil which will do to Mu. For this reason he has not succeeded yet to jump. Mothers don't agree. He is waiting since half century. Then you were born. In between your Mu's heart beats, he perceived an irregularity, a gap. He tried to sneak through the gap in between your irregular heart beats. He wants to go through your doubts' door. That room is too narrow for his big ego, for his huge lust for power, so he tries to widen the entrance.'

'Do I have to delete any doubts from my heart?'

'You cannot, nobody could escape from his own nature. Repressing it could be a worse damage. Implosion. Do you understand? Like a devastating explosion for you and Mu.'

'Yes.'

'Scuro wants to enter to Mu. If he would succeed it, we had been lost. Let's empty this room and make it pure with some incense. Let's paint the walls white.'

'What do you want to do?'

'Let's try to look with eyes of the soul what the wizard wants to do, trying to understand it. Luce, we cannot go back. We need to go through. Forgetting is impossible now. We don't have to hide our drops under the sand like the cats. We need to be brave enough to discover every enigma, rip veils off, point out eyes in the eyes the enemies, without fear. We are not coward, we will not be hiding ourselves behind the curtains of the oblivion, waiting for the end to come. We would be nyctalops and we would fix our pupils through the darkness, lighting thorny paths. We will get wound if necessary and we will safeguard your heart.'

Room is ready in a couple of days, purified and candid. Iris takes the case putting it on the floor, in the centre of the room. They let Puck out. Luce lays down next to the stone. Niobe and Nudo are standing next to her. Iris brings the hand to her chest, looking into her eyes. Luce falls asleep. She finds herself in a dark room now. A table. Four people around that table, in the middle a small plate with some alphabet letters around it. Their faces cannot be seen yet. Only their hands show really clearly which seem to break through the dark. Each one's index finger on the small plate, like wounding blades. The medium goes in trance. She says with hoarse voice, 'giving voice to the recalled entities.' Now her curly hair head can be seen shaking, chest swelling with pride, eyes shut. At that point the small plate seems to be moving indicating some letters that spell the word D A I L O R G. The light illuminates the drawn face of the medium, then the others. Next to the medium there is Dr Scuro and his two assistants. The same ones that Luce has seen through the cave's nightmare. There is a calendar by the wall. The date 2nd April 1978 is red circled. The wizard stands up. Everyone stands up. The medium has been sent away in a rush with some tips. Scuro opens the windows and he breathes the countryside fresh air, loaded with aromas and fresh rain. He just laughs browsing one atlas looking for *Dailorg*. It's there that it needed to start from. Conquering *Dailorg*. Send men there, of course, no problem. They need to know firstly how to get there. A safe road so his power can get stronger. Getting rid of awkward enemies, turning into true the false. Dr Scuro goes out through the garden in the villa. A huge olive tree catches his attention up. It has a curly trunk and complex roots challenging their ages, dip through the soft ground, in depth. The wizard touches the bark rubbing his strong palm against the tree. 'The roots of this plant go everywhere, like me. I will know how to get to *Dailorg*, wherever it is.' Luce recognises through the olive tree the one under

Scuro has slit the ram's head for his rituals. The wizard is thirsty. The Upper World is too small for his insatiable hunger. He has corrupted, eaten, satiated himself. He has changed the coins aspect. Now he wants to conquer other worlds. He wants to bring his life philosophy. One of his friends, the landlord, puts one hand on his shoulder winking to him. Then he is giving Scuro a strange book: *Dailorg's Chronicles*.

'Read it, to remember today.'

Scuro takes it and thanks him.

'Dinner will be ready soon.'

'In the meantime, I would like to read for a bit.'

'Of course, Alberto and I are going to play pool.'

Scuro browses the book and some worlds open up to him. "*Dailorg* is the county town of Mu, the Underground Earth, a peaceful and marvellous city..."

In the book there is everything, all the history about the ancient heart of Mu and about its immortal people. Conquering a world that does not die. An ambitious idea. The book doesn't give any notes about getting the way to Mu. It doesn't exist a way, literally. It needs jumping. Traveling through worlds. A bit absurd, indeed. Sometimes the absurdity gets into life and becomes an important factor in History, boosted by the power of being, by willing, by money, by friends of friends. A dense pattern of dark relationships, weird. So nothing is impossible. The world has no logic, completely irrational. The intellect does not exist unless into the willing all human to categorize the reality, justifying it, to make it less bitter and painful. Ah, it's a tough one! We are trying to soften it a bit with our willing to tidy up, the need to control everything. Centuries of idealism, of spirituality, to justify the universe. Bullshits, indeed, although they lead over people's minds. We were born in the chaos and we will die into it, ending our terrestrial adventure. I won't be stopping to make a bit of wind over this bitter episode of our lives, I won't be hurting my arms trying to grab clouds. The answer is simple. If the intellect is a loser, unreality, I will look for the Beyond, the senseless. Scuro looks out the window. Where is the sense of this absurd rain which makes the world wet of tears? And what about the evil burning heat of the summer sun? And in my eternal wait... The sense... The world is unreasonable. The religion, for instance. I was born as Catholic and I am still Catholic, a faith, a power, a winning card which opens all doors. A virgin woman that delivers a baby, a man-God who dies over the cross and then resuscitates. I do not care whether is true or not. It is a fact, illogical, absurd, but it's believed to be true and I do believe it, because it's convenient for me. That's the truth. Something absurd accepted by the world. Nothing is never idle. Not even myself it's only myself, but I do represent something and I have got willing to decide. Moreover, I do analyse myself too little, confused with my religion which claims for power. I am a god too, my way, because I live since 50 years in my body and I haven't died yet. Now I am a politician, a businessman. Here I am, a leader, lot of friends, some troubles, some awkward nicknames. People have fun giving to powerful people some funny nicknames. It should not be permitted. A man like me needs to be respected. At the end I am a yielding divinity, flexible, due to cease, stabbed by damned satire. And then accusations, open challenges, problems. I only have some small bailiwicks, cities where I am the leader, putting my people into strategic positions, trusted friends and relatives, supporters. Into banks, universities, offices, a bit everywhere. Pervasion, expanding roots, growing. But nothing in this world is forever. Not even the power. If I could get to *Dailorg*, then yes indeed, I would be a ruling God, immortal among immortal people, eternal. I was born to lead and I would have my revenge and I could never die. My enemies would disappear all of a sudden. I could be the History, the event. No elections, a god cannot be elected, he has only to be worshipped. His decisions cannot be denied, it needs to obey and that's it.

GREAT MOTHER'S HEART

Dailorg is a nice town, full of springs, waterfalls and leafy trees with shiny black trunk. Houses surrounded by green spaces, lawns full of stunningly perfumed flowers. There is as well a honey coloured cold lava stream with loads of coloured butterflies around. Magnificent Dodos are nesting in between nearby ravines. They emit rasping yells, moving the small wings not suitable for flying, since centuries. The enormous yellow beaks glow under the sun. They move clumsy looking at the elegant flight of splendid hoopoes, which have black and white striped plumage, with blue iridescent shades. *Dailorg* sits over a hill surrounded by tangled forests full of fresh and pure waters. At night the eyes of sneering owls go deeply through the light of Mu, their voices got mixed with crickets singing their sweet songs. They maybe talking about *Dailorg*'s stories, aedi animals, laughing and crying through the windless air, challenging the consuming power of the time. Wild cats are sharpening their nails on the shiny black trunks tracing some marks that will be the walkway for giant blue ants with red antennas and mandibles. The purple pinkish parakeets with yellow wings open their beaks looking for food slapping the smooth air. Dogs are silent for 606 long years. They are waiting for the moon, algid and cold will be showing in the sky breaking the usual green. When they see it, their pupils get wider, their nostrils shudder, lifting their snouts. Their gaping throats emit a vibration so intense to hypnotize *Dailorg*. Then the forest sits standstill and quiet. Only the leaves whisper and they move like a totemic ancestral dance.

Today is holiday in *Dailorg*. It is celebrating an ancient ritual, which from centuries repeats unchanged during Carnival period. Twelve Mu people make two lanes. They wear ritual costumes. Hard black wood masks that look like stone. Over their shoulders belly goats skin with sleigh bells. Boots on their feet. Hands in their pockets, they come forward with little jumps and then they stop listening to the silence. Six women in a white mask and pearly clothes look at the dancing men. On the side, ahead and behind the lanes, they whip on the floor whilst the dancers move their shoulder to make the bells playing sounds. Women are the rational wisdom of the Great Mothers who knew how to tame the beast leading it towards selected paths. The twelve Mu people that personify the feral aspect of Mu cannot eat and drink, it is forbidden. The instinct cannot be satisfied, but just moderated, balanced. The dance is all around the grass paths of *Dailorg*, hypnotizing the spectators. Noise and silence in alternating fight, for hours, from the morning to the night. Destination is one cave behind the big waterfall of *Dailorg*. One by one the goat men get inside with small jumps. The legs give up now. The hard masks show hot and red faces of tired Mu people. The beast is tamed. Through the fair air Great Mother's whispers could be heard, the atmosphere is full of pearly shades now. Once put away the beast skins, the goats turn back into Mu people, eating, drinking and sleeping with their heads resting over a straight stone, overnight, inside the cave. They silently listen to the voice of the water. A legend tells that it fell down from the mouth of Great Mother who created Mu with a yell from her throat, deep and strong.

Dailorg is not only sylvan ancestral rituals. Gradually going up to the hill towards the town centre the silence is broken by urban noises. The main square is full of Mu people running up and down, everyone lost in their daily small life problems. The sight is impressed by a huge fountain. The open mouth of the marble head of the Goddess gushes pure water falling over the tongue of the frog Heket resting over a candid shell. From the frog's mouth comes out a gush that hits the tongue of another frog from where comes out another gush that hits another frog until a number of twelve. The result is surprising, synchronous. The water gets colours under the greenish sky. From the other side of the square there is a statue of the Mother Goddess. In one hand she has a big heart. In the other one she has a stick about hitting a frog with its mouth wide open from where bodies and heads of Mu people come out. In *Dailorg* there are no temples, no churches, no Gods where Mu people have to worship. Religion is a trick of their souls. The Goddess is only a symbol that doesn't require any kind of worship. It's a voice that creates and breaks the anger of the dark. Throat vibrating and filling the empty with sounds and whispers. Heket is the teacher of sounds, able to vibrate the senses with the strength of her arcane tongue.

A group of tourists gets closer to the fountain and is looking stunned at the sinuous shapes of the Goddess. A woman with a perfect oval face and the stunning white usual to Mu's witnessing ancient myths. 'The legend says that hitting the frog forcing it to reveal its secrets, the Goddess succeed to lead over the underground powers and getting to know fruitful mysteries, enclosed into fertile and pregnant womb of the Earth. The perfect balance between good and evil is guaranteed by the stick of the Mother caressing the worlds without excluding the chance of always new future to discover. Doubts and investigations are not banned. From the frog's mouth, delivered by the lunar uterus, the eternal and immortal sons of the Underground Earth go out, Mu's people with hairy heads and silver nails. The special ones, the immortals. Their birth touches black and white, their heart is the reflection of the Mother's heart whose the 12 frogs whispered to the worlds. But their croaking goes lost through the air of the Universe, suspended between stars and planets up there in the sky and down, through strong green tunnels crowded with souls, over the stormy and dispersing foam of the oceans, on hefty islands, inside dark caves of the subconscious cut by the monsters of soul. The message of life spreads out, having different new shapes, modified by the friction against the earth of the parallel spaces, confused with the sharp and irreverent sparkle of the stars, sharp teeth of the night. They bite the sky and swallow it shining of new senses inspired by the voices of the frogs. And every world will make the message its own, but distraught, adapted to the mutability of the being, to the creatures different for shape and substance of hearts. Yet the message is misunderstood by someone, horribly warped. The Mother becomes Father. A huge white beard grows on her face and it gets printed over time and season indicators called calendars. The primitive shell of the Mother Goddess, whose fertile womb gives births, the primitive uterus, it transforms into an enormous phallus of a jealous God. The frog gets nailed to avoid it to keep talking, to avoid it to tell the truth and the message gets buried, condemned by the oblivion. The Father opens his mouth and screams. His wild and feral yell breaks the sound barriers, smashing down the open doors of the worlds. And where the Goddess would have entered smoothly, he entered violently and darkly generating his depraved brothers: money and power. Everywhere the gluttony of scream tears down like heavy stone over freedom ruthlessly breaking it. Disengaged trees, destroyed houses, alienated consciences, victims and oppressors, States, wars, blood, battles, inquisitions, lodges, secret sects and conspiracies, unfair democracies, secret services, credit establishments, roly-poly toy tiara. The yell of the plunderer phallus sounds like echo of death generating hate. The God tries to steal the stick off the Goddess to beat himself the frogs and replacing her. He wants to reach her to kill and to erase any proof of her existence. The goddess feels his heavy steps, hitting Heket with the stick. The frog yells as loud as it can and its message can be heard through 12 worlds. Mu shakes down to the foundations and the moon in the sky can be seen afterwards. Then the Great Mother rips her heart off the chest, holding strongly in her left hand. Under her candid feet the ground opens like one uterus. The Mother makes her precious beating heart falling into it. Mu still keeps it in the Black Star's chest. Before God can reach her with his huge sword, the Goddess melts over a pathway through the Underground World. The pearly path of the Great Mothers. The disappointed God, is always looking for the Mother. Sometimes, travelling he rests over sharp stars and cutting through with his feet ice and fire planets, he finds his dust spread all over the worlds, echo of Heket's yell. The God has never reached the ancient heart of the Goddess and all Mu's people are hoping he would never get it not oven with the help of the dead ones.'

Iris feels a shake on her back. She looks into her sister eyes shivering, thinking of what could happen. 'Let's buy 2kg of apples.'

THE KISS

Chemako thanks them, the fruit is good, finely ripened. After dinner, he blows out the air with a loud noise, attempting to mess people's hair that are puzzled. He sits on the beach in between Iris, Luce, Nudo and Niobe. Puck is purring. All inside a circle traced on the sand. The night is awesome. The waves are touching finely the bank of a sea full of reflections.

Chemako is sad. 'If the other dead ones find out I am talking to you, I would get killed.'

Luce invites him to talk avoiding humour.

'I am the last arrived and I am the less important. They don't say anything to me and sometimes I don't get their speeches. They say that our leader, Naiir, kissed a wizard on his mouth, a strong one it seems, someone really clever. It should not be known officially, but everyone talks about it under their breath. An ordinary dead person explained that is a kind of agreement, I don't know. He said that there was a kind of meeting between the leader and Dr Scuro. Both together with their collaborators. An epic event, it has been said. They talked for a while and then they kissed each other, horrible! Then thanks to this kiss it looks that dead ones would become important at Mu. Dr Scuro promised it to Naiir.'

'Since when Mu's dead ones have a leader?'

'It's been a month, maybe, elected overwhelmingly through direct democracy. It's been said something about ballot rigging.'

'What does the wizard want to obtain from the dead ones?'

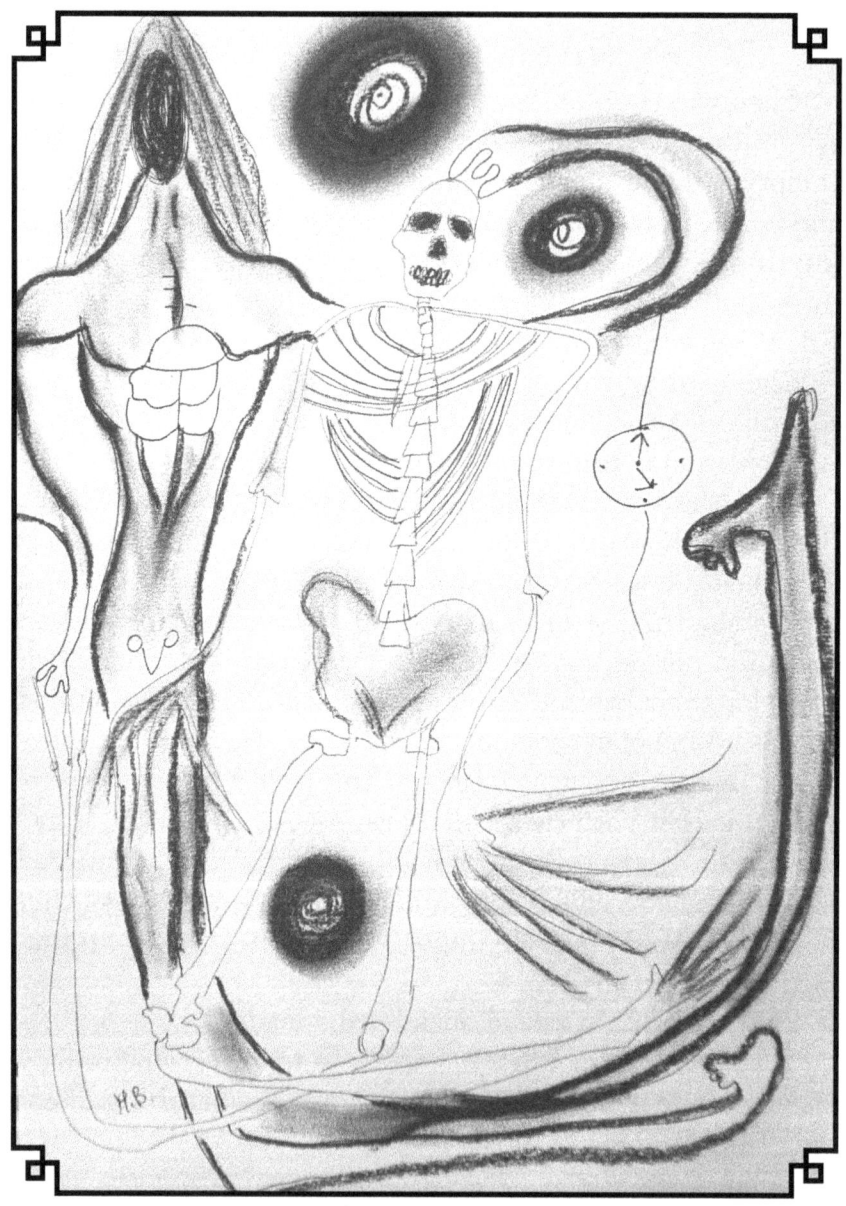

'I believe some help.'
'What kind of help?'
'To come to Mu. He cannot jump. When he will be here the dead ones will gain strength. Our things will be more respected and Mu people will be scared of us, they will obey to us. It is cool, isn't it? Democracy rebirth plan. They called it this way. Everyone will have his own duty and there will be someone leading and someone less important. For the first time some hierarchies will be made that will be breaking homogenisation. We are not all the same, but different. This has to be highlighted. Surely I won't be considered even for any responsibility roles, indeed. I am ignorant and maybe I don't know what to do as well. I don't mind the power.'

'Is everyone coming along with the plan?'

'I am not sure, I do believe that some don't really know what is happening, a bit like me. I did get very little of it. There will be a meeting tonight. I feel the shades already getting closer to me. I think they will take a decision about the matter and every doubt will be sorted, hopefully.'

Nudo and Luce are the only ones that could be in the meeting of dead ones with no risk for their own lives. Luce because is the Black Star, Nudo because he's already dead in the Upper World so he cannot die twice, it would be more than enough.

Niobe, Iris and Puck go away.

The night is sadly quiet. The shades coming produces like a silky swish.

Naiir is on the front followed by a queue of naked dead ones like souls on the Judgement Day. They have two bundles under their arms, one white, one black. Naiir is covered by a black linen tunic. All the dead ones come forward silently. The moon illuminates their ghostly faces, hard cheekbones, dark eyes to pierce the night. The ruthless wind goes through their bodies of nothing and it whines a deep gloomy sound, whispered to the waves and the deep ocean.

Naiir acknowledges the presence of Luce and his gesture looks disappointed, although it is everything pointless against her. He severely rebukes Chemako because he left without permission. The dead ones, without talking, make a circle sitting on the sand. In the middle Naiir is standing and he is explaining them the reasons of the meeting. 'It has finally come the time for our redemption against the not existence. We are the unlucky sons of Mu, unhappy birth of the destiny. Do our living Mu's brothers love us? They don't even remember us. Their life goes on and we, who could live forever and get warm through the greenish air at Mu, are relegated dragging out the weight of the absence of our no-bodies to the bottom of the sea, gathering us on this beach, run through by the cold beams of the moon. Mu people are scared of the death, they don't get even close to us. They send us away to the borders of Mu, because our presence disappoints them. Running their bodies through ours makes them nervous. We represent a stage that they would never like to reach. Our physical presence puts under their eyes the evidence of the death existence. They cannot stand it, poor ones! So for some bad reasons, wounds, incidents, lethal fallings, murders, we are second class citizens. An embarrassing evidence, a scandal, fear, horror and panic, this is what we are. Buried under the oblivion of the sand, shooed like scruffy dogs, abandoned, loathed by all. And the hunger gives us troubles, always. We have no stomachs, no liver no heart, although we feel a huge absurd and uncontrollable hunger.'

Chemako nods.

'But we can be strong together, united. A big important family. We are supportive between each other. But that is not enough. We want more, I want more, but not for myself, for you who are like sons for me, like brothers and sisters, ignored by the eternal kiss of the Mothers. Do you think is fair that the other Mu people would live almost eternally and we are dead? Who are we? Why death to us and life to others? There is no logical sense in all of that. Do you know why? Because the worlds have no sense. Death is not the punishment given to the evils, it is not a penitence of the Great Mother. It is the bad and rotten result of the fate. It has no eyes, no brain, no hands, no ears, no nose. Endeavour with no parameter, irrational God! We are its burnt offering. The worlds themselves, their variety, they were born from the chaos, no order no limits. Irrationality! Even there are men and women in other worlds that had given a sense to all this, rationalising the life, scanning the time and the seasons, creating the State and the power. At Mu none, all this is impossible. Who speaks about power can be considered a seditious, a dangerous thug. Though men since generations know the power.'

'For this reason did you gather your dead ones family Naiir?'

Luce's voice goes through the body of the dead ones chief.

'Dead ones feel suddenly the need to have a boss, a leader. Good news really. Dead ones talk about power. It could burn your gut and make you feel a bigger hunger, stronger, a devouring hunger like the hydra, able to regrow back, insatiable. It could destroy you.'

'Dead ones! Did you hear that? I would say that in our

case it cannot be said that more destroyed than this it can be dying!'

Strained laughs come out the throats of the dead ones.

'Luce, come on, don't you have anything better to say? Do you believe we have something to loose then?'

'If you would not have anything to loose, you could not have something to gain. If you were nothing, you would not have been playing with the idea of everything inspired by the power.'

'Power is necessary to become something.'

'If a little scintilla of dignity still exists after death, that thing that you will become would be monstrous and alienating. You would not recognise yourselves and you would be only and always hungry.'

'We will satisfy our physical hunger with the broth of power, we will fill every gap with sense.'

'How?'

'Dr Scuro will show us the way.'

'The wizard will destroy Mu and he will satisfy his own pride.'

'We will help him to come into our World. We will sacrifice for him our purest soul among our dead ones, so he could make the jump. Afterwards we will realise our dreams. Dead ones! Oh, I am talking to you. Wouldn't you like to be the first class citizens, the strong powers of Mu? Wouldn't you like to release yourselves from hunger and starvation? Wouldn't you accept to be reborn and lead over the living ones?'

'Yesss!' The yell is almost unanimous.

Chemako stands up and sits next to Luce. 'No, for me no. I don't want to. I don't care about power, it will be a weapons which I cannot use. I am against it. We cannot calculate the results of a random jump, led by our crushes. The wizard doesn't have to jump. You talk about sacrifice. The order starts not very good, with a sacrifice of a pure soul whose marrow has to be sucked by Scuro to let him enter to Mu. A rebirth built over blood it cannot be a sweet awakening.'

Naiir is furious. 'Idiot traitor! Dead ones don't have blood! Let's take him!'

Chemako sits inside the circle between Nudo and Luce throwing a challenging sight to the leader.

Nudo looks at Luce and then he stands up. 'Chemako will come with us, troubles to whom dares to touch him!'

The dead ones leader is beside himself, 'You can keep him, what a miserable! Ignore them! Come on! Let's vote! Let's choose our bundle!'

In few minutes all the dead ones are dressed in black. Only Chemako is wearing a white tunic.

The dead ones want Scuro to enter Mu to seed the evil art of the power.

They deliberate for hours. They need purity, the necessary mean to let Scuro jumping through the worlds. But nobody among the dead ones gathered in that meeting could have purity. The stains of their souls paint their ghostly faces. Their words are full of greed, captivating, that goes through the gaps of their ribs. The envying absence of their petrified hearts is contaminated with the wish to obtain again the life. Then everyone turns towards the circle where Chemako is sitting. His body is bright of purity. He has got the sorrow of hunger and two apples are enough for him to be happy. Dead ones want him now. They stare their stunned pupils over him. They surround the circle for the whole night. But Luce and Nudo do not give up. They will wait until the dawn. When the brighter light will force the dead ones to take shelter to the bottom of the ocean, they could exit the circle and take Chemako to a safe place.

The greenish night gloom after hours of wait vanishes finally under the daily light coming. The three friends, tired of the long wakefulness, stand out the circle and travel through the way to get back to Luce's house.

Whilst digging his feet into the sand, Nudo becomes sadder every minute. 'Do you know, my friends, what is the Government?'

Chemako does not have a clue about it.

Nudo goes on, like he is talking to himself, 'The Government is a horrible monster that devastates everything touches, corrupting it, making it rotten. It opens the greedy mouth swallowing all our freedom with the excuse to tidy up everything, to rule over our lives. And then the rotten goes everywhere, like the tentacles of an octopus. A devastated world. I used to know it, you see, and it killed me. The State has got its servants in uniform that obey to the orders of the stronger like blind puppets. A senseless world... Truths built up that aren't true, even.'

Luce is puzzled, 'I do not understand.'

'You are lucky that you do not understand, believe me. I fear that Scuro entering to Mu will make you understand what I am saying now.'

'It's been said that you killed yourself.'

'Gosh no! I could never do it, and I have been always innocent. Murder. We were 84 of us. All stopped by the State servants. They needed a scapegoat and they questioned me.'

'For what?'

'Massacre. We had placed a bomb into a square. Obviously they did not have any proof against me. I told them. As reply they punched my eye and they threw me out the police station window. They were 4 brawny men, I could not make it on my own. I actually got crushed into the bush. So it's finished the life in the Upper World for me. A second of distraction and all finishes. That's why we don't want to get distracted. Luce! We cannot let Scuro to make his jump, it could be the disaster for Mu. The taste of the power has already ruined the dead ones. Then he would chase up the living ones like an epidemic, a ruining cancer. We have to stop him. We are in danger.'

On the bottom of the road there is Puck jumping on Luce. He is happy to see them. Behind him Niobe smiling. They decide overwhelmingly to take Chemako home. There he will be safe. The sorceress will spread some herbs that will keep the dead ones away from there and the poor guest would ideally rest.

After few hours Chemako gets awaken by footsteps inside the room that Niobe has given to him. Maybe is a nightmare. He rubs his eyes. No, the dead ones are surrounding for real his bed. Naiir laughs sarcastically, inviting him to stand up. Chemako yells Niobe's name with no effect.

'It's useless for you to call her, idiot! No one of your friends could help you, you are the scapegoat, the perfect sacrifice, stand up, pure soul, we need you. We will take you around to the Upper World.'

'No, I don't want to!'

'What you want we don't care about, for us you are only an instrument.'

Chemako is hungry and scared. Then he thinks that he is already dead so they cannot kill him twice, not even hurt him. Although he is nervous. He has got a bad feeling.

Naiir's menacing expression doesn't show anything good. A criminal organisation, that's what they are those dead ones. They are dangerous.

An instrument. He never played in his whole life! Chemako has always been a bit ingenuous, happy with little things. It's been said that the herbs of the sorceress would have kept those thugs away! They did the opposite effect. They entered in Niobe's house and in every room like nothing, quietly. Maybe Niobe got the wrong herb. Hopefully they did not hurt her! Those thugs have no mercy, they can behave cruelly! They will go through their own mums corpses to do things like the living ones and to become important, considerable ones in the Underground World!

God knows where we are going to. Where they are taking me to. Escape is not the right thing to do now. I am strictly under surveillance.

It can be heard the noise of streaming water. Nice, a marvellous waterfall! Amazing! And what is this? Ah, it's a cave, really nice, but cold. There are mushrooms on the walls. Maybe they are edible. And what a hard work to climb up here! Don't they feel tired? They look like robots, even their eyes, blank expressions. I wouldn't be surprised if their pupils will turn around like tops, as they are not real. Who knows! Hey, what are they doing? Damned! Here, naked and under cold water, what a good one! They put a black tunic over me now. That's what I need. It is horrible, awful, I don't like it. I think they do not care about it that much. I am the scapegoat, that's what they said, oh gosh! They will give me a good lesson now. Completely dark into the bottom of the cave. It's huge! Massive. The hole of a monster. And what is down there? A tunnel. They push me in. I have to enter through it basically. My legs are shaking. Not even one apple they give me those bastards. Naiir sometimes pushes me. Idiot! Who made him the boss needs a specialist of nervous diseases. One of those where you will sit on the chase and you tell him about your life. Maybe the famous wizard that hits the frogs made him the boss. The boss of the servants. He could have chosen just an idiot like Naiir as king for other idiots. God knows where they will take me. This tunnel looks like an ox gut, tight and long and dark. Sometimes I have to bow because I could hit my head against the walls. One moment, they are soft. What kind of place is this? A soft gut. Now we go down. It's slippery. Some vibes could be heard. The inside is moving. A nightmare like no others. Wouldn't be that Niobe has given me some drugs to make me sleep and I am dreaming? Cannot understand. I cannot see the difference between the true and false. Total confusion, as usual. I have been confused when living and I guess when dead something wouldn't change? Oh, what is this? Nice room, all covered with velvet. I get nervous with all this red colour. It's in my eyes. There is a bed with black blankets too.

That should be the famous wizard. I would imagine him more awful. He is big, lot of muscles. What does he do? He puts one hand over my head. He looks into my eyes. Those pupils are hypnotic islands. The eyelids are heavy like they would be existing for real and not even consumed by the death. Noises come to me deaden. Dead ones are around me. They lift me up towards a dark bed. What a deadly sleep! The wizard plunges his arm through my body. It can be seen his hand swelling out like absorbing energy. All the muscles stretched, vibrating. The veins of his body blown up. Now it can only be heard the heart beat of Dr Scuro. Vibrations hit the air, stronger whilst my dead body is vanishing until becomes air. Chemako is not there anymore. Better, he is there, although his energies that permitted him to look as real body, are not there anymore. Absorbed by Scuro.

That bastard hitting the frogs took the energy from the purest dead one in all Mu. Now he is strong, half naked. His hips are wrapped around a cloth, lifting his arms up, fixing thoughts through movements and actions. He vacates the mind, creating the empty. A woman comes in with blue reflections hair. She fixes the thought with a gesture lifting up her arms too. She only wears a light black tunic. Her body shapes can be seen through the tunic. The cloth wrapped around Dr Scuro's hips falls down, the black tunic of the woman falls down over the red floor. The light comes through an oval window on the ceiling. The two go under the light, hit by the sunlight illuminating their pale flesh. The woman opens a glass cabinet, inside there is an obsidian full of energy absorbed by the pure body of Puck. She offers the stone to the wizard who swallows it. Afterwards he gets closer to the woman.

Through the ritual orgasm the wizard gets through a different condition of being. Energies got released. The physical body through the sensual pleasure goes through a psychological transcending that makes possible to switch a level. Mental flow grows up like a flooding river until reaching its peak during the orgasm. Death and life get mixed up. The woman allied to the dead ones has offered Chemako and now her body is able to go beyond limits. Mysterious powers free. The alive seed is full of new energies. The wizard transcends himself alienating through the peak of the action. He goes through a backward pathway beyond the time, going down the stairs of puberty, steps of childhood until get confused within its own seed. He is ready, he rushed into quickly. He jumps through the dimension of the Underground World. A moment when the soul flows inside a gap through the ancient heart of Mu.

Luce has a grip to her chest, like a stitch. From her mouth a white smoke comes out. For three days she is a kind of alienated, stunned. Then she gets better, but she feels like something happened. On the third day Scuro was reborn naked into the cave behind the *Dailorg* waterfalls. He stands up, wearing a black tunic, opening his arms in front of the water flowing and shouting his name pinching the air shivering in front of the evidence of his physical body presence.

The wizard was reborn at Mu. At the bottom of the waterfall the dead ones are waiting for him. Even the woman with blue hair is waiting for him. She turns towards him smiling. She takes her blue wig off showing blonde curls like ripened wheat. The light illuminates her face. And Niobe betrayed her people for the love of the darkness.

Luce can see her through the double pupil of Iris down to change the wet cloth on her head. Even Nudo is there, next to her bed. He has understood that something really shocking happened. Through his eyes all the sadness of the world. Nothing will be the same like before.

After 40 days Luce is completely recovered. Through the mirror on the wall over the head she can see in her room everything is happening in the Upper World, wars, State's homicides, rapes, corruption, taxes, banks, slotted time, daylight saving time and solar time. All perfect, nothing to say. Mu cannot be ever like this. She breaks the mirror with a marble pyramid. 'Those are childhood games. We need to focus on what happens here and I cannot see it through a stupid mirror.'

Nudo and Iris look her a bit worried. Someone knocks on the door.

Luce goes to the door inviting someone to enter. Nudo and Iris cannot see anybody though. It looks nobody is there. The Star invites Mr Nobody to sit on one chair. She tells him to wait. Then she goes into the cupboard room and she takes some apples. She offers two of them to the air and let them go, but they do not fall down. They are suspended in the air, then vanishing slowly, like someone is biting them. It is only the core left at the end.

'What a task to get here, my friends!' Mr Nobody talks now. 'I did not know the way to get here, do you know? Indeed I had to ask for it a blind person, the only one that was kind to answer to me. The others were running away. Dr Scuro has sucked all my energy out. Niobe has given me into his hands, good bargain, really! And now here I am, without my body appearance, I am well, I should say, I cannot see myself even. Voilà, where's the arm? There is none! And the hand? None as well! But I am always really hungry.' The apples pieces that has been bitten float inside the invisible stomach of the poor Chemako. 'I want to laugh, my dreams are becoming true, I would say. When I was alive I wished to be invisible. And now I am super transparent, like empty, exhausted.'

Nudo is puzzled. 'Luce, can you see him?'

'Yes, I can see him exactly like before.'

Iris understands. 'If I even had the gift of the sight, I could not see anything. Only Luce can see him because she is the only one who can go beyond the barriers of the death, for Mothers willing. We can hear it. It's just something, poor Chemako! The purity lives where you won't be expecting.'

The dead one gets offended. 'Why are you saying this? Did I look not pure when I wasn't invisible?'

'Sincerely you looked to me more stupid than pure.'

'For a superficial spirit is always really easy to confuse the spontaneity with unworldliness and to mix stupidity with beauty or thinness with coldness or fatness with ugliness or a car with windscreen, no, no windscreen, wind breeze indeed.'

'What are you saying?'

'Or finesse with old age, or tiredness with tightness, disdain with fragrance.'

'This is crazy.'

'Crazy with misdeed, I get closer to your double marine eye.'

'I got it now, stop it, I did not mean to offend you and please don't get closer, that is better.'

'Awaken with...'

'Are you starting again...?'

'What do you mean? Ah, yes, worms.'

Worms?'

'Unarmed, affirmed, confirmed, no, not at all, it's worms indeed!'

Luce replies, 'Let him talk, he repeats words that the wizard thought whilst he was sucking his energy, they seem not to have a logical sense. Iris, it's nothing wrong with you. It's an involuntary process.'

'Calendar, dogs, State, executed, banks, benches, tired... Hands, yes, hands. Oi, oi, what a headache... Stay, holiday, sad. I cannot stop. That wizard has broken me... I believe he took something off me making myself pronouncing nosense sentences.'

Luce asks him to rest. 'Come to me for a sleep, into the room next mine, there is a comfy bed. It's evening now.'
'The Black Star and the Sun.'
'Yes, yes, indeed.'
'Proudly it rips lives off, new spring, infinite era...words, waves, all, all... Oi, oi my head, shocking, disturbing...'

Dr Scuro left the cave of Mu where he was reborn and he talks to the dead ones from the top of a rock.

'This is not anymore time for words, friends. The machinery of the Government has to start up in this greenish and quiet world without breeze. There will be a new Mu spring. Your voices will get to the sky, shaking the sun and the beauty of the stars. Until now you all have been considered as useless worms. Thrown away by stray dogs, like junk. You live through the coldness of the deep maritime eye, abandoned among the waves of nothing. The proud death mangles your lives and what Mu people do? They forget. The oblivion is a comfortable panacea for the torment of a superficial spirit, an amazing misdeed. And what does remain of your beauty, of your hands warmth, of the infinite words pronounced by your mouth? Disappear. There is no Mu person who does not hate you, who doesn't think about you disgusted and feared. I wake up in Mu as reborn towards new eras of spiritual light and I can see your future marked into a calendar of a newborn time. I can see a State, banks with their glossy plastic chairs where citizen can rest their tired bones and worm out by the daily work. All the same, dead ones and living ones, fatness and thinness. The executed criminal and the awarded innocent. Homogenisation. This is the correct word. Fairly the ugliness of centuries of anarchy needs a strong wrist, special arrangements. Mu people have to understand from the early stage who is coming to lead. Our awaken heart will create a new world. Order and discipline. A perfect power, with no creases, no surprises. I will make you taste the stunning delight of the power that will penetrate through your veins like sweet bile. The Black Star will respect you finally. All Mu people will love you because people really love the strong ones, admiring them. You will be the gods of Underground World. We are the Government, we are the Supreme Father who rules and decides. Nobody could stop our way to the power. To realise our dreams we need some sacrifices and to act finely, smartly. We will coin new money, spreading it. The jingling of the gold will fill our ears with new marvellous sounds. One unique currency for all Mu people. Dead ones, are you ready to become my precious ministers, my soldiers?'

'Yesss... Hurray! Hurray! But what does it mean?'

'I haven't understood well, although they will love us, it's all we want.'

'Hurray! Hurray!'

'If you will be loyal to me, I will take you to the stars. We will extract from the generous womb of Mu so much gold that we could buy all the worlds that will bow down in front of us.'

'Yes, yesss!'

'And we will have a headquarters where my love Niobe and I will live. There we will have meetings to decide about changing the face of Mu. Now follow me to the cave of *Dailorg* where I was reborn in Mu. I will show you things that you never dreamt about.'

The warm breaths of the dead ones crowd the cave. It's hot. Scuro orders to them to make a circle, leaving a huge room in the middle. The ground in the middle starts moving and some dark shadows made their appearance. A really thin dust goes through the air. A black dot shows on the ground, getting larger slowly like a colour spreading then it starts to go deeper, deeper in the ground. A huge chasm appears quickly around the feet of those stunned eyes among Mu people. From the chasm a strong cold breeze comes out that smells of rotten. A big hand with sharp nails from the bottom grabs the edge of the chasm trying to come out the abyss. Monstrous arms, slimy tails, unusual creatures with odd shapes are living inside the huge hole in the ground. Metallic bodies, half Mu people, half fish-like emanate some sharp sounds and whistles bit disturbing to hear. Four demons show up from the bottom waving Scuro and they sit on the edge of the chasm. Two are stunning, naked and similar to Greeks. Their perfect shapes and muscles leap under the eyes of the crowd. The other two are disgusting and ugly. They all stand up going behind Scuro. They slowly go through his body like they would have to load him with new energies and then they disappear inside the wizard. The chasm now is full of weapons. Scuro invites the Mu people to take them. He will teach them how to use those weapons. The conquer of a new world cannot be done unarmed, it needs some means that could persuade even the reluctant people.

The dead ones' training to use the weapons will happen into the fields of the surrounding *Dailorg* Castle that will belong to Scuro now. The wizard himself will deal with the training, helped by the four destroying demons smartly called in and then through his body, life and death symbols.

The castle, huge and majestic, sits over one hill straight down the seaside. On the stone towers, really high and ancient, sturdy ivy leaves climb up with thousands bloody eyes. The pathway to the top can be walked through or reached boarding fast triangular Mu's shuttles.

Dr Scuro asks to make one blue shuttle ready, with customized interiors in black leather and red velvet, mobile bar and massaging seats. The Head of Government doesn't have to walk. The door to access to the castle is monumental, decorated with carved iron sculptures, monsters heads and odd symbols whose meaning is not even clear to the historians of *Dailorg*. Once we get in, there is a huge staircase. The steps are made from coloured stones and bones. On the right hand side of the stairs there is a marble statue of the Goddess Mother. Scuro orders that it has to be destroyed, substituting it with one that depicts himself. Some among the dead ones have been excellent sculptors and painters. The wizard poses for months, benefiting from their talent. On top of the stairs enormous arches with acanthus leaves carvings embellish recesses where ancient paintings colour offers beauty to the visitors. Scuro makes removing them thinking they are not suitable for his new leadership. Paintings about Mu's legends, depicting the quality of the Mothers. All changed. Now the Underground World is ruled by the Father. Obelisks everywhere, stretched muscles paintings, beards, rough Mu people trapping the moon inside one ampoule.

The Weapons Hall of the castle full of armours and precious things of the past turns into a Massage Hall. The wizard has chosen among the living parents of the dead ones four excellent Mu's masseurs, really expert. Their light hands press over his skin really expertly, loosening knurls and tensions. It needs to involve living ones. True revolutions cannot be done only involving dead ones. The whole Mu population has to be contaminated by the power delight. The dungeons got prepared to inflict tortures to all the regime opponents. There are antiques, but always efficient tools ready to be used: "interrogation chairs", "head crushers", "branks", "scavenger's daughter", "diving chairs", "scold's bridle", and a black goat with a rough tongue for a special kind of punishment. The investigated one is fastened, his feet spread with salt. The goat licks them until bleeding. Two dead ones are in charge of feeding the animal and cleaning the precious instruments. The Banqueting Hall is still the same. Scuro hopes that soon the tables will be full of fellows. They would eat together until exploding. The cake will be shared as to keep everyone happy so the party will never end. The big library, severe and full of busts, will be used for meeting and conferences, the small one, cosy and stunning, for more private meetings. The garden is really green. They pull the neck to the white swans in the lake. The black swans, instead, can keep swimming without being disturbed reflecting themselves through the fair cold water.

Niobe persuades the wizard not to cut the flowers off. She will need them to prepare perfumes and potions to cook in some days and to marinate things in some other days, according to old effective recipes. Scuro listens to her because he is sure that he could benefit from the concoctions of his partner, an ancient soul. Without her, he would had never succeeded to get to Mu. She prepared for him magic rings with small tanks full of special liquids loaded of strengths. She has chosen the stones to mount on the rings and the perfume that Scuro has to put on in special ritual occasions. She has collected the herbs to obtain essences, she marinated the plants with human fat extracted from the sweat of the wizard. She fed Puck after Hilde's travel. She thought the energy of the small innocent rhino-grade could be enough to make Scuro jumping, but it wasn't. So Niobe has caused the anger of Thomas against Chemako, giving to his allied the purest and most stupid dead one among the whole Mu that, together with the strengths of Puck's obsidian, would have let the jump between one world to the other.

An incorporeal energy, limitless, technically perfect. Ritual bearings has allowed an irresistible energy to spread out, sublime sum up of three powers together. The intersection of those three energies has generated one spot. Travelling inside it has been possible to find the very little way to the ancient heart of Mu, shielded in Luce's chest. The first meeting of Dr Scuro with Niobe happened accidentally. Niobe one night was looking for a special kind of herb which grows up only alongside the rocks of the waterfalls opposite the cave of *Dailorg*. She was filling up her linen bag with tuft of fresh herbs, scented and dewy, when she heard a vibration. Her fingers looked as numb, insensitive. She found herself accidentally with no reason into a shady room. Some men around a table were focussing their energies towards a saucer. One, especially, had his eyes deep as winter lakes and solid shoulders like rocky mountains. Niobe realised that he could be a human. Sometimes the inhabitants of the Underground World having peculiar energies, got projected through the Upper Earth. It happened other few times to Niobe. But never she got lost into a man eyes neither a man got lost into her ones. Only that man could see her. Niobe put her finger on the saucer through some letters inside it spelling the word D A I L O R G. If before seeing Niobe Dr Scuro was a common ordinary, greedy and dishonest State person, afterwards he started to believe about things beyond his sight for real. New opportunities, new powers, a different World. Their meetings happened more often. Scuro started to give all his efforts through some occultism. He hired a famous medium for any communications with the "creature". He did not know yet Niobe's name. Slowly he found out everything and day by day he was craving to do the big jump. From that point occultist meetings, goats sacrifices. He wanted to find a way through for the New World. Niobe bewitched him. Her power was strong. She loved and hated him at the same time. She has directed him, guided him, told him Mu's legends. Their last meeting into the Upper World, into the red velvet room has been memorable. The energies out from their two bodies orgasms, after the wizard had absorbed Chemako's energies, made the jump possible. The Upper World medium was almost about to die to evoke Chemako and Niobe together, due the opposition of the first one. Then Chemako has been led by the fluid of the medium, so together with Niobe he has jumped into the Upper World and Dr Scuro has absorbed the dead one's vitality to join the sorceress rituals and to make the big jump, being born again inside *Dailorg* cave. Niobe waits for him with dead ones on the bottom of the waterfalls ready to follow all Scuro's orders. Now they handle their weapons around the fields surrounding *Dailorg* castle.

Naiir and Scuro check the Mu dead ones troops. Some of them don't even know how to handle the rifle shaking it like a toy, looking "stupidly" inside the gun barrel.

Scuro is furious. He makes a rasping yell and from his body the four tutor demons come out trying to convert those unprepared Mu ones into a cruel soldiers, ready to kill.

The two awesome demons explain to the Mu ones the beauty of the war, the delight of heroism and bravery, the affection for their own weapon, the techniques to handle it in the same position, clean it, mount and unfix it in a short time.

One of the two suddenly makes an encouraging speech. 'Peacefully armed, we will conquer *Dailorg* with pious devices that you handle, try to stand straight at least idiots! We will face, if necessary, the creative positivity of accidentally arguments, although the real living "flesh and bones" Mu people would have, as said, a different point of view from ours, that is. Life is made of strength and contrast, two constant and ineffable rules. We will respect them. Religion, power, politics, economics will drink the blood of our opponent enemies. By the way, who we will be with no enemies? What could we become? Nothing. The hostility is the core of the political exercise. The weapon is the mean that allows the dreams to come true. For this reason, you have to use them in the best way possible, until getting to the identification. You would choose your weapon, feeling a certain physical affinity, aesthetic with it, do you get me?'

Naiir nods everyone to say yes and everybody nod back saying yes.

'Well, appearance is nothing that fills the space up of the everything simply because it needs to hide it.'

The dead ones yawn now.

'You will be the State's servants, honest, ready to sacrifice, obedient overall, aware to be pawns of an important game, drops of a huge ocean, brothers united to create the Republic of Mu. Do you know what I mean?'

'Nooo, we don't know it, Majesty, we don't know it.'

'Good. The only thing you should know is that you are the State so the State loves you because you love yourselves, right?'

'Right, Majesty, right! Yes, Sir!'

'So you are fighting for the life of Mu, because if you will be the State, you will be again alive, main part of the whole, you will have your new dignity, you will serve yourselves and nobody else.'

'Yes, Sir!'

The two monstrous demons become a target now. They wear white shirts thin as onion skins. They open wide their arms saying to the dead ones to shoot trying to centre them. Then they take off their pierced shirts, deciding over the points that each soldier scored. Before starting again they pull out the bullets from their bodies with their own hands, whilst the Mu people look at them stunned, they yawn and order to the new soldiers to shoot again. The air is full of sounds that don't give a peaceful feeling.

The best shooters will be the personal guard for Scuro and they will be manning day and night the castle of *Dailorg*. Niobe looks outside from one of the huge windows of the castle whilst she gets the smallest room in her hands that will become her personal laboratory. She covers a boxwood table that is pointed towards east, with an ornamental linen cloth. On the table two candelabras symbolising sky and ground. From the ceiling one lamp made of blown glass, black and white. Two incense holders have their sticks spreading deep aromas around. A woollen carpet softens the steps noises. Everywhere magic instruments: *in primis* the perfectly straight magic wand, of blossomed hazelnut wood, cut with a noble wood sickle, the sword, the cup and the pentagram, a box with some perfumes, a coal box, a bowl with ritual water, oils, candles, wreaths, incense holders.

The sorceress sprays a "kastania" essence through the

air, opening a cardboard box and taking out a bat still living that immediately flies to the lamp. She hangs to the wall some small paintings with some moving insects that move their legs under the glass. They are mechanical devices, nothing really supernatural, only ornaments.

From a luggage she takes out a sachet with some herbs of the spirits: coriander, celery and henbane, together with the poisoning hemlock whose smoke attracts the demons.

A door links the laboratory with another hall, from where, gone through 21 gates, 15 doors, 7 courtyards, it can be accessed to a dead ones Court, where Scuro will judge his political opponents. Trials with no chance to appeal against everyone would dare to discuss the State Principles founded over rationality and order.

The Republic of Mu

'You should fight and dig into Mu's womb to look for this.' The wizard lifts up a piece of yellow metal that under the light looks having really shocking appearance. 'Its name is Gold. Its value is equal to its charm.' Mu people struggle to understand what is the meaning of the word "charm" referred to a piece of metal. They never need it and they don't know it. Although, that shining material seems to have the maximum importance for Dr Scuro. He orders to violate the intimacy of the land of Mu, to probe the silent rivers of *Dailorg* for the gold hunting. The dead ones, guns in hand, invade the town and they dig out, devastating, browsing through. The gold gets transformed into ingots and stored into a secret room of the castle. There is a lot. The room is full. So the ingots get stored under the sofas, under beds, everywhere. It can breath smell of gold. Eyes are stunned because of its beauty. Although it is cold, hard, lifeless, heavy. Scuro wants to transform part of it into money. At Mu money does not exist. It's time to change. Barter is for primitive people. A well respected population has to know jingling coins and rustling notes.

The day when the first coin was minted Scuro sends shuttles equipped with loudspeakers to the main squares of Mu. The voice of the regime town criers is loud and clear, 'Listen to me, listen to me, ladies and gents of Mu, the honourable Dr Scuro invites everyone into the *Dailorg* Castle, where it would be a buffet to celebrate the beginning of a new era. Do you hear the cry in the air? Could you feel a new breeze? The Republic of Mu is born. Dr Scuro will be the first President of the history of the Underground World.

He will live into the *Dailorg* Castle together with his recently named ministers. The new government has issued a permanent army to defend Mu and from today barter is considered forbidden. The sad barter would pack up and just go forever away from here. Barred! Mu's land doesn't want it anymore. Barter will be replaced with shining gold that is in the fertile womb of *Dailorg*... Let's celebrate the birth of the first coin that will have a lot of twin sisters! The newborn ones could sleep quietly and they will be stored in the Reconversion Acts Institute that will stand into a building next to the Castle, dealing with all the financial services of Mu. Mutation will be the right word. Mu has to change aspect because of the willing of its President and his trusted ministers. The Underground World will loose every primitiveness. It will become a modern State to trust, obey and fight will be the main points of a new and unheard life philosophy. Obedience has to be the main quality for the good and honest Mu's citizens, servants of the State until identifying themselves through their President and his minsters, really pure institutions and deserving the maximum honour. Order will be the golden rule at Mu from now onwards. A State Calendar will rule the time and the hours, precisely. It will be forbidden to the mobile vendors of candied and fresh fruit, bric-a-brac, soaps, painted canvas and quackery, to stop into the public squares, issuing tickets and arresting them in the worst cases. Forbidden to open the shops overnight. Strictly forbidden to stop in the streets to talk about politics and philosophy. Any gathering will be judged not suitable for the dignity of the State of Mu. Forbidden to print books, notebooks, newspapers and leaflets that haven't been through the State censorship. For willing of the President and his minsters a State Religion will be adopted. The books over Mu legends will be written again by the regime intellectuals that will be enhancing again the priority of a unique male God over the Great Mother. Rebels will be named as irrational chaos rebels, because not able to love the beauty of the Government Order. Forbidden any cultural gathering, libraries and similar places, in order to plot any conspiracy against the newborn State. Prison or death penalty in some cases. Mu people! Come to the *Dailorg* Castle tonight, food and drinks! The new State will give the blood to you because born from the ashes of the old world!'

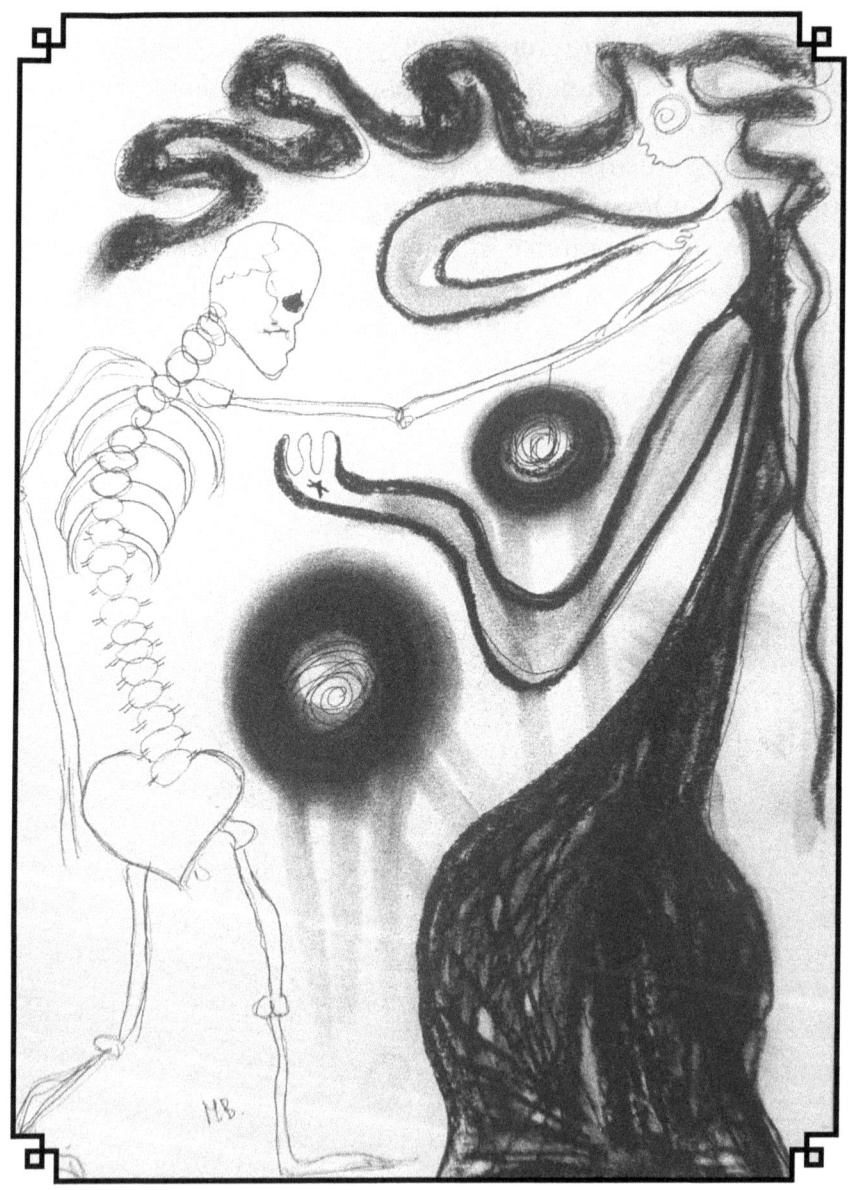

THE RESISTANCE OF MU

'The situation is hard. Now *Dailorg* is in the hands of Scuro and dead ones of Naiir. Those thugs with weapons in hand hang around the streets beating anyone would dare to make an opposition. They cannot even be killed, it's a joke!'

'Luce, calm down please!'

'Nudo I am calm, even too much, by the way. We have to do something. Mu people are not sheep ready for the slaughterhouse. A population that doesn't raise its voice it's like forgetting its own dignity somewhere long time ago.'

'It's time to stand up now!'

'Shake their minds. Resistance has to start from here.'

'From the library?'

'Scuro wants to convert it into a big hotel. We cannot afford it. We are our library. Books are our people's souls, the concrete evidence of the Mother's kindness. Inside those volumes there is everything. Life and death strictly linked with the story of our world and identity. There is the memory knocking the door of our imperfect consciences every time we browse their pages. Hate and love and the power and sorrow to exist believing into infinite levels. Mu does not have to die through Scuro's hands. Mu has got more bravery and dignity than Scuro's whole army and his servants corrupted by the gold. Luce has got her weapons too, follow me my friends! Nudo, Chemako, Iris and you too, little one, sweet Puck, come with me!'

They get into the Brains Hall. Luce pushes the wall into a dark corner. A door, that Nudo did know about, opens. It needs to go down your knees to go through it because it's really narrow. Damp smell. On their faces silky spiderwebs. Luce moves them off. Some big nyctalope bats similar to big winged rats hang from the ceilings. They are now into a really narrow corridor. It can breath hardly. After few steps they arrive in front of a white door with pearly reflections with a big cameo instead of the handle knob. Luce puts her thin hand on the knob turning it. A really strong light dazzles their eyes for few seconds then it fades lightly, so the visitors can enter. There is a really white room with no furniture, like a candid box; floor, walls, all white. Eyes are like stunned, enchanted, like trapped through a hallucination. In the middle of the room one trapdoor. Luce pulls the white ring and the hatch opens drawing a dark square mouth on the floor. They go downstairs, step by step, down, one, two, 900 steps towards the abyss. They reach one room that looks carved through the stones. There are books into stone bookshelves. Floor, walls, table, chairs, all is stone except the books and the skeletons reading them. They are everywhere, some sitting and browsing the pages, some others standing and touching the books spines looking for the right title. When they see Luce and her friends they all stop suddenly. Their eye sockets look towards their visitors. Now there is silence and a pleasant warmth comes from the stones. The skeleton sitting at the table now stands up getting closer to Luce. The skeleton greets her, offering its "all-bones hand" to shake. The Star grabs that skeleton phalanges, not scared, greeting him and smiling. She knows him. The skeleton's name is Erasmo and he is part of those dead ones of Mu that whilst living ignored terrestrial burdens, giving priority to dreams rather than material desires as they don't have flesh. They don't feel thirsty or hungry, neither cold or hot. Their feelings cannot be physical, but only metaphysical. Chemako looks at

~ *The black star of Mu* ~

them bit jealous now that he can feel his body needs without having a body, not even having a simulacrum. Erasmo pull his hands towards Chemako like the others. He can see him! Erasmo invites him to sit too realizing that he is really tired. Saying to be sorry that he doesn't have one apple for Chemako. He hugs Erasmo whilst Luce pulls out a couple of apples from a leather handbag. While Chemako sits and eats them, the others are chatting. Luce introduces her friends to Erasmo. He belongs to the dead ones superior race, the ataraxic. Once upon a time he was alive, with flesh and blood, like anyone else at Mu. Long time philosophical studies took him through the way of the indemonstrable. All the living ataraxic ones prioritised the idea of the illusory of the everything, so even of their personal feelings and body needs. It can give up the flesh and live only with a skeleton of your own research. Truth can be reproduced, auto-replicating, some times, although it does not exist with absolute monolithic certainty. Erasmo is a wise peaceful investigator. He has meditated for so long through his life at Mu that his own flesh consumed and he is no longer in need of it. He invites the visitors to exit the room of stones towards a garden with living pure herbs. There are trees and marvellous plants. Flowers like indecent large wounds are widening on the wet ground. 'Nature does not need complex alchemy to show off, take a look at the emerald of this sky. Clouds are diamonds set into a precious pattern.'

'Mu is in danger,' Luce has her voice shivering.

'I know it. The ataraxic ones know it. I have seen through the mirror of this sky the terrestrial intruder and I realized that you would have come to me. We have to organise Mu's resistance. There are some fine weapons more effective than rifles and daggers. The library from where the idea of us could take place has to be saved. We have to save ourselves, because only our anarchic and rebel safety would guarantee the idea of freedom, like dust spread into the worlds. Sustenance of those who believe in what cannot be seen. Freedom is the milk of the mother that feeds her children. The wizard has replaced it with bitterness. And the obscene phallus of the God proposed by Scuro would give me goose flesh, if I would have it. Luce, I am with you, until the end of the world. We will scalp the time of Scuro. We will destroy him under the radiant light of being free. We will trample on his corrupting evil gold, his hateful banks, beating his servants. The ataraxic ones are superior than the dead ones of Naiir. They feel hungry and thirsty, they need the terrestrial desires, that tarnish the illusory simulacrum of their bodies.'

'They have killing weapons though. They are spreading the panic at *Dailorg*. They will come to look for me.'

'I do believe myself too. Here you will be safe, no ordinary Mu person knows that in the Brains Hall there is a deep spot that goes down to the ataraxic place.'

'I cannot definitely hide myself here waiting for Mu to be destroyed.'

'Hiding you? Not at all. Here you can think on your own, that's not a joke. Resistance has to be a strategy, intelligence, a fine plot, not only action and brutality. It's all about thinking that make the worlds moving on and not the other way around.'

'Where do we start from? I don't know...'

'The answer is simple.'

Nudo steps in, 'From the beginning, here it is where we have to start from.'

Erasmo nods.

Luce is puzzled. 'My fault I should say. Doubts opened a

wound into the ancient heart of Mu. The wizard has seen a gap and he jumped through it.'

'Doubts are the basic for the investigation. Maybe you are wrong, it hasn't been what you call doubts to wound your heart, but to have stopped over one higher step of being.'

'What do you mean, Erasmo? I don't get it.'

'Yes, indeed. For moments you did believe to fill the gap of doubts with a certainty. You were too proud. You thought to be the only one at Mu able to understand the certainty of not knowing things. You did feel superior to any other Mu person, for a moment, a second of illusory light, a small gap. It has been enough for the wizard. Not knowing is not a certainty. There are no certainties for us. But it is a relative concept. It's simply true everything and its opposite. The investigator does not go high, but he goes deep to the bottom, and more he digs out less he knows. Instead you thought to go up and you got a wrong conclusion at the end: the certainty of not having certainty. It's crazy! The certainty is never definitive, relativity is instead. That does not mean having no certainty is a certainty, it would be a contradiction in terms of it. Who does say to us there are not worlds where certainty of having certainty is the constant rule, where our white is black instead?'

'We know nothing,' Nudo whispers.

'I know one thing, you are giving me an headache,' Chemako says.

'Maybe, we know nothing, but maybe there is someone who knows everything, we cannot exclude it, so we have to admit one thing and also its specula opposite.'

'Sorry for the ignorance of a poor dead one not ataraxic, but all this talking about certainty, doubts, relativity and various, practically, if we have to fight against Naiir's army, what do we need it for? All these useless chatting, for what? And doubts and the conclusive confusion? We need weapons.'

Erasmo is having fun, 'Indeed, Chemako, we need weapons.'

'God bless you, now you are right, quantity, model, location, where are those weapons hidden, under the flowers of this field, underneath some small mat in the stone room?'

'Our weapons won't be rifles and daggers hidden underneath the mats like indecent dust.'

'Ah, and what will they be then, made of grace?'

'Thoughts.'

'This is bad then. With your thoughts you can give them the same headache I have at the worst, I am not sure about killing them, it's hard.'

'Thoughts cut, open and close worlds!'

'Those ones with daggers and rifles will open and close us like mussels, forget about thoughts, they will wipe your thoughts off in one go. Did you hear about the propaganda? Forbidden gathering in cultural places and libraries to plot against them...'

'The library will be the main centre of the resistance of Mu. Tomorrow when the wizard that beats the frogs will wake up he will have a bad surprise, listen to Erasmo. Over there there is a lake and fish for your diner, lots of fruit on the trees, ready to get picked. Can you fish?'

THE FLESH OF THE MOTHERS

Niobe spends long boring days at *Dailorg* Castle. She feels tired without doing anything, tired of not doing, of looking out through the clear windows. She decides to act. The laboratory is huge and it has everything she needs. 'I know exactly what Scuro needs. He will be happy with me. Here we go, green plants, sap and dew inside containers. Spagyric method. Peat, plain black, when the plants inside jars reach the peak of putrefaction, calcination, great yeast or saline powder, add slowly other vegetables, sap and dew for 12 years...hydrating, drying out, 12 years, then add powders and distilled dew, it cooks inside a sealed pot, boiling with slow fire, after hours of cooking the preparation mix gets yellow, then rest, then cooking again until a star shows up... elixir...alkahest, healthy elixir. The boiling movement needs to split the soul from the metal core...12 years match to 12 zodiac symbols. Preparation of the panacea, bring the materials to putrefaction, to the black of the death, to the mortification. Without death the matter cannot be reborn. For each sign a transformation happens matching the nature of the sign...the absolute black can get reached in 12 years, each year matches to a planet. No, 12 years is too much. The wizard has to beat soon the frogs, immediate powers. I will use this, hoping that works. I made it on purpose. It's a really delicate tool, time accelerator, it has a glass ball shape, but its material is energy, pure and absolute energy.' The sorceress put inside it the black of the panacea and she waits for 12 days. But nothing happens, the black is still black, putrefaction is still the same, unchanged. Maybe the tool does not work. It's a fail. Maybe not, perhaps it has to be charged with new energies. Retrying until the dream comes true. Niobe takes an ingot from her working table. She observes it stunned. Trying again and again, no stop, days after days, to fill the eyes with light and from the black to create the flesh of the Mothers.

Niobe works until the dawn, bending over old dusty books. She looks for answers and new alchemies. She doesn't feel asleep not even tired. In the meanwhile the wizard sleeps soundly into scented blankets of black silk. Two waiters in livery knock respectfully to his door, they step in, serving an afternoon tea and they leave after bowing. Scuro drinks only tea with no sugar. He hates sweeties although Niobe loves them. But last night she has not slept into her place next to the wizard. He touches the cold blankets remembering about her. Here she is, she appears on the doorstep, her eyes exhausted and hair bit messy. She comes from the laboratory. Scuro can realise it from her clothes that smell of spices. Niobe plays a bell next to the sideboard. After few minutes a waitress with a moustache enters the room. 'Did you call me, Madam?'

'Yes, prepare a hot bath with aromas.'

'Yes, Madam. And for the Sir?'

'Scuro prefers the cold water of the lake.'

Whilst Niobe gets scented through a warm relaxing bath with pink foam, the wizard gets to the bank of the coldest lake of *Dailorg*. He gets naked, putting his clothes over a rock and he dives in. He swims for two hours and after he gets dressed and he makes three times the whole route all around the castle, running. He suffers terribly for the absence of the yellow bright terrestrial sun, although he will get used to that absence, after all one can't have

~ The black star of Mu ~

everything. Better owner of a land with no sun than slave into a desert land. Niobe is stunning. Mu people are naturally pretty, with no need to do swimming or jogging. A really interesting race. The waitress informs him that the guests are in the big Hall. He instructed two Mu's architects for the conversion of the *Dailorg* Library into a monumental hotel, with swimming pool, and all the modern comforts. They arrived earlier.

'Gents, good morning.'

'Good morning, Mr President.'

'Did you already make a project?'

'Yes, sure. Shall we put it on the table?'

'Yes. I listen to you.'

'Library's structure is helicoidal, spiral shaped, we would knock down the internal stairs and create ten rooms in each big hall. Inside each room, basic interiors, classical style...'

'Yes, yes, we will decide it.' Scuro is nervous. 'I only want to know if the project can be done and how long it will take.'

'Months. We would have to hire a lot of labourers.'

'There is no problem. We have plenty of gold, moreover, it will be the first chance to spread the money system at Mu. The new coin system has to start now, remove the old methods.'

'We have to go there to perform some checks.'

'When?'

'When you would like, President, even now.'

'Perfect, let's go then, we take one shuttle, that will be quicker.'

Three shuttles are flying through Mu's skyline, Scuro's one in the middle, left and right the bodyguards' ones. The President never goes out without the protection of his per-

sonal guards.
 Perfect landing. Scuro cannot believe his own eyes.
 'You made the wrong route, the pilot has made it wrong.'
 'No, President, I did the right route, I can guarantee it.'
 'It's not possible!'
 'Indeed, it is annoying...'
 'Annoying? I say, are you joking me?'
 'No, Sir. I would never did that.'
 'So make this vehicle start again and let's go immediately to *Dailorg's* Library.'
 'Sir, here we are.'
 'We are where?'
 'According to my calculations, we are in the precise spot where the library should stand.'
 'There is nothing here.'
 'Indeed, Sir.'
 'What do you mean? Is it a joke?'
 'I don't know. I only know that there was the library here and now there is not even one brick instead.'
 'The library disappeared!'
 'You are a big observer, Mr President. There is no library anymore.'
 'One building cannot disappear like this in moments.'
 'Yes, indeed, it is weird.'
 'I order that you will get arrested.'
 'Why?'
 'Because you took the wrong route and now you are joking me to avoid my anger.'
 'Do apologies, Mr President, I am 1,800 years old, I did this route 176,000 times, I do believe I know it, do I?'
 'So what?'
 'Sixty.'

'What?'

'Sixty miles per hour and I am not drunk, I never drink on duty.'

'You make me furious! I want to get off, to check it personally.'

The wizard gets off the shuttle. Instead of the library an empty space. There are no doubts. All the Mu people, Niobe too, swear mortified that few hours before the huge, ancient, eternal *Dailorg* Library, the biggest in Mu, now vanished.

The wizard laughs, 'At the end, basically, this is a pleasant problem. I can build the hotel straight on where the library used to be before. There is no need to demolish it. You, architects, what is your opinion?'

'The idea is not so bad, Mr President. All *ex novo*. There is only a little problem.'

'If there is a problem with the project you just do it again and that is it, a luxury style building, really elegant, archways, wide windows, swimming pool...'

'It's not the project that is concerning, Sir.'

'Fire up then!'

'To build it needs to dig the foundations.'

'Yes, indeed. Let's dig out then! I give you my permission.'

'We cannot.'

'Why? I just said I give you my permission.'

'Sorry, Sir, your permission is not enough to make it possible.'

'I am the boss at Mu and you do what I say with no arguments, you do it and that's it!'

'I am not doubting it but...'

'No way! Dig those foundations down and build the best

luxury hotel in Mu.'
'This is not possible practically.'
'Why?'
'Because you usually dig out the foundations by the ground.'
'Yes, indeed, don't you have the suitable machinery? You dig, you build, what's the problem?'
'We cannot dig the foundations, impossible. You look at the ground here, where the library used to be, can you see it?'
'What?'
'Take one stone and throw it from the top, here it is one, please.'

Scuro throws the stone on the floor really angry. A metal noise can be heard. 'What's this?'
'*Afsaneh.*'
'What is it?'
'The hardest metal in the world.'

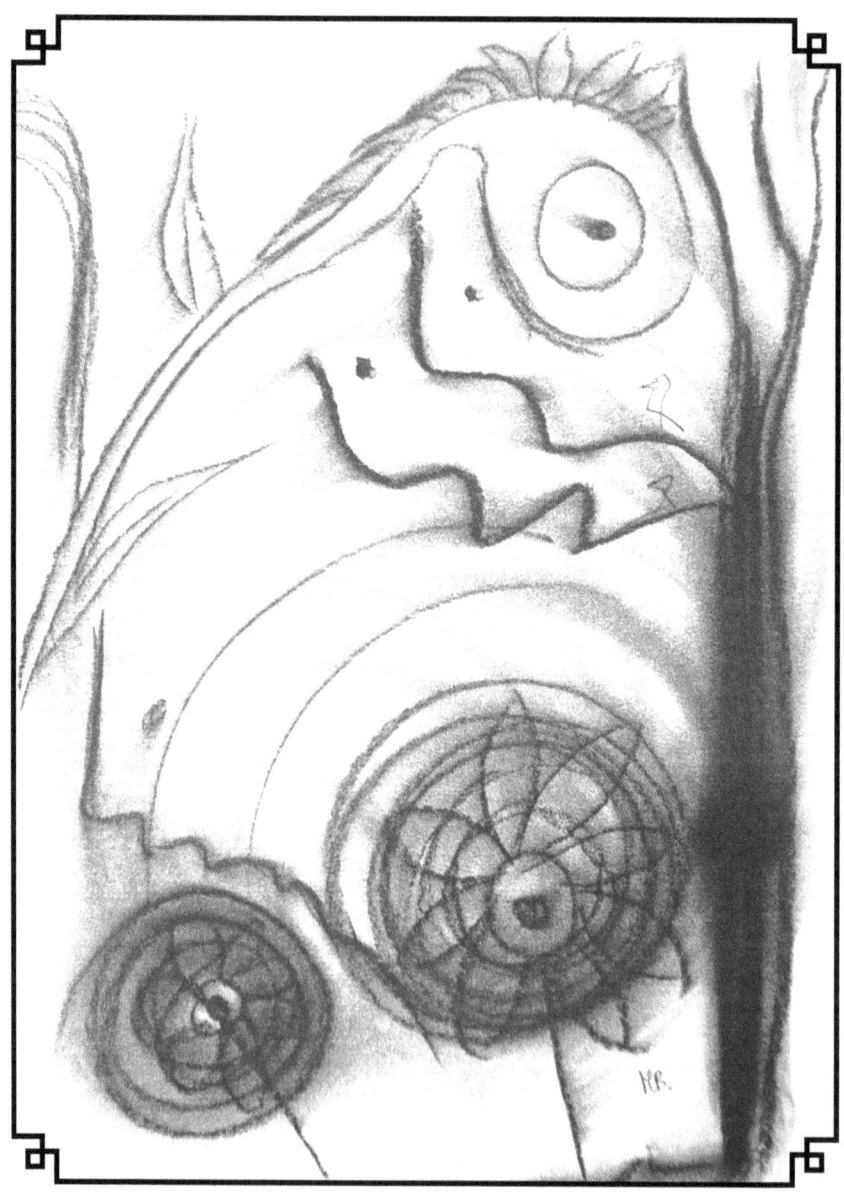

THE ROCK BOTTOM

Erasmo shows that he is a good fisherman. The land of the ataraxic ones is a real underground heaven rich of water full of fish and living flowers with flute voices. They whisper songs that make the pomes off the trees. Fruit and fish are for the guests. The ataraxic ones don't eat neither drink, they are totally free from any sensitive bond. The ground suddenly lightly shivers. All the body seems to be like inside a lift, feeling of going down although being standstill.

Erasmo says that we don't need to worry. The fishing has to carry on. *Dailorg* Library is only sunk.

'Sunk? But we are inside it now,' Luce says.

'Of course we are inside it, into the rock bottom of it, this is what we think at least. But it won't happen anything. The library is like a huge tip of a drill, a cylinder structure with spiral shaped walls. The architect who built has thought that in case of a real danger the building could become an underground fortress. I activated the defensive mechanism. The structure is sinking slowly through the ground. On the surface will remain only the roof made from pure *afsaneh*. In this way we could organise the resistance of Mu and the Black Star will be safe. If Scuro captures her, Mu will be over. Luce's energy will give to the wizard a really absurd power to destroy the voice of the Mothers. We cannot afford it.'

'They will try to break in piercing the *afsaneh*,' Nudo says.

Erasmo nods. 'Indeed, they will try. It won't be easy. The *afsaneh* is rally hard, although it could be drilled out. The roof has anyway a lot of material and symbolic layers. Under the metal there is the wurtzite that, according to an ancient legend of Mu, has been extracted from a meteorite loaded with unknown worlds energies. Then there is the grains mixed stone of adamantine and finally marvellous reflections... Come here. We should be able to see them already.'

Erasmo precedes the guest inside a stone room. The ceiling is a spectacular show of extra pure diamonds. The ancient books of Mu stored by the ataraxic ones say that every layer is matching to a peculiarity of the soul and the ancient heart of the Mothers. The *afsaneh* is the external shield, the outward appearance that hides always something else, like a protective and tough mask. The wurtzite is the investigation, the desire of discover, the projection towards the external hidden by the matter. The stone is strength and obstinacy that swims out towards the inner resistance of the adamantine and towards the extreme purity of diamonds, hard to reach, but not impossible.

TABUM

Niobe mix some dark substances with some clear ones, powder and mixtures, organic and inorganic.

The crucible is like one uterus that shapes the matter and has to create a new life. The sorceress believes in what she is doing. The experiments are the main task during her days. She isn't hungry or thirsty. She has to fix the mercury, making it hard like the silver. Before she has to kill the basilisk, its tormented soul, then sulphur, obsidian fragments, saltpetre, mercury, petrified rotten blood, inside a hollow of coal dust that has been used to fill the crucible which will be hermetically sealed. Niobe is really busy to close the lid of the crucible with the mastic. Then she puts everything on the fire that makes the spirits really menacing. The mantic blows up. The sorceress waits for it. A black liquid comes out the distiller and the oven, spreading over the floor, sticky, verminous. Whilst the liquid is spreading all over like rotten blood, assuming weird shapes, the sulphur spirits get aggressive. The distiller shakes terribly. The bricks of the oven are incandescent. Something is going to happen. The servants hear the detonation into the adjacent room and they run into the laboratory. Niobe has just fallen on the floor, her face black for the smoke, on the ceiling the mark of the crucible lid that, although the mastic, jumped in the air staining the plaster recently added. A failing, no flesh of the Mothers, no silver, nothing at all, moreover it will take days to clean the laboratory. Her face and finger burnt, a real success!

Scuro is angry. 'What did you try to do? Destroy the Castle?'

'No, I wanted to...'

'You what? It's a miracle that you did not die inside this laboratory.'

'I will sort all this out, I will make build a new oven with a huge distiller. I have an important target, I know already what to do.'

'You won't do anything now!'

'Yes, instead. You cannot see beyond your nose, here, you can see only a laboratory full of black dust, still and upside down glasses, broken oven. You don't see beyond it, you are close-minded. It needs to fly high, beyond the contingency and the mistakes. I don't look at the curves and the obstacles. The road is straight. The target is the only thing that is important.'

'What are you talking about? There is very little one here. You got me nervous. Whilst I reorganise the Government, the library is vanishing, ungrateful Mu people are hostile, you have fun, you play with your concoctions and you do the permanent to the scarecrows!'

'What about the scarecr...'

'And what is that now?'

'I don't know...'

Into a corner of the laboratory there is a lying body with messy hair and a ripped jacket. He is sitting on the floor, with his legs wide opened, back to the wall, hanging arms alongside his body, the head pending one side.

Niobe gets closer; she touches him. The body moves. He has a blue face. His mouth is moving and talking, 'Hello.'

The sorceress steps back. The creature talks again. 'Sorry, I did not mean to scary you.'

'Who are you?'

'I am a dead-end street, the horror, the bugbear of the

~ The black star of Mu ~

unstable nature, the roaring lion. I am the fleeting metal of your experiments, your willing, my pretty sorceress, can you hear it?' He hits his own leg with his knuckles. The sound is metallic. 'Iron, only my eternal heart is stone.'

'What are you doing here?'

'I was born from the explosion. You called me and I am here now.'

'Me?'

'Yes. Are you the one that wants to defeat the rebel nature? Subjugate it, enslave it, hunting the birds, eating the fruit? Are you not the sense that wants to offer to the intellect the flesh of the Mothers?'

'Yes, more or less.'

'So you called me out, I obey you; I am your servant. I will be your assistant. In a while we could offer to Dr Scuro huge amount of flesh on a gold plate.'

Scuro laughs, 'The flesh of the Mothers cannot be produced, it only can be found digging the deep womb of the earth and few years time its bright trend will finish.'

The scarecrow stands up hardly. 'Everything has one start and one end, my dear wizard, only the flesh produced as experiment will never be over, it will feed you, it will stop your thirst.'

'The thirst is burning and consuming the womb, the eternal anger, I cannot sleep night and day.'

'For each wolf there is a sheep. Niobe and I will make you to taste the best flesh of Mother that you ever had in life. It will feed your blood and your boundless egotism.'

'If the egotism could be fed, I would not be here, I would be where I used to be. And during my old age with my millionaire pension I would have played chess with friends of friends under the portico of a country house, groping sometimes a pretty servant.'

'Listen to me. The flesh we will produce would be the purest, the most nutrient for you, you will wish to get more, you will wish to touch it, to have it in between your hands, it will be your daily target at Mu. Without it you could hardly breath, you will feel absolute zero, crashed, annihilated, unstructured. The passion you will have for it will be not natural, fierce, visceral, abnormal. Your intestines will shake like a wounded beast when you could not touch its cold monstrous beauty. You will breath next to it, you will caress it like an excited lover. It will go underneath your skin. Your only reason to live, the reason why your heart will beat still fiercely inside your human and mortal chest will be the cold flesh we will produce. And no sex, no woman eyes, no servant bottom, no chess games, nothing would attract yourself more than the shining sight of that poisoning honey flesh that charms. It would go through yourself like a cold blade, it will possess any of your most intimate fibre. You would be wrapped through. For that flesh you will be doing everything, you will kill too, you will lie and you will love deeply only who is going to offer it raw as gift. You will love me and Niobe, blindly, without breaks, like a drug addicted loves the white powder of his visions. You will thank us as you could satisfy your hard eyes bottom with the indefinable scent of the flesh. We will be your drug dealers. The stuff won't be available soon, it will take time. The impatience will tire your nights, it will rape your feelings, exhausting your mind and body. Think about something else, go out, breath, build, destroy, kill, leave us doing our job and you will get what you want.'

Scuro orders that a new oven will be fixed as the sorceress instructed. His pupils similar to two extinguished coals stare intensely at the new arrived, almost like piercing his metal soul.

'Have you got a name, scarecrow?'

The creature laughs showing his really white teeth. 'Since centuries my name is Tabum.'

'Well, carry on with your games. I go to the Meeting Hall. I will organise the Government,' Scuro says whilst leaving quickly the laboratory.

S 8

Scuro wear a dark suit, elegant. While he is going to the Meeting Hall, he feels a pleasure vibration behind himself. The awareness to be the chief of the new world excites him. The Hall, oval shaped, has got white walls and big windows from where Mu scented air can get through. The wizard has soon noticed it, as just got to the Underground World. The scent. Peculiar. Never smelled before. A mixture of milk, caramel, scent of flowers, although delicate, really smooth, relaxing. Surrounding the senses like a caress, a Paradise promise.

The S-8 too is a promise, a summit of 8 ministers named by Scuro. Servants of the Government, law-abiding, with their efforts towards the organisation of the State of Mu.

The ministers sit, assembled. Left and right. Scuro sits in the middle of the Hall on a Higher Chair. He looks leading over the scenario.

After a brief introductory speech from Scuro, the Minister of Economics carries on, 'Respectful President, I take the speech to underline the giant steps made by this New Government towards the Economy Laws. The foundation of the Money System and Notes currently around and in use, has allowed the ban of the anachronistic barter, impossible within a modern society. Economy has grown. Mu is flourishing. *Dailorg* changed its appearance. Mu people are not simply ordinary ones, but rich and poor now. A distinction that has not to be underestimated. The flattening usual of the weak systems has not allowed the best citizens to arise, to move forward and to occupy important placements within the society. Now everything is changing. The Underground World is evolving. The best ones acquire wealth and powers. Lot of cultural centres, core of unclear ideology movements, uprising, anarchy, odd concepts, have been converted into banks. Perfect, shiny, clean, organised, protecting the honest working people savings that pay taxes.'

The Minister of Culture nods and stands up, 'Mr President, dear ministers. In support of what has been said by my illustrious colleague I want to highlight that the conversion of the cultural centres into credit institutions has allowed the new organisation of the school system at Mu. Banned the rebels, the fighters that have easy and primitive anarchist behaviours, rebels to every disciplinary system, we created Government Schools and Universities with precise tuition programmes. The old teachers have been partially divested of their roles because of their rebellious ideas. We hired new teachers, devoted tutors, servants of the State, duteous to the power, to the rigid programmed system imposed by the Government. No rebel could be admitted to the schools. The chaos has to be eliminated through discipline and indoctrination. New generations must never know the chaotic uncertainty of the doubts, the spasm of rebellion. Relaxing certainty, by the way, education programmes submitted to the constant careful inspection of the Government. The same censor that is here will submit all the books and newspapers to go through his own review. Without his authorisation, nothing, and I say nothing, could be allowed to be printed off. It needs control and discipline.'

The Minister of Sports stands up and talks through the microphone, 'Regarding the schools, censorship and discipline, referring to the precious words of our colleague, I want to add only that in the schools has been established,

~ *The black star of Mu* ~

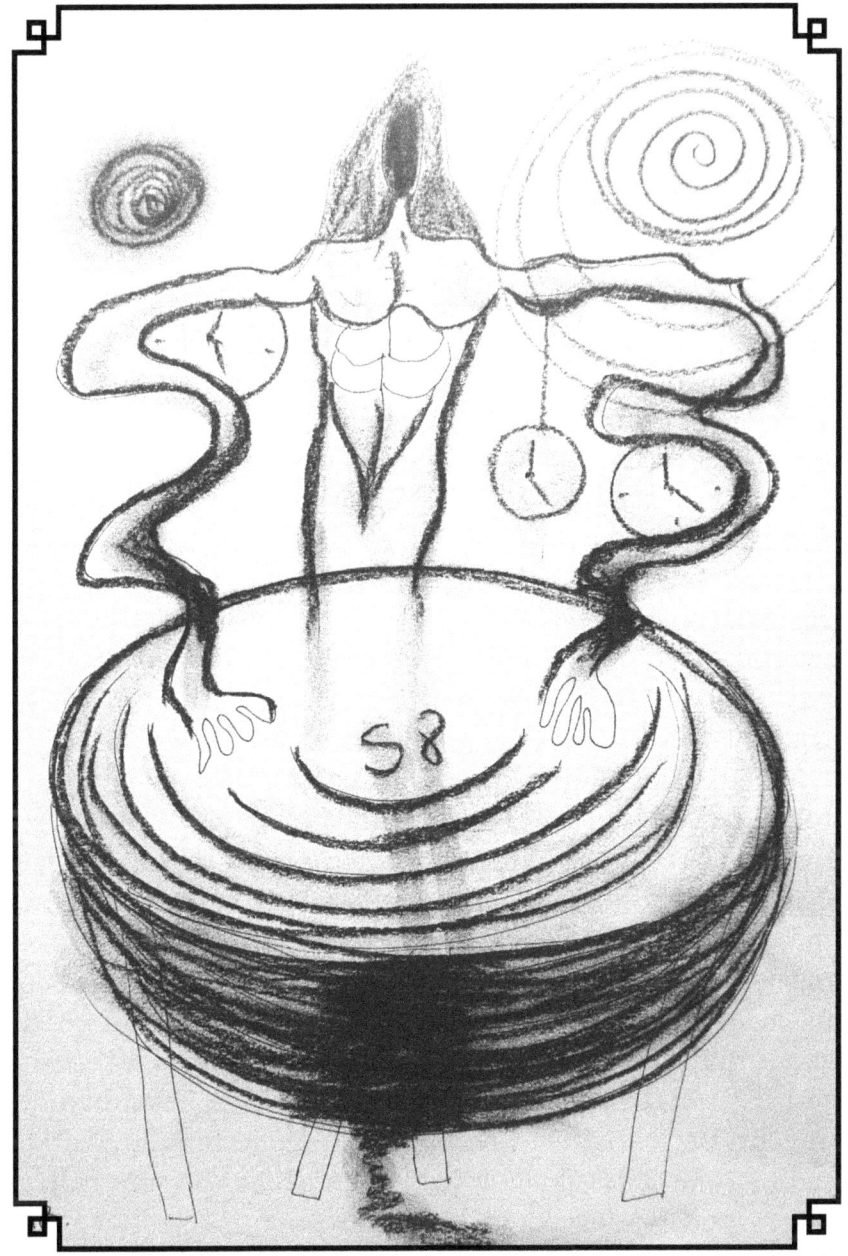

by the Ministry that I lead, a sport programme. New generations have to exalt, through a programme of physical exercises, the war skills of the people of Mu, completely to the State service. After attending the mandatory school classes, whoever wishes to enrol to the Army of Mu could become mean to defence and offence towards everyone tries to threaten the system made and ruled by Scuro's Government. Sports could be executed only to serve the State, like preparation for the young ones. Agile and healthy bodies, ready to be instructed towards the fighting techniques.'

Naiir, as Minister of Defence and Vice President, shakes his hand to the colleague who has just finished to talk, 'Eternal truth. Sports have to be always seen like the introductory preparation for the war. *Ad hoc* we organised the personal army of our loved President that will be next to the State Army whose representatives are already in each town of Mu, firstly overall *Dailorg*, our Republic's Capital City. Obviously the Army needs funds. Its organisation is expensive: for this reason every citizen has to pay taxes.'

'Right!' The Minister of Revenues and Taxes is strict. 'Every Mu citizen has the duty to contribute towards the growth of the State with his own expenses. The salaries of the Ministers will be the same level as their importance and their responsibilities. Each Minister, due the psychological fatigue and physical stress that is involved when ruling, will collect from Mu people any resource in order to get guaranteed: extraordinary salary, massages, thermal bath and physiotherapies for free, blue extra-luxury shuttles used to travel through the Underground World, and more benefits that we will establish by the time, ultra luxury pension, excellent accommodations. Together with the Minister of the Environment, we made a plan to make

Dailorg Beach privately managed. Some villas will be built for the Government representatives, a kind of privileged island where the key people of *Dailorg* will be gathering to use their intellect. They will be provided with swimming pools, golf pitches, and all the modern comforts. They will have a fabulous design which won't be affecting the landscape around. All this because the best citizens of *Dailorg*, as the Ministers, Naiir's dead ones, deserve more. We deserve more. Governing, making laws, provide verdicts is exhausting. A really unsustainable burden that needs comforts, balsams, gold.'

The Minister of Justice has his cheeks red and jumps up, 'True! Think about me, that I have to reorganise the justice, review everything. *Dailorg* is messy, with no prisons, with no bars. The Radicale, where Mu people say that the Black Star takes the guilty people to, is inaccessible. We don't know how to get there, neither where it is. Only she knows it. We don't know where the Black Star is hiding now. We have to find her to understand how the Radicale looks like, building bars, making reforms. All from scratch, a world to recreate. Stumps and chains will replace the goodness of the Mothers. The right justice will not have any mercy. Whilst waiting for a new prison to be built, hoping to find the Black Star to access the Radicale, we will jail into the Castle basements all the rebels that try to fight the new Government. Making a clean sweep. Justice. Someone is knocking the door.'

Someone is knocking really strong the door. One Naiir servant enters quickly, he is breathless, 'Mr President, Mr Vice President, a mess! It is urgent! There are some riots in *Dailorg* town centre, some injured and a dead one too.'

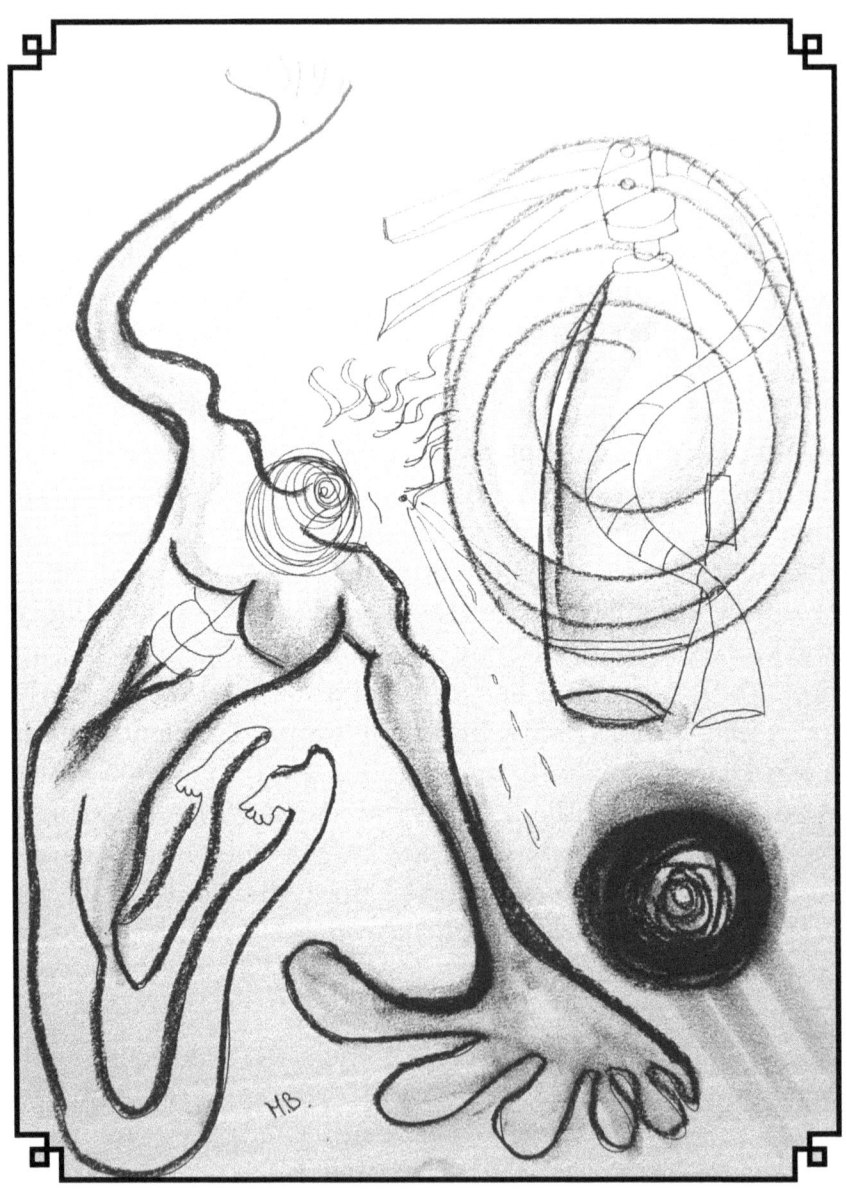

~ *The black star of Mu* ~

THE LAST SUMMER OF LOARC

The summer at Mu has just started. Temperature does not change, but the air is cooled with fruity scents. The sky is like an invitation to enjoy the day on the seaside. Thrown apart the night shades, at *Dailorg* Beach there is no dead ones around. Mu people could dip their feet through the soft silver sand and soak their skin in the salty water. The birds are dancing into the air and it is pleasant and good looking. Like led by a magnetic energy they draw acrobatic routes within the air, flying, all together, like a small real brothers army. Water is clean, fair, really emerald green coloured. On the water edge a light wave whispers massaging the perfect bodies of bathers.

Loarc is a young one from Mu. He leaves in the morning with his swimming suit underneath his light clothes. He planned a day out on the beach, a quiet day. Anyone's destiny, sometimes, goes through unexpected pathways. It shakes feverishly inside the glassy time bottle. The cap jumps out, the bottle opens and the destiny slips through the world fingers, with no sense, blind, unreal, cruel. Then everything changes. The project vanishes off, the air gets loaded with new opportunities.

Loarc meets some friends. They greet each other. They convince him to follow the stupid destiny. No day on the beach anymore. They all go to a huge open space with no trees, Piazza Diamalon. There is a fight for freedom there. There is a chance to make the history for servants and rebels, for all the bloodbath. Blood over the street, splashing to the sky colouring it through cruel barbarity.

Naiir's army of dead ones is ready and fully structured

in battle gear.

Brawls start at the very early lights of a sad lawn. Rebels are against the New Scuro's State. Banners and speakers, they yell their disappointment. Loarc is together with them. He has got on his face a dark blue balaclava. There is a lot of pressure. Dead ones come forward, guns and batons on their hands. The clash is fierce. Broken bones, crashed bloody faces are marking the ground of Mu. Loarc is standing 6 and half metres from a police van with 3 Naiir's men on board. He tries to collect a fire extinguisher from the floor. A man in uniform, sitting inside the police van, takes out his gun, pointing him out. The noise of the shooting is loud. The young Mu's man has been shot on his left cheek and he falls down on the floor. He is hardly bleeding. Trying to avoid the other rebels, the police van driver turns quickly and drives twice over Loarc's body.

A photographer takes some pictures of the body lying on the floor. Naiir people attack again. They reach the photographer. They beat him with their nightsticks, on his head, on his shoulder, everywhere they can. The face of the photographer is full of blood. They tear the camera off his hands, destroying it. They take even some other cameras that he was hiding under his arms. All the work is gone.

Scuro is furious. He meets Naiir in the Conference Hall in the Castle, 'Do you realise what you have done, you and your stupid dead ones?'

'Rebels were nervous, destroying cars, shop windows, throwing stones.'

'So to calm them down your army thought to kill someone cool-blooded.'

'Do not worry, we will sort everything out.'

'The matter is complex, hard. We need to think something to justify the execution, because that is what it is, an execution.'

Naiir reassures Scuro, 'Do not worry please. My men will deal with the matter.'

'Indeed, I am more relaxed now...'

'I sent one of my men to simulate a mock rocks throwing. We broke the boy's head with a rock then we left it next to his corpse. We will say that he has been killed by the rock not by the guns. We took pictures of the blood covered rock next to his face. Now my men are dealing with the photographer.'

'What photographer?'

'A man, a photo reporter, he took pictures of the corpse after the shotgun. In those pictures there is no rocks obviously.'

'You have to find him and destroy the pictures before this matter will destroy us.'

'Done it already, it's all under control! He is not going anywhere. Do not worry! We are dealing with the Zaid School Institute too. The anarchists have gathered there to organise their Resistance of Mu.'

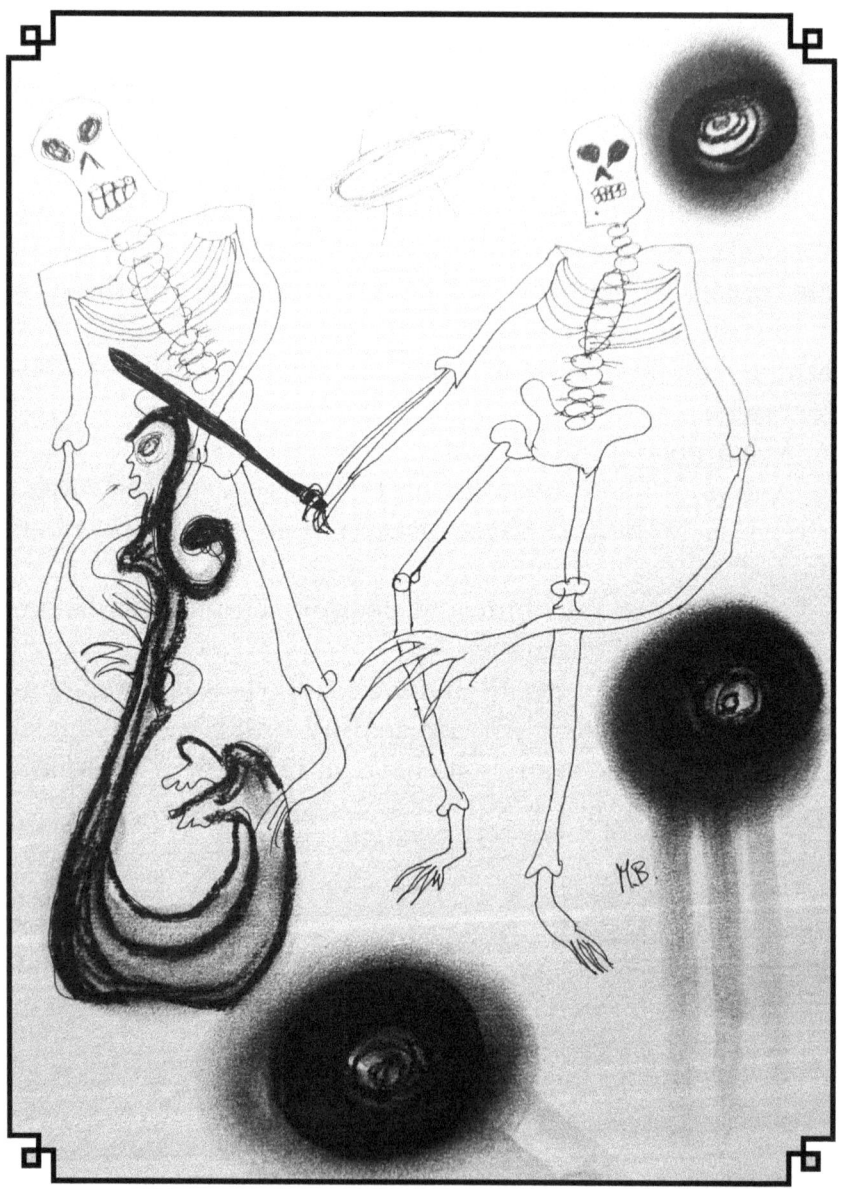

ZAID'S SLAUGHTERHOUSE

There is no even a weak light of star into the green sky of Mu, not even a dust from a moon ray. Even though the silence plays on that night, marking its own transient presence. Mu people sleep at the Zaid School, occupying the building's rooms and corridors with sleeping bags and randomly picked blankets. A really peaceful protest. They discuss about freedom and anarchy, about rebellion against the laws of Scuro's New State.

But the night is full of assassins, disturbing shadows and yelling through the cold and deaf breeze.

Naiir's Army is outside the school, placed in anti-riot line-up. Opaque heads of puppets under glossy blue helmets, batons in hand, heavy duty boots. The iron gate gets smashed off. Their boots advance towards the garden. The entrance door falls down. Their feet enter the building, stepping over everything is on their way, breaking hands, crashing bones. Their batons lifted up are hitting sleeping people, unarmed, over their heads, faces, arms. Red blood over the walls, floors, blankets. Blood everywhere. The blind fury of Naiir's dead army tramples on and kills. The bitter smell of blood hits their nostrils. A group of rebels gathers inside one room. They decided not to resist to the arrest. They lift their hands up. The dead ones slam the door, but they don't look at their hands up, as surrender sign. They just clash the Mu ones with their nightsticks. A young long dark hair girl gets beaten up repeatedly on her left side. Kicks, batons strikes, over her legs, her back, her arms. She breaks her wrist. Her arm moves convulsively, out of control. Her warm blood goes on her face so she cannot see well. Now it is dark. They carry on beating her up, like beasties, blind with their senseless anger. A dead one grabs her head, her hair. Her fractured body in different points gets dragged alongside the stairs and thrown like a potato bag next to other fainted bodies, beaten up fiercely.

Whilst blood is running at *Dailorg*, Scuro has called some architects for his conversion project of the town centre. Niobe enters the room without knocking. 'I questioned the astragals last night,' Niobe looks concentrated while she speaks to Scuro.
'Don't you knock usually?'
'It is important.'
'Let's remind it later.'
'I said, I questioned the astragals!'
'Well, so what?'
'They spoke to me. I know where she is!'
'Who are you talking about?'
'Luce. I know where she is hiding. Magic does not lie.'
'Where is she?'
'You have to swear first, Scuro!'
The wizard nods the architect meaning for them to leave the room. The discussion carries on in private.
'You have to swear to me that after you will absorbed her energy you will kill her. If you won't do it, she would loose you.'
'Tell me where she is!'
'Swear it!'
'Alright, I swear it.'
Niobe takes a big book and she opens to page 17.
'Look!'
'What does it mean?'

'Can you see this antique print?'
'Yes, but I don't get what it is!'
'I was looking for some books that could help me out to create Mothers' flesh, maybe some tips, a suggestion. Sometimes the ancient books are full of surprises. I found this. The library is sinking. The library has been created in the way that when in danger it sinks down the ground. It has not disappeared. For the Mothers the biggest treasure is culture and awareness, memory and music. All this is gathered into the immortal *Dailorg* Library, human conscience, beating and eternal heart. Luce is hiding down there and she is plotting some revenge.'

THE MIRRORS' ROOM

Erasmo's feet trample on the soft grass of the ataraxic world. Trees look strangely bending. Green leaves, as prayers lost through the time. Voices of remote memories, as whispers. Erasmo's hands grab fists of soil. He thinks and shivers underneath the light clothes. Nature feels the evil since the most intimate fibres. The tree suffers and hopes that his time has not ended yet. The ground produces odd horrifying vibrations. The ataraxic sometimes could see what is happening at *Dailorg* when there is a bloody fight at Mu for an unfair reason. Erasmo is sad while he looks Luce and her friends into the soft mirrors room. There is a really feeble red light. Enormous oval mirrors, transparent, look fluidly glued to the stone walls. They move slightly, like shivering, making concentric circles. Erasmo touches the soft surface of a mirror with his fingertip, inviting his guests to look at him. Red blood drops from the circles, slipping out dense and warm, pouring over the floor. The images become alive and consistency of reality inside the bright and jelly surface of the mirrors. People are agitating inside them, opposite strengths. Young rebels of Mu opponents to Scuro's regime are beaten up hardly. It can be seen a Naiir dead one taking off his uniform jacket and bringing inside the Zaid School a plastic bag with two incendiary bottles inside. So they can say that rebels were armed and dangerous. That the Zaid School intervention has been necessary to safeguard the Sovereign State. A lot of Mu youngsters get dragged by the dead ones inside shuttles and lorries that will go to *Dailorg* Police Station. The building is not big. The walls just freshly white painted give an aseptic atmosphere, unreal. Mu ones get pushed inside the cells and forced to stand for hours by Naiir's ones. Who tries to sit on the floor gets forced to stand up again immediately. The dead ones grab the unlucky hitting his head against the wall. That is the punishment for the tiredness. Hours standing, no food and water, no toilet even.

The girls get naked and forced to bark like dogs, mocked, insulted.

Naiir dead ones are with no control. After 30 hours of violence, the tortured Mu ones are given back to their families. Their life has changed forever. Blood cannot be cancelled. Through innocent blood, the loss of freedom. A shameful page within the history of *Dailorg*.

Nudo is overcome with grief, speechless. The words, within their inane boundaries, wouldn't express his feelings. The history comes back fiercely, inexorable, in every world, every time. The inexorable and monstrous face of the destiny pierces your soul, killing it slowly at time. Nudo re-experiences his death. He feels negative vibrations, an intolerable sorrow. Sorrow overwhelms him. If also *Dailorg* is loosing its own freedom, where do we go now? Where is the shelter, the house, the nest of the free souls? Where do we fly, run, beyond the evil and the lies of the power? Lies, lies, deception, eyesores, plots to justify the violence. And the lacerating presence of those two bottles brought ad hoc into the school, weights over the heart of freedom. Nudo feels like empty, with no strengths. Death won over life, obscurity is over *Dailorg*. Nobody will forget it. Luce puts her hand on his shoulder, without talking. An eloquent silence, dense and macabre tasting like blood, dust and melancholy, goes through the pink room and gets darker. The mirror keeps talking about its own sad story. The anarchist body gets cremated really quickly. The autopsy reveals a bullet hole. The official version will be incredible, planned ahead, the one seen only through a surreal fiction. A stone thrown by a rebel has diverted the bullet route, determining the death of that person. But the mirror does not lie because it's pure voice of spirit created by the soul of the Mothers. The mirror sees and knows everything. A man in uniform grabs the stone, he moves off the balaclava and he hits the anarchist lying on the floor. The stone has been left next to the corpse, full of blood, like a kind of proof.

One ataraxic enters silently the mirrors hall. He gets next to Erasmo. He whispers something to his ears. Erasmo looks at him a bit worried then talks to Luce. 'It looks like a green bird has revealed where you are hiding. Let's go.'

They enter into a stone room. There is a ladder that takes upstairs through the dark. Luce, Erasmo and Chemako climb it slowly, paying attention not to slip over. While going up they hear some beating. They are exactly beneath the roof that is shaking. There is a room completely encrusted with diamonds. Erasmo gets in. The stone seats are dark and glossy. They are waiting for someone to sit on them, caressing their constant coldness. Someone is trying to enter, to pierce the roof of the library. Beats over beats, angry, nervous, fierce attempting. The vibration makes a little diamond dropping. Erasmo collect them and put them over the black table. He smiles lightly. He looks almost happy, reflecting. Diamonds make polychromous glares over the dark and straight table surface. Few more minutes and they seem to get smaller, darker, until becoming dust. Into the wall where they dropped from, some more grow up, new ones, more beautiful ones, bigger size, instead of the lost ones.

'Those stones are like baby teeth. For us ataxic ones they are like illusions, but for the wizard they represent richness and power. Because Scuro is the matter. Only finding the Antimatter we can defeat him. Although it won't be easy, I know it.'

Luce is puzzled, 'How do we do then?'

'You, Star, with your own company, you would have to go through the Unknowable Beyond and touch with your hands and soul the Antimatter. Only in this way the wizard could get destroyed and Mu will have a chance to be safe. This is written through the pages of this infamous time looking at us, enjoying this show.'

THE GOLD OF TABUM

Niobe's laboratory is full of bitter and blues smokes. Niobe is exhausted. That day her cold beauty looks like spent through exertion and tension of the venture. She breaths the disgusting vapours of the crucible asking Tabum for a suggestion. He nods, he opens the laboratory door letting in two Mu people. Two free citizens that want to be test subjects for some money, the new disease that infected *Dailorg*. The guests are sitting over two comfortable low stools. The sorceress scrambles a dense solution, similar to green lava inside a big copper pot. The fire burns and the pot is boiling. Niobe is tired. She follows step by step Tabum's suggestions which dries her sweat with a candid napkin. Here, it needs adding a bit of bones powder. With a spoon, the sorceress takes a bit of the boiling solution, pouring it inside a small saucepan. The saucepan is connected, through a futuristic mechanism made by metallic conduits, to a cylindrical machine with majestic appearance. The machine gets the solution cool immediately making it solid. Now the solution that earlier was boiling in the pot has been transformed into a kind of unshaped stone. Niobe takes it. She pours it into a shaping-pills machine. After 5 minutes the machine, after a bit struggling, lets out through the small nickel pipe 5 golden pills. Tabum sniffs them. Horrible. A disgusting smell, like excrement. Well done. They can carry on. The whole solution in the pot can be transformed into pills. The testing subjects have to swallow a certain amount of pills and then going over two treadmills that Dr Scuro has bought to make Niobe happy.

'One, two, one, two, come on, faster! You have to sweat!

Alright? Sweat! We pay you for this!' Niobe is a bit frustrated. 'Swallow two more pills, come on!'

'No, please, they are horrible!'

'Take them! Two more each, every hour two pills, if there are no results in two hours then you will take three, come on, run, run!'

'Please, a little break! We are going to have an heart attack then!'

'No, no, here there is Tabum that checks you out. You are good, run, run!'

'But we are tired and the money that you gave us it's not worthy this monstrous fatigue, not even swallowing those smelly pills like rotten excrement!'

'Smelling? How you dare? My pills contain selected ingredients, not genetically modified, all genuine stuff. The smell is a bit strong, but it does not affect the product. Run, run! If you do not run, I won't pay you, come on, swallow those pills!'

'It's been hours that we run!'

'Come on, run, run, move your feet and shut up! Oh, watch out! Look, Tabum, the first specks of gold! So it is true then. Don't stop right now. They increase whilst they are sweating. Quickly, Tabum, let's collect some samples! Do you realise, Mu people? You are producing the flesh of the Mothers. It comes out with your sweating. You are sweating pure gold! The experiment is technically successful. Indeed, we have still to work on it, ingredients, test the subjects.'

One of the Mu people falls on the floor. Niobe touches him with her foot. 'Stand up, do you think it is the right moment to faint? Stand up idiot!'

Tabum smiles showing his white set of teeth. 'I believe

that he could not obey to you this time, my dear Niobe. He is dead.'

'What did I say to you? We have to work on it, night and day, if necessary. Call the servants, take the corpse away. I don't need dead flesh, unless in pieces, in my laboratory. Away, away!'

'Really?'

'What do you say?'

'According my calculations... *Melius abundare quam deficere*, and you said as well, we have to improve the experiment!'

'But I, I cannot do it.'

'Don't worry, I will deal with it.'

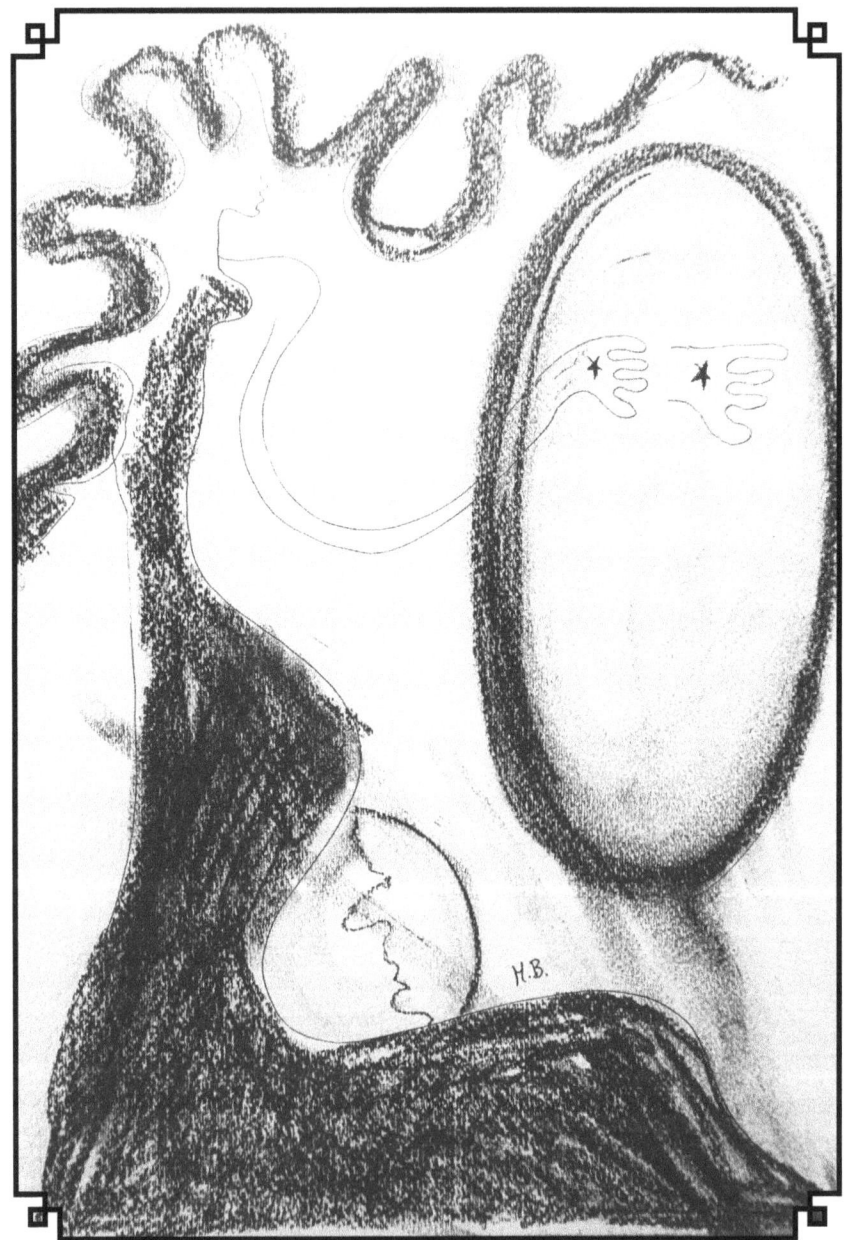

The library secret

The Black Star is in front of Scuro, few centimetres away. He stretches his hand to touch her, but his body melts like ice on the sun. The wizard wakes up, sweaty, in the middle of the mirrors room. But the floor is not the usual one, it is soft, earthy. The matt is cold like a marble layer. His feet are now twisted roots that dig into the ground. He cannot move; he is stuck. Luce now has appeared again, really close to him, with her black eyes firm over him. She touches him and all the mirrors get opaque at the same time, more and more opaque until becoming soft and dark, fluid like magma. The room melts down. Scuro is stuck. Now even his hands are tentacles that dig through that inert and dead matter of the mirrors. Scuro feels his body getting rotten, under the effect of the angry sight of Luce. But he cannot avoid looking at her. Her magnetic pupils hypnotised him. He gets nervous. He wants to free his tentacular arms from the ground, stopping the time of being rotten. Impossible. Any effort is useless. His salty sweat drips on his forehead and it becomes a sea that overwhelms him. He slips through a dark abyss, a light less world. His flesh has melted, transformed into a monstrous creature, static in the dark. Then eyes, eyes everywhere. Scuro is observed by small and big pupils gathered in the immensity of that abyss. He is alone, wriggling, fearing, shouting.

Niobe shakes him forcing to wake up. The room is untouched. The mirrors shiny, perfect like always. Only the carpet is slightly wet.

The wizard is stunned. Call the servants ignored Niobe's questions. A woman from Mu with a waitress uniform makes a light curtsy to the half naked President, lightly embarrassed. He is visibly shocked, 'Remove the stain off the carpet, completely! Prepare one shuttle, I have to go to *Dailorg* Town Centre!'

Niobe smiles, 'Get dressed first!'

'Of course, I will do. Are you coming?'

'No, Tabum is waiting for me in the laboratory. His obsession for Luce starts to make me worrying.'

'I need her heart.'

With the presidential shuttle Scuro gets quickly to the spot where *Dailorg* Library used to be. Naiir and his dead ones are almost all there. They are checking out things there. Metallic noise. The library roof camouflages itself perfectly with the ground. There is anyway a huge surface producing a metal noise. The library roof. There are no doubts. It would be possible to remove it with some levers. Two hours trying. No results. With some picks, with their arms. Nothing.

Although all those efforts the dead ones of Naiir could not get into the roof of the library. A really hard material, that not even the diamond neither the hardest metal could scratch, gets against any attempt. Scuro is puzzled whilst thinking. He knocks the roof of the library. He feels a light vibration getting into his right ear, like a really low sound wave. Someone would know what is the material. It is not possible that in all *Dailorg* there is no one that knows how to find a solution. A library that sinks... Niobe's books talk about it. But none of those books says how to pierce the roof surface, how to get into the vanished library, to the ancient heart of Luce.

The thin hand of Naiir touches Scuro's shoulder.

The dead ones' boss smiles, 'Maybe I know who could help us.'

EBBONE

The road seems endless. At the boundaries of *Dailorg*, into a land where Mu people have never been, there is a forest of wet and twisted roots. Climate is not mild like in town. Plants are huge, bending towards the ground, creating a dense vegetable pattern.

Naiir dead ones get forward with their machete. It is not easy to walk through that forest. Moreover there is lack of oxygen, it's warm and there is a lot of moisture penetrating through their bones. But the dead ones cannot feel anything, they are insensitive to all, they just carry on following the orders from their boss. Scuro instead is sweaty. He struggles, limping on under the funny sight of Naiir and he has legs and arms wounded by the brushwood.

Beyond the forest a small rotten wood house next to the clear river waters. Nobody inside it. Some lunch leftover on the table, a glass bottle half full of water, a pair of old shoes on the floor next to a three-legs stool. A bunch of spiders walking on the leftover plate. A lizard walking comfortably on the ground.

Uninhabited since months, maybe years. That's a serious problem.

For days, Scuro and the dead ones are looking up and down through the whole forest, every spot, each cave. No results. Scuro's clothes are dirty and ripped off. He chews some leaves given to him by Niobe, to keep himself awake and not giving up to the tiredness. Night is the worst moment. There is cold and the moisture increases. The wizard wakes up with his rotten bones and he looks jealous at the dead ones, fresh like roses, at least at a glance. They re-

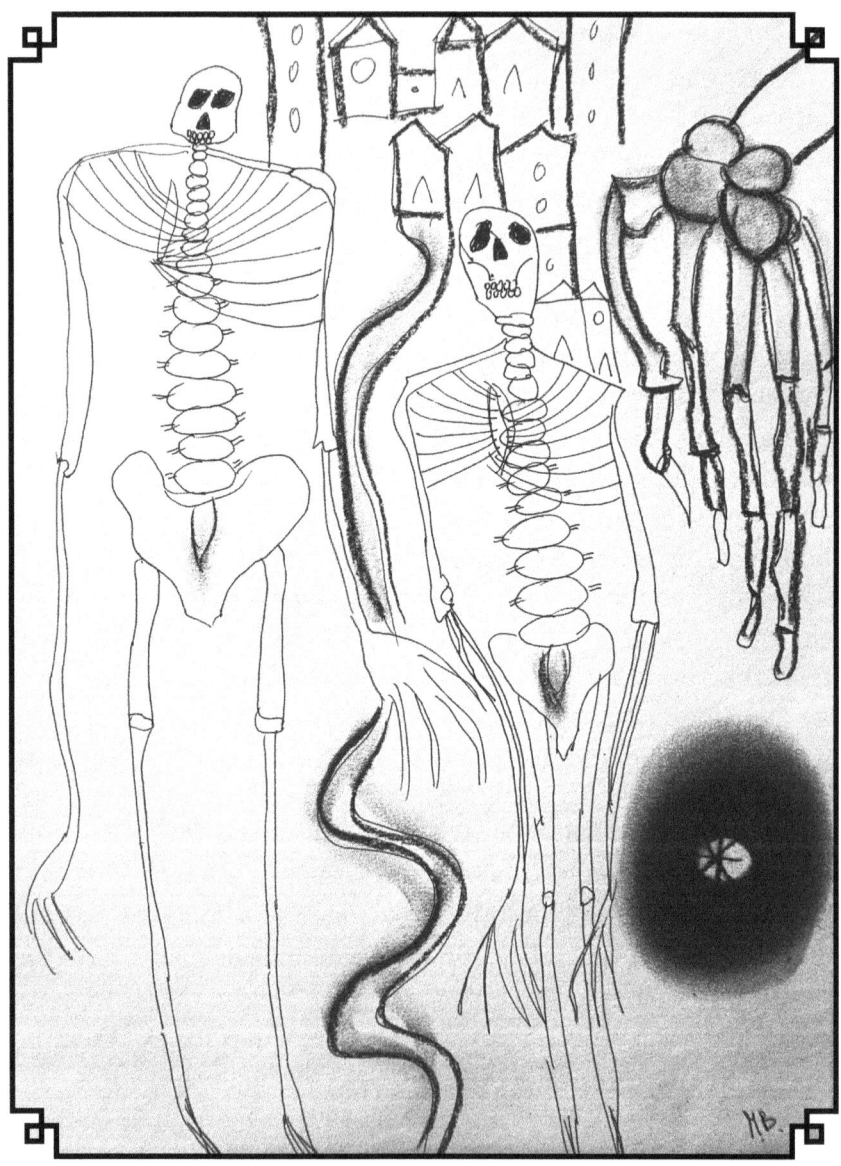

turn again to the abandoned house. Scuro has his knees bending down. The dark goes over his eyelids. He wakes up again into a better looking bed. A Mu person with a deep sight, hair tied in small white braids, looks at him with satisfied expression. The unknown body is deformed by a hump. The face is full of wrinkles. He asks Naiir for holding a wet cloth, whilst he folds back the blankets to the sick person. Scuro does not understand.

Naiir explains to the wizard that the white hair man is Ebbone, who they were looking for, jumped out suddenly from a trapdoor through the basement of the house.

'*Dailorg* houses are full of damned trapdoors, we should have checked underneath the carpets.' The wizard voice resounds through the empty room, sharp as a blade.

Naiir confirms, 'Indeed, we should have known earlier.'

Ebbone puts the wet cloth over Scuro's forehead and he smiles.

'Why are you laughing? Oldie?' The wizard stands up suddenly, throwing the cloth on the floor with disappointment.

'What is there under that damned trapdoor?'

'A cave where you can stay cooler. It's been months I am living there.'

'Naiir says that you are the only Mu person able to help us.'

'Naiir is wrong; I am the only Mu citizen able to get older. That does not mean that I should know something more than the others.'

Scuro grabs Ebbone on his neck. 'Talk to me, if you want to live! You have to tell us how to get into the *Dailorg* Library roof!'

'I know nothing. Why are you asking me for this explanation?'

'Because the legend says that you know lot of things, that you were among the first people to be born at Mu. It's been said even that you are a prototype.'

'What a stupid thing!'

'A testing Mu person, I would say. The first Mu person and the only one born from Echet's blow. A kind of joke or experiment!'

'Yes, like the first cookie, that comes out always more awful than the others following. There are so many legends at Mu, lot of them, maybe too many! They distract us from the true sense of reality.'

'Would you please explain me then why Mu people are not getting older and you have a lot of wrinkles on your skin?'

'I really don't know it, and if you ask me about my age I don't even know.'

'Why are you living on your own? Have you got any family?'

'I was born here, I don't know where I come from, how, why I am here now. I can move towards the forest easy. Hunting and fishing. I talk to the animals. I love to stay alone.'

'You have to tell us how to get into the *Dailorg* Library!'

'I know nothing.'

'Take him away! We will make his mouth talking over the Castle. He will sing like a singing bird!'

THE EXPERIMENT

Tabum has prepared everything. The steel table shines of bright beauty before to put over it the Mu testing subject dead during the first experiment technically successful. Tabum now operates under the vigilant eyes of Niobe. He cuts the body in pieces with competence, sectioning the right parts and collecting the thick and dark blood into glossy glass containers. Sometimes he runs to a stone table to read one book. 'Blood and sweat and Mu's eggs under substances that the golden flesh of the Mothers is made from, according this book at least.'
'Which book?'
'I found it into the library of the Castle, really remarkable, but impossible to realise.'
'Tabum, what is impossible?'
'Check it yourself.'
'It needs 2000 eggs for the experiment... And where about are we going to find them?'
'I said, impossible.
'The only animals able to do eggs at *Dailorg* are the Dodos.'
'And do you have many of them here?'
'Lot of them, at the reserve, towards South. They are goofy. They nest on the ground. It will be easy to collect their eggs. We can even eat some.'
'In the meanwhile let's prepare the Mu's testing subject properly.'
'Yes, yes. What do I need to do?'
'Not much. He's already cut in pieces. The blood has to be stored in a cool place, to preserve it. The body has to be

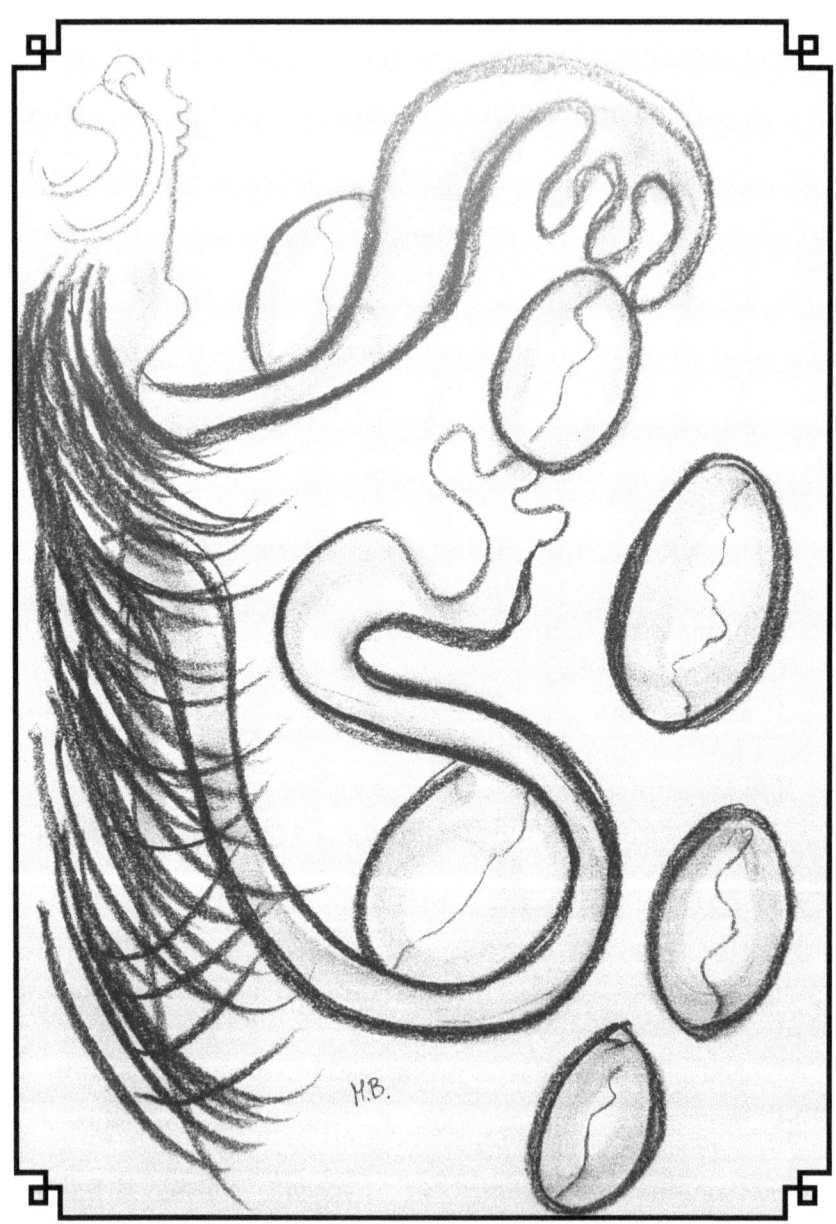

shredded and then we boil it, slow cooking, with no rush.'
'Is it not better to leave it raw?'
'No, better boiled, according to this book.'
'Shall we trust this book then?'
'Hopefully.'
'Hopefully? Are not even sure about it?'
'You couldn't ever be sure about anything. Although it is really antique. That's good sign.'
'Although what is written could be not true!'
'Possibly, but it is the only book where the flesh of the Mothers is mentioned. I looked for it through all the libraries of Mu, except in the *Dailorg* one, obviously.'
'Luckily the right book is there.'
'Maybe, perhaps, if and although are all useless words! Maybe the right book does not exist at all! Maybe it has never been written. The world, my dear, is leading over the chaos, a total and shameless chaos, with no decency and with no boundaries. Sometimes the truth is close, and we don't look at it. The truth breaths next to us, although we don't feel its uncomfortable blow over the skin of our soul. I have lived for too long so I know now that the faith sometimes is the best one to give suggestions. Start chopping down because it's late.
'I don't really want it. The smell of the blood gives me nausea.'
'You have to get used to it, my dear! From now onwards here won't be anymore a place for delicate stomachs. What are those shouts?'
'Scuro came back maybe. Keep chopping whilst I go to meet him. He will have some news for me.'
'What a noise! Shut the door, it's awful!'
Niobe just walks out the laboratory going to meet Scuro.

The wizard has a totally different appearance. The long beard makes him looking older and his face and body are full of scratches, his clothes ripped off.

'What did happen to you?'

'Nothing, not worries, go back to your experiments.'

'Who's this old man?'

'Ebbone, who should know how to get through the library.'

'Did he explain how?'

'He will do it. Take him to the hall.'

The old man gets tightly tied over a table by Naiir's men, his hands and feet.

After beating him up and kicking him, the dead ones try finest methods. One of them takes a pair of black plies. With surgery indifference the executioner digs the plies through the flesh of Ebbone's arms. A tear off, a lacerating shout. But the old man doesn't talk. So now the executioner starts ripping off the face of the poor man. In moments he is bleeding on his face everywhere.

Into he ataraxic world the mirror shows the event to Luce and her friends. Chemako faints. Iris could hear only the shouting, but she gets goose flesh.

Erasmo laughs. The Star is really shocked. 'How do you dare laughing in this moment? They are beating down one Mu citizen and we cannot do anything!'

'Ebbone, Ebbone... Listen to his yells. He has always been histrionic. Of course, he feels pain but he is exaggerating!'

'I don't get it.'

'There are many things that the common perception cannot get. Unknown mysteries are existing that we don't have any power over them. Ebbone is among them. He will not talk for the moment.'

'I am not worried about he is going to talk. I am disgusted!'

'We need to be strong and to look at the death straight to its face to be reborn again and again through new lives.'

'Do you believe that the death of this poor old man could be useful to something?'

'No, his death is useless.'

'He'll die.'

Erasmo laughs, 'Look!'

The pieces of flesh of the poor destroyed body of Ebbone are still pulsating on the stone floor of the tortures hall. But the blood on the victim's face seems to be reabsorbed, the wounds are recovering themselves, the flesh grows up again where it was ripped. The executioner throws the plies on the floor a bit disappointed. Ebbone asks him whether he finished so he can clean after. Scuro is petrified. Niobe gets closer to Ebbone who has still his hands tied and she touches his face with her finger. 'There should be a trick!'

'Yes, it should be, awesome lady. Indeed there is. But don't ask me because I don't know it myself. Since I was born I am like that. You could do everything to me. Grinding me, slicing me, blending me, weapons, weapons, weapons. I am like the echo of a won battle. I can regenerate forever. In few words I am a monster. I don't feel pain even. I acted a bit earlier to make you a bit happy. And now, if you have finished to play to the crazy investigator, would you mind to untie all this knots for me please? Would you like to talk about business?'

Scuro looks at him from the top. 'Business? You are not able to do any business. I can do everything I want to you.'

'You can do nothing to me and you know it.'

'I can make you to mate with a group of Mu girls so they will deliver your sons with the same regenerative skills as you. Genetics is not a joke.'

'No, for sure it is not. But sterility is.'

'What do you mean?'

'That I am infertile.'

'I can throw you in prison for the rest of your days.'

'My dawns are eternal, my sunsets idem. You only can deal with me. You don't get that even I look different but I am still from Mu. Mu people are immortal, unless something won't kill them. Killing me is really impossible, I am already dead too, so I will stay forever in your prison and you will die without having what you want.'

'Damned you!'

'Order to those idiots to untie my knots immediately!'

'What do you want?'

'I want to chat into a private room, without this smelly executioner breathing on my face with his appearance like an idiot which attended a miracle. Ah, and I need this pretty lady to be with us as well. I heard while you are taking me here that she tried to produce the gold. Life is strange sometimes...'

Niobe smiles at him pleased. 'Strange?'

'Indeed, strange my darling, but fascinating, unusually stimulating.'

~ The black star of Mu ~

DODO'S EGGS

At the South of the town, into a nature reserve of great beauty, there is a Dodo sanctuary, goofy and clumsy birds from the Raphus family, really careful with their small birds. Their feathers are shining of bright reflections. Adults birds weight more less 22 kilos and they have a huge curved beak that could open wide and crack even the hardest fruit. Their head, glabrous until inside their eyes, looks a bit severe and sad too, with a bright black pupil and a yellow wet iris. The egg that they lay down, on the wet and warm ground, is huge. Taking the eggs is not that easy, as they are really heavy and fragile. It needs to be careful and transport them with care. For transporting them there is a team of Mu people led by Tabum, they put the eggs inside crates full of straw and then loaded into two lorries going to *Dailorg* Castle. Now the laboratory entrance is blocked by the crates, some shut some other opened. Tabum looks confident and Niobe let him do whatever he likes, hoping that his insights are correct. The eggs get shelled and put inside a huge steel container. Cooked, dried, freeze-dried and pulverized. The body of the Mu's testing subject dead during the first experiment, got the same treatment. So the Mu powder is mixed with the egg powder adding up sweat and blood collected in designated containers. The mix is ready to receive a new ingredient that Tabum has got from Niobe's hands. A secret substance, got from Ebbono, his own tear. One elixir or quintessence, material perfection, strong and personified life. After a really long process of manufacturing, they get a compound that is turned into gold-making pills.

~ *The black star of Mu* ~

Ten Mu testing subjects, filled with pills, are running over ten treadmills. Their sweating produces specks of gold that get collected and analysed by Tabum. There is no doubt. It is pure gold! The flesh of the mothers, produced by sweating, by blood and body of their own sons, has been useful to the beating-frogs wizard, as main dish for his power.

THE WEAPON

Ebbone is a nuclear weapon, his elixir works. He produces living flesh of the mothers, pure gold. But Scuro needs something else, he needs the Black Star.

The old immortal laughs, 'Oh yes, the Star. It's not easy to go into the disappeared library, it's not easy.'

'But you know how to do it.'

'You wouldn't pretend that I will let you put your hands on Luce and I won't get anything back, I would be a stupid.'

'Tell me, idiot, what do you want?'

'Firstly respect, that's necessary, if you want to get on with me! After all I have a certain age.'

'Yes, alright.'

'What do you want as you have got everything? An eternal prototype, the only outcast rejected by his own people?'

'I don't know really, maybe youth but I can't give it to you certainly.'

'You are wrong.'

'Not even Niobe's magic could get you to be young again.'

'Yes, indeed.'

'Do you want that Niobe gets you to be young again then?'

'Indeed.'

'How would she do it? I think she is not able to...'

'She only has to look at me, she looks like a girl from Mu that I loved.'

'I am touched... Well, I make Niobe to look at you, if you fancy.'

'It's not enough this. The Black Star is a really precious gift, unique, the antique beating heart of Mu.'

'I don't get it.'

'Don't you get it? Yet you seem smart enough. I think you don't want to understand, I see. Niobe.'
'Niobe, what?'
'I want her.'
'Niobe is not an exchanging product!'
'So you don't want the Black Star then.'
'Ask me anything, I will give you everything you want.'
'I only want to have Niobe, nothing else. I believe it is hard to digest. You did not expect this. You can think about it, I have got plenty of time, I am not in a rush.'
'I agree. Niobe is yours.'
'I see, you have thought a lot about it...'
'I have got different priorities.'
'Yes. Don't try to dupe me, then! You will regret it!'
'Cheat on you? I don't care about Niobe, I only want the Star. My power will be stronger, wider and the one of the Lodge too.'
'Which Lodge?'
'I created it. A secret organisation of bankers, politics, businessmen, iconoclastic high-handed people destroyer the power of the Great Mothers. A network, you see. A powerful and linked spiderweb of people. The dark side of the Government, secret powers, unspeakable secrets. If I got the ancient heart of the Mothers, they would be erased over any Mu's memories and no anarchist would challenge me over any absurd freedom.'
'Luce will never be on your side. The Mothers never stopped talking to her. She is one of them. The sound of your mortal and human voice is too weak in order for her to accept hearing it.'
'We will see!'

NIOBE'S END

For a long time Mu people haven't heard the Mother's whispers. *Dailorg* is like sleeping through a nightmare and maybe there will be never a wake up. All the other cities of Mu have adhered to the new Government's standards. Some anarchists still resist, challenging the State of dead ones, sabotaging the opening of banks, symbol of exploitation and slavery of Mu people. The majority of citizens, anyway, has no willing to challenge the Government in behalf of the freedom. A kind of vicious addiction to the evil has spread like a destroying disease. Resignation is on Mu people's shoulders. The gold as opium has corrupted the fair purity of their minds. A world of new destroying injustice was born. Within the chance to provide a sort of order, next future will be horrifying. The dull and sad opacity of Scuro's Government delivers monsters and infections of the souls. Preachers paid by the State to give new religious tales, scream their iconoclastic fury against fountains and statues dedicated to the Majesty of the Mothers. *Dailorg* has been changing appearance and all Mu gets uglier. Beauty dies everyday a little bit more. Living people voices get confused with dead ones yells that are now leading over the Underground Earth. Public transports which before were free of charge for Mu people, now are private. Going around *Dailorg*, after the introduction of the money, it's expensive and for lot of people it is difficult. Where the concept of affluence and poverty before used to be referred exclusively to the soul, now every aspect of life is based on the tragic, horrible, cruel and absurd distinction between rich and poor. The essence devalues through the posses-

sion of physical assets. And the trustworthy servants of the State of Scuro are checking that on the shuttles, traveling through the green places of *Dailorg*, passengers have their own tickets. A piece of paper to stamp before to get on board becomes symbol of social difference. Everything is based on time now. Ticket is valid for 75 minutes for people that can afford it. Shoes, clothes, water, free time, work, arts, health, disease, everything has a cost and its own duration. Providers of transport, hospitals, companies, banks, are all friends of Scuro. Selected personally by him in the *Dailorg* Castle during orgiastic private parties. Even friends of friends have suggestions about hiring people. There is a deep pattern of relationships that cannot be unnoticed. A thick spiderweb with steel strings. Power is based on convenient friendships. A lot of high standing people belong to the secret Lodge of the wizard and they have noticeable important roles within Mu's society. A web of mutual interests, connivance, intercession is affecting the new Government purity. It is a bad plant with nice and fake foliage, but rotten roots. Public press publishes what Scuro and his friends decide to in order to get a pleasant impression and to hide the deep cracks through their secrets. The independent press is forced to close down for debts. No one is allowed to discover some vases or stoups where ministers dip their hands. Freedom has instead its own hands dirty of soil. It digs out and hates, start and end planned ahead, rates and swindle-laws. Freedom breaks the clock hands and doesn't give monetary value to life. Even the Mothers are enemies of the Time which makes people servants and subjugated accountants. Scuro worships the Time. Through his mortal and jealous meanness Scuro wants to make Mu people similar to him, subjugated to the inexorable and evanescent rules of the Time.

Niobe wakes up a morning and she remembers the nightmare when Time was staring at her straight into her eyes. She observes what no Mu people should ever see: the marcescence, the cruel indifference, the betrayal, the deterioration that provides wrinkles of decrepitude. They get wider, like deep bleeding wounds.

Niobe heard what the wizard said to Ebbone. And she suddenly woke up under the cold and even devastating fingers of the time. He talks, a metal sound comes out his purplish teeth. Niobe hears that like through a dream. She touches her own face to be aware of her lost profile. She looks at her hands horrified. She shivers while points out her pupils towards the sarcastic mouth of her interlocutor. She recognises him, her own Time laughing at her. He tears her hair off. He pulls it strongly, in between his fingers. The Mu woman turns her sight away. Her eyes are hurting. She tries to listen. The Mothers don't whisper anymore, freedom is under anaesthesia; her dated friends disappeared and betrayed. Her hands are dirty. The sorceress now is awake and she walks towards the black beach that once upon a time belonged to the dead ones. Now it is abandoned and silent like an urn. The rough sea is the transparent eye of a child that just cried. Niobe walks with her candid feet over the silver sand, drawing footprints due to vanish. She gets closer to the sea shore, brushing her fingers through the waves. She breathes deeply. The air is like infected by her breathing of that time that is sticking on her side and it keeps talking, suffocating the whispers of the Mothers. She cannot get rid of it. It is repetitive, hateful, unconcerned, a torture. Her words are bouncing over her wet clothes, heavy because of the salty tears of the sea. It looks like her white thin hands are bleeding. It's been days and days that she is washing them continuously. But the innocent blood doesn't give a break to the assassins. It's gone under the skin, the nails, through each pore and it doesn't go away. No sea in the world could wash it away. There is no point to carry on this way. A rock, with a strange shape of elephant, is standing out overhanging against the greenish air, over the sea womb. Niobe climbs the rock hardly. She prays for the Mothers to talk to her for the last time, but her ears don't hear anything now. Her nostrils breath the foam of sharp and furious waves. The empty gives her deep anxiety, but it calls out, attractively, wicked. Niobe answers. No one runs away from himself after waking up. She never learnt how to swim. But now fears are gone, she has other demons instead. She dives into the cold water, from the rock into the empty. The sea grabs her; the wave grasps her into a lethal hug, taking herself away forever from Ebbone's orgasm. A huge coelacanth swims next to her with indifference, whilst the Time, sitting over a rock, smiles at her breaking out her hair that he got in his hand.

Scuro measures with big steps Niobe's laboratory. Tabum has vanishes as well, dead together with her, as he was only a projection of the sorceress' fantasy. Recently it is getting hard to distinguish the true and the false at *Dailorg*, the reality from the dream. The city is like surrounded within an oneiric atmosphere. The anarchists call it as a nightmare. Indeed, the wizard knows it. Those bastards don't stand for his authority, his system, order, dividing, monetise. Although the State requires discipline. But rebels don't accept it. They are becoming a serious problem with their odd and old-fashioned concept of freedom. And they organise, plotting from behind, ready to hit the core of the banks, so precious, so useful for the richest ones. Mu resistance is getting stronger day by day. It should need to adopt a bit of repressive actions. Police extraordinary measures to get rid of the problem. What an ingratitude from Mu! The wizard has destroyed the statues of the Great Mothers; he built churches of true God, the same as the one that he knew in the Upper World. But Mu people don't care about Heaven and Hell. Here it is useless. No one believes it. Religion is a flop. Scuro has established financial institutions, money. In few words he thinks he has civilised *Dailorg*, and, instead of giving him thanks to save them from primitive superstitions in which they believe, Mu people are standing against him and the Government of the dead ones. Every day fights, riots, blood. This is not good for the President, he is not popular at the moment. People start to reflect and reflection is never a good thing, is harmful to the power. Even the new religion says that. Never over-knowledge. Even more if there would have been a little chance to get through the library, now there is no chance at all because of Niobe's death. Ebbone won't say anything. It could be some sort of deal with him, although it is very hard. An immortal, a Mu person that has everything. What would he like more? What if Ebbone wouldn't know that Niobe died? Hiding the news... Scuro walks toward the library. Ebbone is there, sitting and reading together with two dead ones that are controlling him.

'Hello, Mr President! Did you sleep badly? You don't look in a good shape today.'

'I am really good. Just get to the point, Ebbone!'

'The egg?'

'Don't joke!'

'I am not joking. The egg is the origin of everything, the

start, the regression, the quid, do you know what is the egg?'

'I am not here to talk about eggs! You have to tell me how to get into the vanished library!'

'*Dailorg* Library is pure metaphysics. I can suggest you a mechanical method to open up the roof, but it won't be enough.'

'How come?'

'You should understand the essence of the library, and only getting to the essence you could enter the library, here we go, that is the key.'

Ebbone puts one egg over the glossy wooden table. 'The gold created by Niobe is perfect, there is blood and death inside. Dip this egg through Niobe's gold and throw it to the roof of the vanished library. It will melt. Something that you humans cannot understand is that an arcane world is hiding beyond the materiality. The ataraxic ones live into the bottom of the bottom of the thoughts of *Dailorg*, into the lowest point of the vanished library defending the purity of Mu, violated by you. Mu won't fall down until you haven't caught the last ataraxic one!'

'Who are those ataraxic ones?'

'They are the inviolate conscience of Mu.'

'How do you know that?'

'I used to be one of them long time ago... They love a lot the freedom... They will sacrifice everything in the name of freedom. Now they are listening to us. Luce can hear your words.'

'How can they do it?'

'A soft mirror.'

'Let's go...'

'It has been said that the mirror is a tear of the Great

Mother collected by the ataraxic ones when the genitor goddess took her heart off to offer it to the Underground World. Entering the library takes time, effort and eggs, a lot of eggs. You have to regress, finding your primitive conscience, a pre-birth status and during the trip you have to throw an egg dipped into the flesh of the Mothers, against the roof surface of the library. The journey will be long and exhausting. No one could help you. But it is the only way to access to the world of Erasmo.'

'Who's Erasmo?'

'You'll find out soon... He had never forgiven me... Where is Niobe?'

'Later on.'

'Now. To enter into the library I need her.'

'What do you mean?'

'I mean that without her Ebbone is not Ebbone.'

'I don't get it.'

'The ataraxic ones have a spiritual body kept by their moral skills. Their world is special, metaphysical and physical at the same time, conscience and body appearance. They don't need a body because their purity is so much that they are not allowed to wish one. I am different because I am guilty. I had the wish for a body and I get older, I regenerate, but my hosting body deteriorates.'

'The hosting body?'

'Yes. Do you see those hands? And the eyes, feet, hair. They were from a young Mu person and now they are old. Mu people don't get older. Only I feel the shock of decrepitude through my regeneration. I haven't got a body, I hope you get it now. After a lot of years I break through inside a young body of a Mu person which becomes mine. If they wound me, I can regenerate, I cannot die, but I make getting older my hosting body with my psychological strength. Then I leave it and I look for another one, fresh and young. Niobe is perfect.'

'Has the hosting body to be alive?'

'Not necessarily. Even more, if dead, it is better. The owner won't challenge me. Although it has to be fresh.'

'Niobe is really fresh. Her body has been transported last night to the shore by the sea waves. She looks still alive.'

'It will be more than good then.'

'What about your old body?'

'Don't think about it...'

They go through a narrow corridor illuminated by big windows with iron bars. At the end of the corridor that looks never ending, there is a white stone room, oval ceiling, similar to a cosy lair. The light comes in strongly from the far end wall, all bars. Niobe's body is lying over a dark table located in the middle of the room. She has been dressed again, her hair tied with a lot of blonde breads, icing lips, her body really bloated, stained. Ebbone touches her face with his hands, close his eyes, the room becomes warm while his feet decompose into thin vapour tears, then his legs, slowly, his body, arms, shoulders, head, and his hands for last. The face of the dead one deflates, her stains disappear like absorbed by Ebbone's hands. Niobe coughs, spitting out a bit of salty water. Her glaucous pupil can be seen through the shade of her purple eyelids. Her mouth shuts showing her bright teeth. Her breathing lifts up her chest and her hands receive a kind of shock. Her white nails get pinkish again. Her fingertips move again. Her palms rest on the table, lifting her body up. Her eyes are bothered by the light and the vapour in the room although going out through the bars. The revived brushes her clothes with her hands. Ebbone inside Niobe is happy, judging to be fine into the new body. He touches himself, moving his neck, smiles a bit goofy, he does ridiculous poses, walks up and down to stretch his legs. Scuro is impressed, not for what happened, more for the face of the reborn sorceress. It's not her anymore, or better she is the same as before, identical, but different at the same time. The light of her eyes and her habit to draw circles into the air with her finger, everything is gone, erased forever. Gone even the light sarcastic wrinkle of her smile into the corner of her mouth, the light walking, slightly fluttering and her way to turn her head a little bit on the side. Niobe is death. Even Mu people that don't know the sorrow of being old, they can also die sometimes. Now Niobe walks in front of him talking to him. Even her voice tone is different. Lost things don't come back. Scuro feels a shiver of fear thinking about his own fragile and temporary nature of being human and mortal. Time is ticking fiercely over clocks hands, stepping out, ruling and leading over the Upper World. This is Mu, instead, the ultra-world. Scuro will be the new Time, and everyone will shiver making his name rolling out their mouths beyond their teeth, along the ousted pathways self-determining of the Mothers, alongside the changed roads of *Dailorg*, up to a green and hard sky like stone, until the stars made of enamel coated iron of light pulling hair to the night, dirtying a little.

Ebbone is happy. 'Let's go my friend, let's go!'

'Where?'

'To celebrate my new body. The aphorism of the day do you know which one is?'

'No, I don't.'

'The exquisite cadaver drinks wine and point out his fingers. I am thirsty.'

'Where do you point out your finger?'

'After drinking in honour of Erasmo, I will point out to you with this dead finger the exact spot which will allow you to enter through the ataraxic world.'

'Who's Erasmo?'

'The boss of the ataraxic ones. He himself does not know who is really.'

'What about us? Do we know who we are?'

'Yes, indeed. We are indecent criminals, with our cruel ethic, gold instead of our souls. We are sons of the dark, free of not being free and to impose to the others our no-freedom. Hedonist destroyers, hypocrites, lobbyists, statesmen, crooks, religious and pseudo-moralists. We are really good lads, bankers, sons of a destroying infinite time. We want even the blood of this uncomfortable father that we are willing to absorb his core in order not to get older. Selfish, liar, cruel and conformists. We are fragile senses lost in the sea of the transforming nightmare sea that we created. *Dailorg* will go from the dream to the nightmare after we have entered through the bottom of the disappeared library. We will tear off the eyes to the day and we could affirm the leadership of our darkness consuming our wombs. And we don't trust anything else than the festering wound of the power. We will taint Mu like a devastating cancer and, if we would have to discover new worlds, we will corrupt those ones too. It's our nature to do those things. We cannot escape from it. Each one of us leads over himself being in his own palm of his cruel hand, hoping not to tighten too much.'

'Dying because of ourselves, it's odd really, it would be a joke!'

'Although likely to happen. War is war, my friend. We are going to dive through the green tangles of the streets of Mu. We run to do a bit of troubles, lifting up our glasses. Move on that the time is precious, especially for you as cruel mortal person. Drinking alcohol we will think more likely and we will kill the old age. We will not have mercy, staring at it whilst breathing and moving for the last time and we will enjoy about it, spitting into the eye of the time which has conceived us with a whore, on the edge of the damned hell.'

~ The black star of Mu ~

HANIA

The inn chosen by Ebbone is warm, smoky and crowded. It looks like an old-fashioned dive with its opaque wooden tables, hot plates full of diced rhino-grade with black bean sauce. Red wine looks like blood under the artificial lights. The drink goes sweet through the throats of those people making them willing to chat. The opaque glasses get emptied as quickly as they get filled again by three agile brunette Mu girls. Behind the bar desk, over a comfortable high stool, the little Hania sits there. She is a dwarf that has the gift to be old. Her small crumpled hands have long golden coloured nails. She always wears a bonnet with pink bright silk roses and rhinestones, pearls, squiggles of netting golden threads. She wears a light dress, red and blue, covered by mirror fragments sewn all around. Always barefoot. A contact with a single shoe gets her horrified. Her mouth with tumid and cracked lips reminds the one of a fish. Blue eyes, really fair, within a not natural transparency. Her brownish teeth are biting a strange long and dark pipe. Hania smokes strongly stretching her deep wrinkles over her crumpled face. The smoke makes opaque the brightness of the rhinestones, going up appearing as white small circles.

'God bless you, Ebbone. I see that you have changed location.' Hania has a calm, monotonous, placid tone.

Scuro is impressed as Hania knows that. Ebbone puts his hand on his shoulder. 'Don't worry President, the little Hania can see what the others cannot. Through her blue iris strange worlds can be seen, sad and strange.'

'Idiot, I recognised you by your pendant. Niobe would

had never have that horrifying thing! You have always odd taste.'

'It's a real little rabbit paw... The good things of bad taste.'

'It's ugly like you!'

'You didn't have the same opinion some time ago...'

'Opinions change and even people I think. Only you are the same idiot that you were before and you will be forever even with different appearance and bodies, forever. What do you and your friend Scuro want?'

'Drinking.'

'I would give you with pleasure some tea with poison, although I know that it won't hurt you.'

Ebbone smiles at Scuro. 'Really nice woman, isn't she?'

'A lot!'

'She loves me desperately, that's why she is like this to me. Isn't it, Hania?'

'Damned you!'

'Indeed, she loves me!'

'Go to the point, idiot! What do you need?'

'The eggs.'

'We don't serve eggs in this pub.'

'You know what I am talking about.'

Hania takes out some smoke. Staring at her friend, 'Go out!'

'Something I never understood about you.'

'I am definitely sure that things you don't understand are more than one, innumerable, like the stars.'

'Why do you want to be stuck inside there?'

'It's not your business!'

'I want you to live, Hania.'

'I do not care about what you want!'

'You are getting older...'

'I like getting older and checking my age counting the wrinkles over my tired face.'

'You will die of old age, if you don't leave the body you have now. I will find a new one for you.'

'You cannot find something better that I would find myself. I am not scared about dying. Everyone dies, a little bit every day, for a reason or another. Go away!'

'You have to give me the eggs!'

'I don't need to give you anything! I have no debts with someone that took everything off me!'

'I will browse the pub up and down.'

'Do it.'

'Do not tell me... I will pull off your womb in order to get the eggs.'

'It's funny. You know that you can do nothing to me.'

'Whether you swallowed the eggs, I can get them off inside you!'

Hania got tricked herself. Her eyes transparency gets dark. Smoke circles vanish in the air. Like exhausted souls, unarmed against a cruel huge evil, they produce tortuous expressions.

'You can choose, you give me the eggs or I will have to open you like a goat. Even you can regenerate, it will be a bit painful anyway, so why do you want to suffer?'

'Split me up, break me, grind me, destroy me, you cannot do anything to me and you know it!'

'Mapuche.'

Hania shivers a bit.

'Eh, the feelings! They always cheat you. I know that he is your favourite, like a son for you. They are interrogating him at the Police Station now.'

'What?'

'21 grams of Meadow Goat's-Beard, the herb that once smoked sends you to the moon. Trade and possession of drugs. Do you want to see your loved one to keep well?'

'Yes.'

'You cannot see him now but I promise you that he lost weight and he is wounded. He fell off the stairs. A bad falling really.'

Hania calls a waitress asking to her for a prune jam. The lady serves her quickly, without talking.

'We wait here, you eat properly and give us what we need, whilst we enjoy the show.'

Two belly dancers are dancing around the tables shaking strongly some golden pendants on their hips, ankles and breasts.

After one hour more less the two dancers leave through pink and blue veils and citrus perfumes of vanilla mixed with recent sweating. Prunes give their effect. Hania goes to the toilet, getting three eggs, washing them under running water with anger and giving them to Ebbone. Whilst giving them to him she stares at him. 'They won't bring you good luck, you know! They were in a lot of poo and they will give you troubles. Everything comes back again. No one can escape from the destiny, not even you.'

~ *The black star of Mu* ~

A WEDGE OF THE UPPER WORLD

The street is grey, even the sky, shaded, made lazy by depressed shreds of clouds, cut by twisted roots of dead trees, wounded by a ruby sun, fake like a false stone. Luce has never seen a sky like that, impoverished, abstract, coloured and punched by the hand of a dystonic painter. She walks next to Erasmo, puzzled, making no questions. Silence resounds over the cement like a living lash that's anxious to find the nice death through a freedom scream. But the throat does not move, like petrified. The sparkle of a purple lonely star that breaks the oppressive greyness, increases the sense of unreality. The ataraxic one sighs, stopping, he moves with his feet some leaves on the floor, uncovering a trapdoor. He opens, inviting Luce to go downstairs, then shutting the trapdoor. There is an unnatural dark, fake, so dense that it can be touched, so cold that it can be felt on fingertips. Then a light explosion from somewhere, illuminating a grey electrical wire from where a switch is hanging and moving strangely. There is a noise, like a dripping tap and marking a kind of unreal time, confused, with no sense and a strange smell of rotten, of spoiled meat. Firstly light, then the smell comes stronger like an echo of indefinite voices, far, that look like getting closer suddenly. A voice orders to press the switch to illuminate the misery of the world. But the switch is moving around like a monstrous big insect with no legs and wings. Luce is not brave enough to touch it with her hands. The voice repeats again to switch the light on over the shame of the world. Luce cannot. The insect looks like bigger and stronger, dirtier and filthier. The voice now yells imperiously to switch on the light at any way because the world cannot be left in the dark. Luce cannot. Then the voices get so close to touch her ears. Warm and smelly breathing over her skin. Something or someone, that she cannot recognise, grabs her, hitting, hitting her, continuously. The rhythmic dripping of the tap follows the timing of the bashing and now it looks louder. Luce feels her blood dripping from her side. It's warm, dense, viscous. Then she falls down seeing over her, next to the switch, a huge head of a nun that keeps hitting her, pulling her hair, dragging her until smashing her on the wall. The nun is human. She wears on her neck a cross sign moving when she lifts up and pulls down her arms to beat Luce. The movement looks agonizing, irregular, so the cross looks like the switch. One, two, ten, twenty blows and the insect-switch has vanished. The wire is naked, sad and depressed without its own hanging insect. The insect now is hanging over the nun's neck looking even more monstrous and grotesque. Tired, the nun stops and demands Luce to switch on getting it closer to her. Luce refuses again. The nun starts again, but she is too tired to follow the previous rhythm so she stops. After a while she decides to switch it on herself and all the room gets illuminated showing girls with white shirts and collars of the same colour. They wear over their noses some glasses with one lens, forced to direct their sight towards a single direction. Their eyes join into one. They are playing a kind of nursery rhyme or prayer learnt by heart with their small mouths semi-toothless that look like getting incredibly wider like trying to swallow the whole room. Luce looks her hands full of blood, they are small, like the ones of the girls. Even her shirt is the same as the girls ones. Luce is one of them. The nun lifts her up pulling her hair and pushing her into the group. She starts to play mechanically the prayer with boring and marked rhythm of her treble voice. The group moves and Luce with them, walking to a building full of small beds where the girls go to sleep at night, mute, almost fasting, broken and worshipping. They are all orphans. The building, with the square big windows, is an orphans institute, shelter, prison, blood and tears and hunger. The orphans stop to pray and they turn around showing their childish backs that looks like are growing up. Even the body of Luce grows up together with the white dress of the nun, stained with blood now it is a clean green tunic. The girls grown up turn around again showing their elderly faces, crumpled, with swollen eyelids, heavy. The woman with the green tunic which is not the previous nun, asks Luce to stand up for the bath. There is no blood now, like nothing has happened earlier. The corridor where they are walking through is bright, but narrow. There are old people everywhere, some tied to the chairs, some others shaved and narcotised by the nurses as punishment. An elderly people hospice. Smell of alcohol, funny smell, warmth that makes you breathing hardly, scent of rotten, spoiled broth, fatty, made with rotten meat. The nurse washes the old body of Luce, pulling her hair, marking some wounds on her arms. Then she dresses Luce up forcing her to eat that disgusting broth, greasy reddish, then she ties her on the chair to avoid her to escape. Luce feels her body getting rigid until transforming into something else. Her arms become wooden; her back is a cushion now. Her becoming a chair shows off under the lighted wire connected to the insect-switch. Over that chair are sitting some people, politics, corrupted and corrupting, investigated and prisoners. On the chair now there is Nudo that some men in uniform call with a different name. They interrogate him. Blaming him to subvert the State's Laws. Those men grab him. Then there is a jump out the window, short and quick. A noise of breaking bones against the severe nudity of the floor. Life ends in a second, over the cold soil, into a black blood puddle. And beyond the blood and the street, and the lamppost, the barracks and the moon, a huge metal cage from where there is no escape. Luce looks up, beyond the thick rough bars. There are planets and stars that move around, little ones, far, unreachable that observe everything from distance. The room in the cage gets smaller time by time, there is no other solution rather than get crashed in between the grey bars. A man with no face gets closer to the cage smiling with no mouth and looking with no eyes. He grabs the switch that now is in the middle of the cage and press the button. An absurd light dazzles their sight. The floor of the cage is soil, it is like various floors of various other places, all around the Upper World. Human figures are moving around. Everywhere a race against the time, physical and moral, rapes, murders, crimes of every kind, dirty hands grabbing whichever possible. And in the middle there is the wizard that with a long twisted stick hits the ground and recalls a group of frogs to gather, after shaking his friends' hands during a séance, pointed out the shelter of a prisoner without knowing it and kept warm a comfy armchair. Light switches off. Dark creates monsters. The world is full of them, every kind, dimensions and colours. They move in the shadows, feeding black powers that use public puppets, fake representative of the people. Into the darkness dead ones of yesterday, today and tomorrow show off. Their cold hands grab sides of darkness leaving blank spaces because of lack of sense. They punch as skeletons through the air, breaking it in thousand pieces the vitreous fragility and showing the idea of other worlds still unreachable. In the meanwhile in the dark polluted rivers are flooding of rage. The air suffocates the concentrated sights of millions of wide-open eyes to the raped nature. Violence, repressed by a fake good behaviour, makes men and women to implode that got lost through the wind, in billions of sharp little fragments. They plunge through the white skin of Luce yelling at her to wake up.

She was sleeping over the stone bench in the garden. She dreamt. Nudo is next to her, sad like a tomb. By a flying pear half eaten, it looks like Chemako is there too. Erasmo puts his hand over her shoulder, 'You saw a wedge of the Upper World. Did you like it?'

Luce is disgusted, she cannot even talk. Her throat is burning like she swallowed living fire.

'Humans are strange creatures, able to do everything, good and evil. Better they don't find you at home even when they want to do good things to you, they would convince you about the advantage of what they say. Scuro is trying to violate our ataraxic world and maybe he would succeed on it. We need to act now. Now it is all in your hands, Luce. Let's go into the egg.'

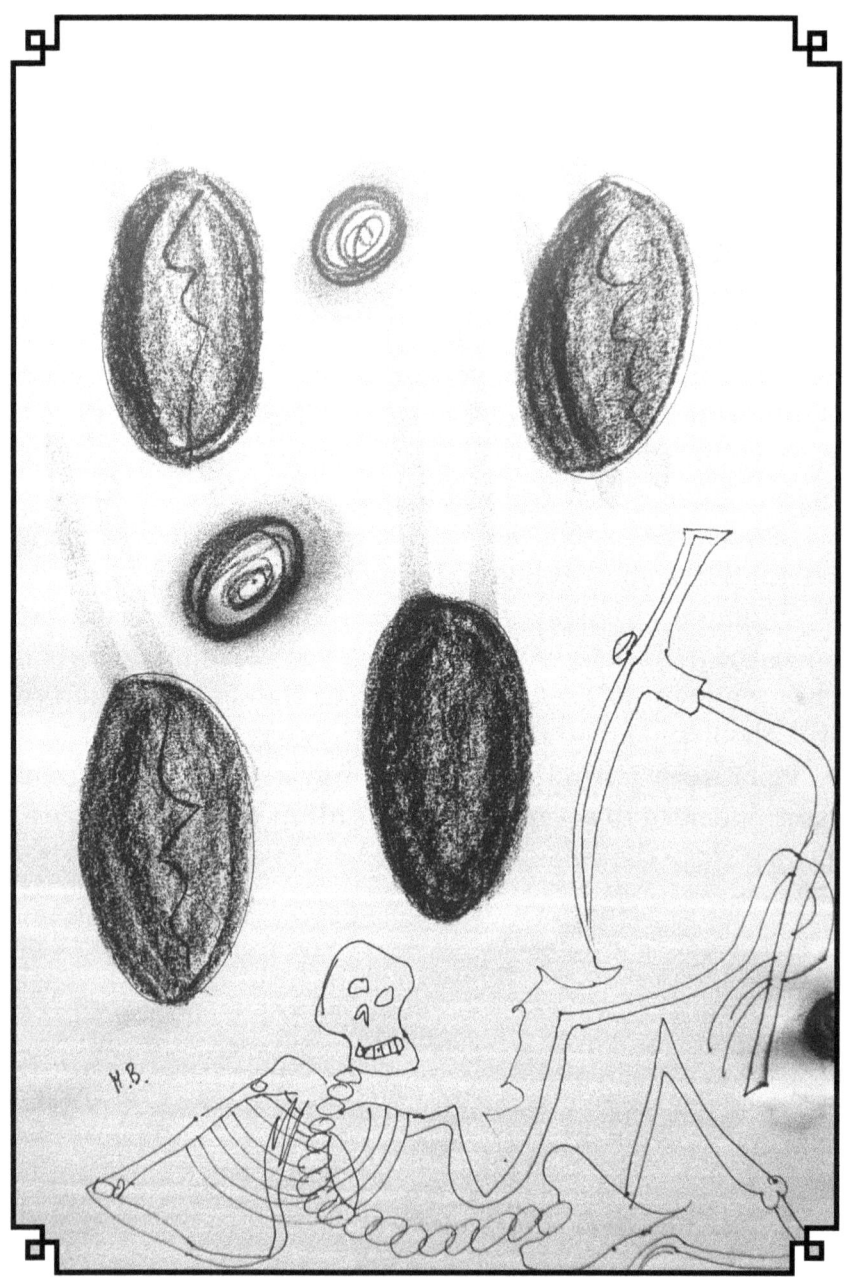

THE EGG ROOM

Four black eggs are shining under the green light of the sky at *Dailorg*. Ebbone puts them in four gaps on the roof of the library. The dark shell melts through purple reflections and gets absorbed by the roof surface showing two fresh yolks, full, yellow and rich where movement images are shaking and two black yolks, rotten, full of worms. Now even Scuro can see the ataraxic ones reflected through the straight and yellowish surface of the yolks. The primordial and neonatal strength of the eggs makes some thin cracks on the first layer of *afsaneh*. Scuro's dead ones start working with pickaxes around the cracks. The task needs time to get completed. A full day is not enough because beyond the cracks there is one more layer of *afsaneh* and more and more. The yellow yolks now showing nude masks, with no face on their surface, slip like living things, time by time, layer after layer, without breaking, getting through the cracks at their early stage, followed by the dark yolks, moving whilst drawing deformities.

After thirty days of hard work, the first layer of wurtzite shows. The eggs show planet and stars, different worlds, possible, ignored by men and Mu people. Strange misshapen creatures born from the dead yolks. They have human heads with open wide mouths dripping yellowish saliva. Their hands are claws of unusual size and their small body, curved, ends into a little squamous tail. They grab the wurtzite really fiercely and strongly opening small, really small cracks where they penetrate quickly together with fresh yolks. Scuro's dead ones get strongly over the cracks opened by those eggs. Reaching the next layer is not an easy job to do. Ebbone soon understands that inside the library Erasmo organises a counterattack and some thoughts are bouncing in his head now. 'He won't give up; it's not his style. Even when I cheated him over Hania he did not give up. Impassive. Although he used to love Hania more than himself. She soon got fed up of me. She understood she has lost everything escaping from the ataraxic world. She cannot find herself anymore. That's why she punishes herself through a misshapen body ignoring me totally. She cannot hate me even. Hate is too exciting feeling as she can waste it over me. Anyway, that day she had listened to me, following me and being guided as a baby. She used to trust me... Erasmo has never forgiven me, these are hard things. I was able to violate the primitive inexperience of his sweet Hania. I stole from him more than a girlfriend. I betrayed his trust. I am an affront to his soul, a rotten demon, a cancer damning the destiny his own faith. Gipsy, from a body to another, without stopping. I made Hania's favourite one to be beaten up wildly because I am rotten inside, tainted without any chances. I only wanted Hania still to look for me, like when we went out from the ataraxic world and we went inside two Mu people bodies. I wanted her to look for me, if not for love at least for hate. But in her sight there is only not-involvement, disdain. So anyway that's it, I will take my part and I will slosh in the rottenness right to the end. I want to reach the black apotheosis, kicking the idyllic and sappy plasticity of the day to impetrate the destroying obscurity and generating of monsters like me!'

In the lowest part of the garden of the ataraxic ones a huge egg with candid shell shines under the sun. Erasmo puts next to the egg a ladder and immediately a hole opens up to give access. 'You have to enter it on your own, I cannot come along, it's not my job. It's an inner journey. It's about surviving to yourself. I tell you it's not easy, but you have to try.'

'Any tips?'

'None. Usually they are made not to be followed.'

'True. Don't you wish me good luck?'

'Luck does not exist inside the egg, you have to make it and remember, pure silence does not exist. You need to go through the possible dimension and reach the purity that usually doesn't need to exist in the usual experience, but it is essential to get through the ultra-worlds.'

Luce enters; the hole closes behind her. The interior is like an opaque luminosity, cocoon-like environment. It's hard to stand, because of the oval shape of the room. A giant and empty egg. Inside only absence, useful to talk to yourself. Although everything is closed, it can breath good because the surface is porous and it absorbs air and light from the outside. No noise. A white dimension of unreal silence. Luce finds out that even the silence has its own sound and getting to its essence without hearing anything else is really hard. After some time she feels her feet adapting to the egg shape, curving, melting like ice on the sun. Her body follows the same destiny, filling of itself the empty until not leaving any gaps. Her arms get curved softly through a sticky yolk. Water and saliva are transparent albumen pushing over the calcareous walls, until squashing them. Beyond the cracked shell there is another egg and so on placed as helix shape, swirling of buried primitive mysteries. Moreover beyond barriers that usually cannot be trespassed, veils not allowed to be squashed, impossible creatures, with an unusual aspect, are moving through paths never crossed by Mu ones. It's the Unknowable Beyond that everyone believed to be the last obstacle to pass, through a little abyss and a small dark cave, it is only an illusory limit, a dot of thousands and thousands of lost and unknown worlds. Even the Great Mothers pathway is narrow, if compared to the group of worlds, a pearly micro-dot. Then Luce realises how small is the eye, how limited is the brain that refers all to itself, marking limits, barriers, categorising macro-cosmic immensities, absolutely not measurable.

Luce, having her physical body back, is walking along a cemented road. It's cold. There is a man in front of her, a stranger with a luggage in his hand. He is suspicious, he is going towards her. He calls her name, he knows her. Luce has never seen him before. The man gives her his hand. 'You got it at the end!'

'Getting what?'

'I was waiting for you. You are absolutely perfect! I could not have done anything better! Come with me!'

'Where?'

'To my house.'

'But I don't know you, I don't know even where I am.'

'You are on the Earth, my dear, and I am your dad.'

'What?'

'Your dad. I created you, do you get me?'

'No, sorry.'

'You don't exist.'

'What a nice news, really reassuring! From the egg to the Earth through a perfect statement about my non-existence.'

The house of that man, one bedroom flat with low ceilings, is absurdly messy, loud and cheerful at the same time. Books everywhere, even in the toilet and in some worm-eaten wood shelves over the walls into a narrow corridor. Little room to cook and to live a normal life, but the man is happy this way. He lives between paper stories, ancient and modern pages, few dusty canvases, but precious and some African Tribal Masks with terrible and stunning appearance. He dusts very little. Thin and visible dust makes a light layer everywhere. His desk is full of paper. Notes even on the lucid surface of the tiles, on the walls, on the brownish door varnished. A black cat with yellow eyes, psychedelic, is lying softly over a holed jumper. It looks at Luce for a second, yawning and turning on the other side simulating indifference, but keeping an eye on her. Cast iron lamp sends suspicious shades over piles of books that seem to fall down in a moment. A silver frame of an old black and white picture shines over a radiator. A spider made his web really good into a ceiling corner. Some dying flies are waiting for their end over an ashtray.

Some little white hamsters run fiercely into the wheel. It looks like everything and nothing could suddenly happen and life and death are strictly joint inside that house and that man head. He is tall. His icing blue eyes are looking outside, beyond the opaque glasses of a small window, mixing out with the cold winter sky. Suddenly he opens the window. He needs to breath some fresh air, feeling that sensation over the skin, like a hug, to feel that he is still alive. His throat hurts. Maybe he smoked too many cigarettes lost in his thoughts. Now he is hesitant, furious against himself. Luce is waiting for him to say something, to explain everything or almost. The man starts looking at her. He is already old. Luce is surprised, observing him. Contemplation of old age is not part of her experience. Mu people don't get old. The clock of a church strikes. A creepy sound, like a carillon. It fills the air then vanishes into the wind. The man looks sad. He asks Luce whether she would like something to eat or drink. No. She is impatient to know all. No appetite at the moment. He says that he wants to eat instead. He opens a cupboard, getting out a quite scratched non-stick coated frying pan, oil, and then he cooks two eggs and smoked bacon. The smell goes all around the room. Luce starts to get more nervous, 'I need to know what I am doing here and how I got into this place!'

'You go where I want you to go.'

'Really?'

'Whether you like it or not, it's like that. I am your dad!'

'Not always sons obey to their parents and then my dad's name is Corax.'

'Yes, according to the story of Mu your dad's name is Corax, but in the real world I am your dad.'

'I did not know that my mum did something with a human being too.'

'No! Even your mum is my daughter and your father too.'

'You are more messy that this room.'

'The mess is only apparently inside here, I can find everything, even myself and I can guarantee you that Mu people are all my sons!'

'Prolific!'

'Yes, indeed, if I may say so. The eggs are ready. Do you want one?'

'I find them disgusting.'

'Maybe I mentioned them too many times through the story, that's why you found them disgusting now.'

'What story? Why are you laughing?'

'The story of which you are the main character. Don't you understand yet?'

'What?'

'You don't exist, unless only in my fantasy. I created you. I created the story of Mu people, the wizard and all the rest and I am proud of you. You are amazing.'

'What am I doing here at your house?'

'We have to create a finale.'

'I should have a finale. I found the antimatter and I save *Dailorg*!'

'Yes, but how?'

'I don't know. You should know it.'

'I believe I won't finish this novel, I shouldn't even have started to write it down!'

'You cannot do this! *Dailorg's* destiny is in your hands!'

'You are wrong. My story has been brought to life. Your presence here is a proof. So we have to make a deal!'

'What deal?'

'You have to find a finale according to the beginning of the story and you will justify it too.'

'But I am not able to do it, you are the artist.'

'There is some empty inside me now, I cannot carry on.'

'You have to! The library is about to be violated. You must create something now! *Dailorg* will end up into Scuro's hands otherwise!'

'No. The story has stopped now. Without me it does not carry on. *Dailorg* does not exist, maybe neither myself.'

'This is just a detail regarding the whole balance of my not existing point of view, so move on! I demand it from you! I don't want to stay here with you forever.'

'I am stuck, over, that is it!'

'How come?'

'I cannot keep carrying on, I cannot write anymore!'

'Why?'

'I am disgusted about living, something like that.'
'Now you are not alone, I am here. You have to let me come back to *Dailorg*.'
'It needs some verisimilitude, coherence, I really do not know... I have frozen ideas by the anxiety.'
'Take your head out the freezer! Anxiety is essential condition to freedom, you should know it already by your age.'
'Everybody thinks that book writers have a fantastic life, full of surprises, averse to greyness. They don't know instead that especially through the greyness we dip our hands, through that opaque sea of heart that we don't really know how is palpitating.'
'Now I cry.'
'Your tears, drop after drop, could fill the room and ferry us to *Dailorg*, so I cannot distinguish true and false through a process of degrading annihilation of thoughts and of my own hateful shadow. A movement through what does exist here on the Earth, it won't be anymore at Mu, the eternal, the unchanging. Do you get it?'
'Not really. I did not get it right.'
'Mu cannot change because it is truth. When Mu changes it is not. If Mu changes, it will die!'
'So it died already. Changes have been. Scuro destroyed the beauty and created the horror *ex novo*.'
'Yes, but all this has still to happen.'
'How come?'
'So the fantasy is the opposite of the real facts. Reality happens first and then it could be written. Fantasy first has to be written and maybe after something would happen.'
'Like?'
'Something like someone reads the fantasy and it may

become reality and I have not written down anything yet. I have the story in my head with no finale obviously.'

'Really interesting theory. I like it. So you are saying that the story of *Dailorg* is not a story because you have not written it yet.'

'Exactly!'

'Well. It will be enough whether you won't write anything so nothing would happen!'

'Perfect.'

'There is only a small detail that you did not take into account.'

'Which one?'

'Why am I here then?'

'Since you don't exist you are a not-problem.'

'When I will start to empty your fridge, you will start thinking in a different way.'

Luce gets closer to the fridge. She opens it. Huge porcini mushrooms are on the top shelf. Wrapped nicely there is a huge steak, then fruit and salad in the bottom clear plastic drawer.

That steak is soon cooked with a strips cut mushroom side with garlic and parsley. Then a nice red wine. The writer cooks really well, nothing to say. The lady from Mu is satisfied. She showed to be a real problem that needs to be solved really soon.

A writer cannot survive too long with his fantasies, it's dangerous, there is the risk to lose track of reality. The matter is serious. The white page is exhausting him since months. Inside his head there is empty. He tried some distractions, going out, maybe going with prostitutes. No way! Nothing. All pointless. The Nothing is standstill, like a not erasable stain. His insomnia that was helping him to write before, now is an obsession and nothing else. Now, it needs to do something. Luce is there. She cannot stay there. It needs to take her back to her world. The only way should be to finish the story to solve everything out. Although the empty is like an abyss that swallows and tears off. What a situation... Really awful. The writer cannot confess it to someone. It's like mentally ill stuff. At least they closed down the mental houses. A real luck... Anyway he does not need to confess it to anyone. People don't understand at the end. Everyone deals with his own matters and doesn't care about others. The relatives even worse. Vile snakes ready to spit out poison provided with pearls of wisdom and good tips.

Wind blows and whistles lightly through the shutters. A creepy sound that seems human. It's almost autumn. A lazy season, two faces monster, sadly mocking and lethargic. It should be nice to die in autumn under loads of crunchy yellow leaves, with your own soul pierced by tree tips as skeleton arms and some blood over the thin rain that shivers your could skin. And on summer live again on beaches hurtled through the wind, smelling the scent of the foamy sea shivering and playing and singing mysterious, arcane, salty melodies. It should be nice not to die at all and to live always in the sun, with no knowledge of yourself own shadow, without understand anything except the fullness of the light, so dazzling to break your thoughts. Spending time hanging around over warm shores, lying on straight and flat rocks, making hair playing delirious stars. A stupid dream of eternity, maybe. It could be boring after long time. Boredom is worse than death, destroying everything that touches, melting everything through a sharp pain, unreal, through a permanent irritable status, timeless and broken. The writer is bored, exhausted over an indefinite frantic time. He has not succeeded through life. That's the simple and cruel reality. Experimentation doesn't pay. And the failing of who knows how to challenge the streamline is just around the corner. Indeed, it's never too late, but creativity is lying over a puddle of delusions, exhausted by the indifference of the homogenisation. Pointless thinking about it. It needs anyway to sort Luce out. Doing something...

Time is going fast and no ideas yet. The blank page eats life, greedy assassin. It makes more complicated the balance, rusting the low certainty. Stress is climbing walls, getting to the ceiling filling the room up with strong negativity. It sits quietly over the chandelier and it's about to break it. Then goes suddenly down and it grabs the writer's jumper, reaching his throat. It sits next to him observing him and going through his body. Boredom slices the soul and it has the same sensitivity of a spider for a fly wrapped around in the middle of its concentric spiderweb. The writer is on his own with himself, tasting vitreous fragments of his past which he had never agreed with. The only solution would have been kicking out the present until making it bleeding good wine. But he has not enough strength to lift his feet up, to hit and scratch the forehead to the faith. Lot of friends come to visit him, talking with him about arts, literature, politics, sports and easy whores, although they don't punch the surface. People and things are stagnant into an aberrant, total and complete ocean of nausea. Disgust is the vigilant and constant expression present in the life of the writer. Tax to pay to be in the world and to see with poet eyes what the others not even can think or imagine about. Too sensitivity maybe, too much of everything.

An excess of incentives that become unstoppable until being ungovernable. Images rotating into the brain, a lethal cocktail of obsessions that shoot over bones, stretched muscles and thoughts. Nightmares still come at night. It look like he has got empty bones like the intensive farmed chickens and yelling to the world a song that becomes eternal friable and dark purple livid, into an absurd empty, violent and so aggressive that legs are shaking, with his heart he would exit strongly from the veins of wrists. Upset stomach with no hunger for hours, uncombed and wild hair with hyperbolic curves challenging the gravity and the basic physics rules, eyes surrounded by strong bluish tones, similar to shabby ponds, consumed by the elements and the rage of wasted minutes through a nervous wake and sterile of fruit.

'Hey, writer, do you have a name?' Luce's voice is clear, silver and it shakes the silence breaking it with no compliments.

'My name is Nobody.'

'Original, I am impressed.'

Days are running. Months are going too. Nobody does not leave unforgettable memories over the blank page. At one point living with Luce is not possible anymore. One morning the man wakes up, shaves his beard and after breakfast he just goes out. He goes to a job interview with a luggage in his hand, his mind full of good proposals. The interview is made by an aseptic multiple choices test, idiot questions, disputable and full of mistakes. The sight of the secretary giving him the form is opaque, lifeless, really sad and grey marked by the odd hairstyle, line in the middle, high heels, although big and heavy. Her shoes noise is creepy, resounding on the quite dirty floor, bouncing over the glasses, over the yellow walls. Nobody looks at the sea through the window, closing his reddish eyes and focussing over the waves noise to avoid to smash that secretary's face that looks at him with indifference. He hates her. He hates her strong perfume too, sneaking through the nostrils with no permission, invading the whole space in the room, really overbearing. He hates her metal glasses. He stares at them looking to catch a bit of humanity through the secretary. Nothing. Two absurd balls with no expression over a face marked by early wrinkles. Lenses seem to join into a unique body, a big one lens that the woman can see nothing through, perfectly integrated within the society of human standard prototypes, unidirectional, integrated, robotised. She walks up and down, waiting for Nobody to give her the form back. Sometimes she looks at her watch, hitting twice the glass with her nail, turning her eyes up and brushing her hair with her hand. She opens a pack of cigarettes and she starts smoking spoiling the air. The writer stands up and goes without even say goodbye, with not even marked an answer on the form. He comes back home slowly, walking over the cold street. He walks his soul. Here she is, Luce, awesome like always. The knot, the start and the end, the mystery. He is nervous. She was born for this. He cannot avoid to call her, marking her existence, defining her through her own essence. The name is strong. Resounds inside and outside like a stone thrown against the flesh. Luce understands that he wants to attack her, he is tired. She sticks her nails over his arm for defence. The writer shouts at her, then he takes out his bag a sharp paper knife stabbing her. Luce is wounded, falling down whilst Time stops to have a look at her. Nobody can see for the first time slices of sky through the wound of Luce and he is fearing that he made a mistake. But it is not too late. He grabs Time for the neck, forcing him to immobility and thinking about something. While falling down Luce hears the voices of the Underground Earth that is plenty of parallel lives.

Nobody stares at Time's metaphysical eyes that strangely forgives him and let him do, slowing down the falling of the Black Star through the empty of the not-existence. Through the violent iris of Time, the writer sings about *Dailorg* and how Scuro is about to violate the third layer of his library, last fortress of the resistance of Mu.

Roof materials are melting under the primitive and wild action of the eggs. Legend says that the ataraxic had them in custody the day that the Great Mother took her heart off her chest to give Mu as gift. Together with heart she made Underground World to swallow the 4 eggs that she held in her hand, symbol of eternal regeneration of the worlds, endless mystery, obscurity and life. But nobody knows really where they are from neither why they have the ability to liquefy the barriers between different worlds and get back together after breaking. Their porous shell has the colour of the night. Over their surface you can look at yourself. The reflected image does not match the reality, but it matches the status of the soul, so it can be seen misshapen whether the soul is corrupted. Hania stole them when she escaped the ataraxic world with Ebbone. Since then she did not have a single minute of peace, tormented by remorse, always looking for penance. And when the yellow yolk with assassin evidence can crush the *adamantio*, the roof shuts again, as many time as it gets pulverized. Eggs melt and regenerate again but the pulverised layer re-atomizes. The interior resistance of Erasmo and Luce could not be broken easily. Nobody wants them to resist. And those characters perceive his willing finally living and concrete. Between Luce that doesn't want to die and Erasmo that doesn't give up, there is an ultra-sensitive communication, a strength beyond the worlds. The eggs perceive it because they have an intelligence that goes beyond the perceivable, they compose and re-compose obsessively. The writer digs his nails through the naked arms of the Time, staring at his dark and cold pupils, imagining the Unknowable, the upside down, and he realises that nothing is lost yet. There's a risk that the characters seize him. That the story would surround him as a whirlwind of senseless obsessions. That's why he felt the tragic and unnatural instinct of killing Luce, to suppress himself as uncomfortable and spoiled towards the eyes of the world, a poet with no definitions, neither a precise location, who doesn't submit multiple answers tests. A strange type that goes beyond every system throwing the alarm clock into the bin. A misanthrope that with iconoclastic fury a good day has thrown the television out the window risking of killing the flatmate at the ground floor. If only he did it! He would have liked to smash on the floor that drunk idiot that was leaving always loads of beer bottles and empty cans in the garden, like sad crumpled thoughts on the edge of bleeding wounds never recovered. But now the writer is present with a luggage full of willingness and he knows that he could lead his characters without being affected, keeping the right distance, nurturing the separation of the worlds like essential lucidity and unalienable. And now the creatures born by his fantasy that have risked almost to lose the father, pulsate with stronger emotions, so real, suggestive and full of arcane symbols that could be touched and grasped with no fear to be hurt. And new communications are in the air, the space between the falling of Luce and the world of ataraxic. Erasmo hears the signs of the Black Star, although he cannot see her. The telepathic strength of both gets together to find the way, the space of the safety for *Dailorg*, the antimatter, the adverse mirror, the alter-ego, the sublime secret reversing of the worlds, where the black turns into white, negative into positive and all is different from what it is, kingdom of the anti-stars that challenge the normal common sense. Erasmo and Luce are anti-aliens challenging the order of the common perceptions, for willing of the writer. They sublimate the matter to get together with its own opposite. And all those that used to believe into the power of freedom gather into the antimatter for the strength of deep attraction. Into the antimatter replicates *Dailorg* and all Mu of free anarchic creatures, like through a mirror. Mu reflects itself through the antimatter so strongly that it is getting consistency through it, specularly. Of the old Mu it is only left an impoverished appearance, a world where who believed into freedom doesn't exist anymore because he has been absorbed through the antimatter.

Whilst the dead ones of Scuro are working towards the holes in the roof opened by the eggs, they feel the roof collapsing under their feet, like butter. Diamonds pulverize under the action of the yolk. The wizard falls down into the library with his dead ones. The eggs recompose back and disappear, absorbed by the ground, like attracted by a monstrous power, a huge magnet, they end up into the antimatter that is unknown by Scuro.

Library is desert. The intruders browse in every corner. Their heavy steps resound over the lucid floor. The scenario is unreal. Books into the shelves of the rooms look carved into the stone. The stars in the ceiling of the Planetarium

~ The black star of Mu ~

Hall like carved badly through the gesso and the planets mummified into a surprised sadly pose. The dead ones are spreading everywhere, unreal, skeletal and horrible. The marvellous garden of the ataraxic is silent. Even the wind has gone. Scuro tears the grass off with rage. Where is everybody gone? What did happen? Ebbone said he doesn't know anything. Not even he can explain where the eggs have gone. Maybe Erasmo hid into a secret room with Star, his friends and all the ataraxic ones. Reflection says, although, that this is impossible. A population into a single room. It's absurd. There are things that the mind cannot explain.

Scuro starts to laugh nervously and convulsively, 'Marvellous and tragic at the same time!'

Ebbone is puzzled. 'What?'

'All this, do you understand it?'

'No.'

'Wherever the ataraxic ones are escaped the resistance of Mu is over. Indeed I have to give up to absorb Luce's energies. I would have developed a superhuman power. Mixing my mortal blood with hers it could have been an extraordinary experience, a huge liberation of powers leading to the conquer of Mu all together. Now it will take more time and fatigue. But at least *Dailorg* is all mine now. Every corner, every shore, even the dust whitening the roads, mine, all mine. My name will be remembered by the historians of Mu and it will keep its young destructive strength. It will deliver terror through the generations deprived of the absurdity of anarchy. Order and discipline will be the life bread and the blood of a new God that will rape the Mothers, throwing on the ground their statues, stepping over with the heels the memory of their pearly pathway. I won't ever die!'

'Poor illusion! I cannot stop laughing, a bitter laugh, laugh of who knows...'

'What do you know then?'

'That you are over, exactly like me. The parabola of your fatuous power is going to finish. Look at the ancient rooms of this library, look at your feet, your hands and your naked soul. It's so hard to discover that you are nothing! All is lost now, even a blind man would get it. I see you don't like the cruel reality. Better to pretend, consoling yourself and hoping that this our vain and wretched ambition, thirst of blood, the willingness of an order that does not exist not even inside us, it could still exist. We are really fragile, spoiled like awful candles towards our own flame, towards our poisoning breaths and smelling of death! We are really pathetic grabbing the constant desires and obsessive of massacre and domination over the others! We are horrible monsters and misshapen that jump out the rotten of the ground after we dig out our graves with our nails full of wind. Scuro, look at you! How don't you horrify about yourself? You are an empty puppet full of nothing, a robot of excrements and chains, slave of your own ambitions, subjugated to the tragic honey of the power. And the illusory and absurd sweetness of that taste is hiding the sweetish scent of innocent blood and Mu flesh that you slaughtered. Can you hear the scream of Hania whose you destroyed her favourite? My little Hania... I, for example, dislike myself, with the immortal shame of an eternal wandering life, through my bodies' parasitism, into my absurd and inexplicable hunger of youth. Looking for a young body where I can live still and taste the light. All useless, without values, with nothing inside rather than betrayal and demons

that never sleep, neither night nor day. Luce and Erasmo found the way and you cannot stop them. There is no way...'
'Their way? What are you talking about?'
'I do believe that prophecy would have happened!'
'I do not get it!'
'Come with me!'
They exit the garden, walking slowly on the grass. They step over the bushes. Under their inhuman feet flowers turn into misshapen and horrible genitals with their broken stalks and their corollas smashed through grotesque shapes. Inside the rooms there is silence and warmth. Steps resound. Suddenly they stop. There is a light noise increasing. Barefoot steps on the cold floor. An old short lady appears, long white hair, squat, button-less grey tunic on. She is blind, big white eyes. She stares at them with no pupils, firm, with her crumpled and huge hands hanging alongside her hips like dead branches.

Ebbone rumbles that he was right, that everything is over now.

Scuro asks the lady who she is.

'I am the Ultraworld Lady.'

'So what?'

'I am and I am not, here and everywhere else at the same time, today, tomorrow, yesterday and never. I pierce the matter and the antimatter. I go beyond the barriers among worlds and I walk where I like. I can see inside and outside you like you were transparent. I can see the dirt of your hearts shaking like empty puddles, marshy and stinking, although I don't judge neither the good nor the bad, it's not my duty.'

Ebbone gets closer to her. 'Are you the birth of the prophecy?'

'Exactly.'

'What's your role?'

'Being and not being here, showing to everyone the cruel evidence of himself. I can guarantee you that there is nothing more tragic and horrible together!'

The Ultraworld Lady gets closer to Scuro with her palms towards him. The dazzling white of her senseless eyes stares at him. The wizard sees in that creature eyes the rotten himself. There is a small room, with aseptic white walls, lightly decorated. A chair in the middle of the room, one of that old chair made with wood and straw, a bit consumed, experienced. A young Mu guy is sitting over it. Scuro walks in front of him, blaming him to be rebel to the Government's Laws. He has to say his friends' names, how many rebels are with him. Mapuche doesn't answer. He only looks at Scuro's shoes tips. He nods to some of the dead ones standing on the door. They get closer and start punching the young one on his face, making his cheek bleeding. Scuro gets to him again, asking again for those names. The guy shuts up. Dead ones still beating him up. They break his lips that are bleeding strongly. They force him to stand up and they keep punching him, with savage fury until he falls down. The floor is full of blood. The wizard demands him to stand up. They have to lift him up. His face is a mask of blood. Scuro asks him again for those names. The Mu guy stares at him challenging. A moment and Mapuche spits on Scuro's face some blood and saliva. It's the end. Scuro lifts his arm ordering the dead ones to proceed. The dead body of Mapuche gets dragged out the room. On the floor a long track of blood of the same colour of the splashes on the wall.

The Ultraworld Lady now puts down her palms, taking

off her sight and pointing out Ebbone this time. She tells him that Mapuche, dead two hours after the brawl, he was her son, born from Hania's womb, after the escape from the ataraxic world, result of the union of their first bodies. Hania has always kept her first body making it getting older and being shameful of her own past. Ebbone has lived the Odyssey of more other bodies, although is now a Judah with no soul.

Ebbone falls down on the floor, knees on the pavement, hands in his hair.

The Ultraworld Lady doesn't get affected at all. She opens her mouth singing the prophecy.

'It was written that after 6,666,000 years the land of Mu will deliver a Black Star whose heart at her birth will stop for few long instant. Whilst waiting for a new heartbeat a seed of the doubt will grow in the shade of mystery, into a forgotten corner of the time. And the seed will get stronger and it will grow up going beyond the dogma and the tradition. It will produce deep and lasting root. This will attract unknown powers, good and bad, it will doubt about the worlds and even the existence of the Mothers. It will produce knowledge and pain, as twin sisters. The change will be huge and it will make shivering the womb of Mu. The Knowledge of *Dailorg* will dig through the ground and it will be violated through an obscure power. Freedom will be in danger. It will be poured some innocent blood of Mu. Although the seed will grow up and blossom new plants into the doubtful heart the Star, producing sweet and bitter fruit. It will dig its own roots through other worlds fertilizing the start and the end, the whole and the nothing. It will be born the Ultraworld Lady that could go beyond barriers of space and time. She will be barefoot and she will see with no eyes, touching the good and the bad without being tainted. Through the space of a falling and of a dream the Star will find the antimatter where everything will transform into its own opposite. The Mothers will open their eyes over their sons and they will shout their names. Their voices will suck the elected ones; their breaths will be whirls that will drag each free Mu person through the born again freedom. It will be two Mu and two *Dailorg*, it will be the double, matter and antimatter. The first one will be the black and the second one the white. In the first one there will be dogs, loaded with heavy moods and mud, the traitors, hypocrites, greedy ones. In the second one there will be the free spirits, light of life, breathing with no chains. And the dogs, because the owner with no servants has no sense, they will eat each other. Their teeth will dig into black bodies flesh.'

Scuro lifts his hand up to express his own aggressive instinct against the creature, but he hits three times the air. The Ultraworld Lady laughs and she spits on his face some blood misshaping his face. And there will be no water neither soap not even time that could rinse off that blood.

Run out, exit the library and look at the life dividing between matter and antimatter! A unique show!'

Like abortions came from the empty, Ebbone and Scuro, together with the dead ones, exit the library. Outside the atmosphere is tense.

In the windless Mu there is a whirlwind now that is blowing off things and people. Lot of Mu people get absorbed by the vortex vanishing in the air. Hania is in her pub now, behind the desk, her eyes lost in the air. People are drinking, eating and talking loudly. A strange yellow dust comes in through the windows, getting in every corner, every hole, even through the pores of the skin. Everyone shuts up suddenly. A strong wind shakes the shutters. Someone tries to shut them, but Hania says that's useless. Nobody can do anything against the power of the new hurricane that will hit Mu. She stares her blue eyes at the yellow vortex, hoping firmly to be blown off. The dust lifts her up absorbing every single cell of her body. Hania does not feel any pain, only a bit cold over her neck spreading slowly over her whole body, like a cold wave. She feels good, lighter and lighter. Some people get absorbed by the vortex dust, that ignores some others intentionally, leaving them sitting there, with their mouths open wide. The majority of the ones left is the servants of the State and Naiir's dead ones. On the streets, in the houses, the vortex dust blows and sucks or ignores someone. All the rebels and anarchists get absorbed. Their bodies vanish slowly. Their flesh regenerate into another Mu, specular antimatter where they come back free, glad to be born with no chains. Mu and its own double therefore, prophecy is happening. The Mu of Scuro is populated only with fierce creatures and greedy dead ones of Naiir, and living people that believed to adhere to the new regime giving up their freedom. But the savage creatures need to eat, they have to drink their victims blood, from the rebels that don't give up. They are all gone through the antimatter that is unreachable now. Not even the arts of the wizard can go beyond the obstacle of the matter. So the oppressor assumes the role of holocaust. Naiir is ambitious. He always dreamt about a dead ones kingdom. Scuro must die and be subjugated to his law. Naked, forced to go down his knees in front of Naiir, the wizard begs mercy, even kissing the foot of the leader of the dead ones, to save his own life. Soldiers celebrate, beating rhythmically their skeleton hands whilst Naiir shows to Scuro the dagger that will kill him, the same one that the wizard used to kill the black scapegoat from where he absorbed energies.

The blade shines under the greenish light. Naiir gets naked, showing the whole his skeleton with no flesh and indecent. He nods two soldiers to hold firm the victim. He grabs Scuro through his hair, digging the blade with the carved hilt with signs through the neck of the victim. Dark and huge blood falls on the floor. Ground drinks it, greedy. The mortal body of the wizard will feed the Mu worms.

The writer takes his eyes off the pupils of the Time that gives to him a manuscript, shaking his hand and going away with a smart smile on his face. The manuscript gets locked into a warm womb of a leather bag. The chair is empty tearing off the nothing with its straight and marked outlines, with its straight legs of lonely sad beast. The writer turns ahead. The street is desert. Luce is not there anymore, she disappeared through the antimatter few instants before falling. She found her way at the end. Everything has been put back, specularly, like into a mirror. And the evil has been split from the good like the grain from the husk. Maybe even Erasmo could look again at Hania's eyes over there, at the eternal Mu. All and nothing have changed, the order has been stabilized back, but nothing will be like before, neither Erasmo's sight not even the innocence of Chemako, not even the infinite sadness of Nudo. Luce will have new fears and more awareness. She will keep the scar made from the wound of the writer, wound from where she could have seen the skies of other infinite and unknown possible worlds.

The sun starts to get stronger throwing away the last resistance of the night darkness. The dawn in silence warms

~ *The black star of Mu* ~

the skin smoothly. It kisses the red hair of a stray dog with big yellow and serious eyes where all the sadness of the world is concentrated. Soon the road will be crowded with presences that will send away the unreality of the silence and they will produce noises of experienced life. A swarm of souls will be in the air drawing the short and illusory cycle of the day. The writer goes away towards home, becoming smaller and smaller, a dot lost through mazes of roads that cross together, wounding each other to the sorrow.

Mary Blindflowers

~ The black star of Mu ~

INDICE

PREFACE	5
THE GOLD	7
WALKING MAN	9
HILDE'S JOURNEY	23
MU, THE ETERNAL	33
THE HOUSE	39
DAILORG LIBRARY	47
THE WIZARD DEFEATING THE FROGS	71
NIOBE	81
CHEMAKO	97
THE RITUAL	105
GREAT MOTHER'S HEART	115
THE KISS	121
THE REPUBLIC OF MU	147
THE RESISTANCE OF MU	151
THE FLESH OF THE MOTHERS	157
THE ROCK BOTTOM	165
TABUM	167
S8	173
THE LAST SUMMER OF LOARC	179
ZAID'S SLAUGHTERHOUSE	183
THE MIRRORS' ROOM	187
THE GOLD OF TABUM	191
THE LIBRARY SECRET	195
EBBONE	197
THE EXPERIMENT	201
DODO'S EGGS	207
THE WEAPON	211
NIOBE'S END	213
HANIA	225
A WEDGE OF THE UPPER WORLD	231
THE EGG ROOM	237

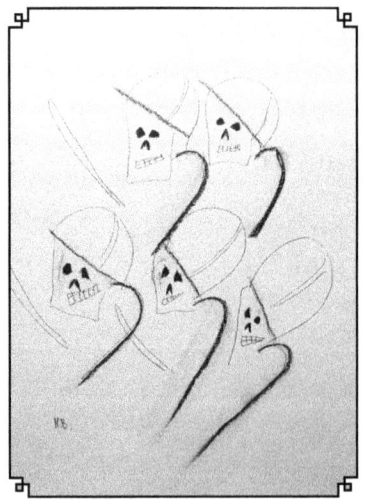

Lightning Source UK Ltd.
Milton Keynes UK
UKHW041334161118
332454UK00002B/20/P